Louise Allen loves immersing herself in history. She finds landscapes and places evoke the past powerfully. Venice, Burgundy and the Greek islands are favourite destinations. Louise lives on the Norfolk coast and spends her spare time gardening, researching family history and travelling in search of inspiration. Visit her at louiseallenregency.co.uk, @louiseregency and janeaustenslondon.com.

Also by Louise Allen

Marrying His Cinderella Countess
The Earl's Practical Marriage
A Lady in Need of an Heir
Convenient Christmas Brides
Contracted as His Countess

Lords of Disgrace miniseries

His Housekeeper's Christmas Wish
His Christmas Countess
The Many Sins of Cris de Feaux
The Unexpected Marriage of Gabriel Stone

Liberated Ladies miniseries

Least Likely to Marry a Duke
The Earl's Marriage Bargain

And look out for the next book
coming soon!

Discover more at millsandboon.co.uk.

THE EARL'S MARRIAGE BARGAIN

Louise Allen

MILLS & BOON

First published in Great Britain 2020
by Mills & Boon, an imprint of HarperCollins*Publishers*
1 London Bridge Street, London, SE1 9GF

Large Print edition 2020

© 2020 Melanie Hilton

ISBN: 978-0-263-08650-8

MIX
Paper from
responsible sources
FSC **FSC˚ C007454**

This book is produced from independently certified
FSC™ paper to ensure responsible forest management. For
more information visit www.harpercollins.co.uk/green.

Printed and bound in Great Britain
by CPI Group (UK) Ltd, Croydon, CR0 4YY

Chapter One

1ˢᵗ September, 1814

If she was in a novel written by her friend Melissa, then this post chaise would be rattling across the cobbles on its way to the Borders for a Scottish wedding and the seat next to her would be occupied by a dashing, dark and decidedly dangerous gentleman.

As this was real life, Jane was on the way to Batheaston to spend at least six months in disgrace with Cousin Violet. Beside her was Constance Billing, her mother's maid. It had become clear ten minutes after their journey had begun that the only thing constant about Constance was her ability to sulk relentlessly and to disapprove of everything.

On the other hand, at least she was not being sent home to Dorset. Cousin Violet was entertainingly eccentric and—so she fervently hoped—Billing would be returning the morning after their arrival.

Jane consulted the road book. 'We do not change horses at Kensington as it is not even two miles from London. Hounslow is the first halt, I believe.'

'In that case, Miss Jane, why have we stopped?'

'Because, as you can observe through the front glass, the traffic has become entangled for some reason.' Jane half rose from her seat to look over the back of the pair of horses. 'Ah, I see there has been an accident.'

The church was just ahead of them on the bustling main road through the village of Kensington and two large wagons were in front of it, apparently with their wheels locked. The drivers were both standing up, waving their whips and shouting at each other, which was not helping in the slightest. Fortunately, they were out of earshot. Passers-by and other drivers had stopped to offer advice, gawk or generally get in the way.

Jane dropped the window beside her and leaned out. Distantly behind them there was the sound of a horn. 'That is either a stagecoach or the Mail is coming through.'

She settled back against the squabs and prepared to be entertained. Travellers complained about post chaises and their swaying motion, but they did have the benefit of a wide front window through which to survey the world. Naturally, Billing did not approve of all that glazing and kept her eyes averted from it. It was neither discreet nor private, in her opinion, and young ladies should not be looking around, risking attracting the roving eye of some rake or sauntering gentleman.

'Do put up the glass, Miss Jane,' Billing scolded. 'There is a common alehouse just the other side of the pavement from us.'

She did have a point, Jane conceded. The Civet Cat opposite looked decidedly seedy and not at all like the well-kept, welcoming inns of the villages around her home.

As she mentally swept the frontage, cleaned the windows and added a pot or two of geraniums, the door of the alehouse burst open and three men rolled out, scattering pedestrians. They were followed by two others carrying clubs.

Billing gave a screech. 'We'll be murdered!'

'No, we will not, but that man will be if someone doesn't help him.'

The fight had resolved into one against four
as the largest of the club-bearers dragged a tall,
dark-haired man to his feet and held on to him
as the others closed in and began to rain blows
against head and body.

'Why doesn't somebody stop it? That is not a
fight, that is a deliberate assault. They should
call a constable.'

The tall man wrenched free, unleashed a
punch and knocked down one of his attackers,
sending him crashing into two of the others.

'Oh, well done, sir! Hit him again, the bully!'

Jane ignored Billing tugging at her arm and
shushing her. She opened the window in the door
of the carriage, gripped the edge and held her
breath because, despite that gallant punch, the
man was held fast now by the two he had fallen
against. He was shaking his head as though to
clear it after a vicious blow and was clearly now
no match for the fourth assailant who was ad-
vancing, grinning in obvious anticipation.

To Jane's surprise the attacker dug in the
pocket of the frieze coat he was wearing, pro-

duced a folded paper and stuffed it into the coat front of the man before him. 'With compliments,' he said, then took a firm grip on his cudgel again.

The first swing of the club jolted the tall man out of his captors' grip, across the pavement and into the side of the chaise. Billing gave another shriek as it rocked on its springs.

Jane threw open the door, reached out with both hands, grabbed the man's arm and the collar of his coat and tugged. 'Get in!'

Whether he heard her, or the momentum of his fall carried him in, she had no idea and she was far too worried about the gap-toothed snarl on the face of the cudgel-wielder to care. The man collapsed at her feet, the door swung in and then, as the chaise righted itself, came back on its hinges and hit the attacker in the face.

Jane took a grip on her parasol with one hand and dug frantically in her reticule with the other for Mama's pocket pistol which was hopelessly tangled with her handkerchief. She was braced for the inevitable, when, with a blast on the horn, the Mail was on them. It swept past, forcing its way through the onlookers around the wagons. Their postilion seized his chance, whipped up his horses and the chaise, door still open, lurched into the wake of the stage and followed it through. As they passed the church the chaise tilted, the door slammed closed and they had left the Civet Cat and its ruffians behind.

Jane considered being sick, swallowed hard and let go of her weapons.

'Miss Jane, tell the postilion to stop, this horrid creature is bleeding all over our skirts.' Billing made as though to drop her own window to lean out.

'Stop that,' Jane said sharply. 'Do you want those bully boys to catch up to us? Help me turn him over. Oh, do not be so foolish, Billing— have you never seen blood before? Put your feet on the seat then; at least it will give him more room on the floor.'

Billing huddled up in the far corner, managing in the process to kick the man who was prone at their feet. There was a groan. At least he was still alive.

Jane bent down and touched his shoulder and found good-quality broadcloth under her hand. 'Can you turn over, sir?'

He grunted, began to lever himself up on his

elbows in the restricted space and swore under his breath as the chaise hit a rut. 'No.'

'Very well, stay there. We will come to a turn-pike gate soon, surely.'

It must have been about two miles before the chaise slowed, then stopped. 'Help me, Billing. *Billing.*'

Somehow they hauled the man up on to the seat between them and it became clear that he was suffering from a knife wound in the shoulder, at the very least. There was blood, rather more than Jane felt comfortable with, and his left arm hung limp.

Jane stuffed her handkerchief and her fichu under his coat and pressed on the wounded area, ignoring the gasp of pain and the subsequent bad language. 'Hold that.' After a moment he obeyed, although his eyes were closed and his head lolled to the side.

She could sympathise with the gasp and she doubted if he was conscious enough of his surroundings to realise that he was swearing at two women. More of an immediate problem was Billing, who had recoiled further into the corner and was hectoring Jane on danger, impropriety, unladylike behaviour… 'And what your sainted mother will say, I shudder to imagine. No respectable lady would consider for a moment—'

Jane stopped listening.

The postilion, having sorted out the toll, appeared to realise for the first time that he had an extra passenger. He handed the reins to the gatekeeper and came around to Jane's window. 'Here, what's going on, miss? This vehicle was hired for two people.'

'I know it was. I want you to stop at the next decent inn that serves stagecoaches and, I promise, you will be back to two passengers.'

He gave her a decidedly sceptical look. 'It'll be extra to pay at the end if there's blood on the upholstery.' But he remounted and sent the pair off at a canter and, as Billing finally ran out of breath, drew up at the Bell and Anchor.

'Billing, please go inside and fetch a bowl of water,' Jane said.

'I'll go in, that is for sure, but to try and get the blood off my skirts, Miss Jane! And I will send out some men to haul that vagabond out of our chaise,' she added, scrambling down and marching into the inn. 'I should be calling the

constable, that's what your mother would say...'
floated back to the chaise.

'Quickly, unstrap her luggage,' Jane told the
postilion. 'That wicker hamper and the small
brown valise there.' The stranger would have to
look after himself for the moment because she
needed to find her purse.

Just as Jane unrolled two banknotes Billing
came marching out again without, of course,
any water, but flanked by two anxious-looking
waiters.

'What's about, Miss Jane? Those are my bags
there.'

'Billing, you are going home to Dorset. There
is your luggage, here is more than enough money
for the stage—you can pay for decent rooms and
food on your way and a girl to accompany you.
This seems a most respectable inn so I am sure
they will advise you and let you hire one of the
maids for the journey.' She thrust the notes into
the spluttering woman's hands and closed the
door. 'Drive on!'

The postilion obeyed, ignoring Billing's indignant cries as they rattled off down the road
again. Jane flopped back against the seat. All
things considered, a silent, if battered, man was

a far more pleasant travelling companion than Billing with her sour face and nagging voice. Jane shifted on the seat to look at him more closely. He was also considerably better to look at than Billing although, even accounting for bruises, dirt and blood, he was no Adonis. On the other hand, she was now responsible for him, she had no experience of nursing wounded men and goodness knew what he would prove to be like when he regained consciousness. The quality of the coat did promise a certain gentility, at least, although, gravedigger or gentry, she would still have rescued anyone from a beating if she could.

Melissa would be deeply envious. This was the kind of adventure she was always writing about and which, Jane was certain, she yearned to experience for herself. She would just have to make do with letters, which were bound to be less enthralling than Melissa would have hoped. On the other hand, Jane could draw as vividly as her friend could write, which should make up for a lack of dramatic description. With a quick check to make certain the wounded man was still unconscious and the bleeding was under control, Jane took her sketch pad and a pencil from the door pocket and flipped back the cover.

Where the devil am I?

Ivo thought about opening his eyes, then decided against it. Everything hurt, but no one was thumping him at the moment, which was a decided improvement, and there was no point in jeopardising that to satisfy his curiosity. On the other hand, he appeared to be in a moving vehicle and the only thing that he could smell was leather and a decidedly piquant floral perfume.

From the motion of the vehicle he deduced that he was in a post chaise and, from the perfume, that he had been rescued by a lady. That was embarrassing, but preferable to remaining with the brutes that Daphne had set on him. The reality of the transformation in the woman who had once told him that she adored him and would wait for him was not something that he had the strength to consider now. What he would feel when he allowed himself to think of it was beside the point, he told himself. All that really mattered was that he could not honour his promise to his friend, her brother, as he lay dying. That failure was a damned sight more painful than whatever was wrong with his left shoulder.

Distantly he could hear the hoofbeats of the horses, the postilion's occasional shouted order to them as the chaise creaked and the wheels rumbled. Under those sounds there was a strange *scratch-scritch* noise, almost a whisper, right on the edge of his consciousness.… It was rather soothing.

The chaise was slowing, turning, stopping. There was noise from outside. Ivo dragged open his lids and found himself staring into a pair of long-lashed hazel eyes.

'Oh, good, you are awake. I was wondering how we were ever going to get you out of the carriage if you were not. You are rather large,' the owner of the eyes added critically. 'And bloody. And dirty.'

He blinked and she moved back, which at least meant he could get her into focus through the headache. Mousy brown hair, freckles, a heart-shaped face. Not pretty, certainly not compared to Daphne's exquisite blonde delicacy, but the overall effect was vaguely feline in an amiable sort of way. A gentle waft of warm female and floral scent tickled his nose.

'Do you think you can get out and into the inn? I have asked one of the grooms to help.' She smiled at him, her head tipped to one side. Smiles were preferable to beauty, just at the moment.

Ivo felt as though he was being studied in order to give an accurate description to the Runners and blinked again. It was possible that he was concussed and imagining this. Ladies did not stare closely at men. Nor did they drag them out of the middle of fights into their carriages, as his vague memory told him this one had done.

'Come on, shall we try to get you out?' She leaned across him, opened the other door and a man reached in. 'Yes, that's right, mind his left shoulder.' He was seized, dragged out and, as he struggled for balance, dropped.

'Oh, dear. Well, hopefully that won't have started it bleeding again,' his rescuer said blithely as the groom hauled him to his feet again. 'Now, what did I do with my bonnet and reticule?'

Ivo found himself in an inn yard, unsteady on his feet and held upright by a large young man who smelt strongly of the stables. 'Where—?'

'The Pack Horse in Turnham Green. Do you want to lean on me as well? No? This way then.'

'Who—?'

'I am Jane Newnham. Ah, Landlord. I would like a private parlour, some hot water, brandy and the services of your best local doctor. My *brother* has been attacked by footpads,' she added clearly, with a sharp jab in Ivo's ribs, presumably so he paid attention to her story. They began to move again. 'Excellent, thank you. This will do nicely.'

'Why—?'

'Because you have been stabbed, I think, and there may be other injuries and my knowledge of human anatomy is entirely theoretical so, although I do not think you are in mortal peril, it is best to make certain. Here we are. Do you want to sit down on this bench or lie on the sofa? It doesn't look very comfortable and you might drip on it.'

'I will sit.'

A miracle, I have uttered three words without being interrupted.

The groom deposited him on the bench with a thump.

Ivo bit back the things he felt inclined to say and waited for the lad to shamble out. 'It appears I am in your debt Miss—is it Miss? Yes?—

Newnham. But I confess I am puzzled. I seem to recall being dragged into your carriage and that there were two women in it. Now you appear to be unaccompanied.'

'That was Billing. I put her out at the last inn and gave her the money to go home. She is my mother's maid and she was driving me quite distracted, even before you joined us—and we had only driven from Mayfair. I do find disapproving people very wearing, don't you? It is like being constantly rubbed on the soul with emery paper.'

From her speech and her clothes this was a lady. Therefore, she should not be out alone on the highway, however unusual and whimsical she might be. She should most definitely not be in an inn with a strange man. Ivo said so. Firmly.

'Nonsense. I could hardly abandon you, now could I? And clearly you are a gentleman or you would not quibble about this. And I told the landlord that I was your sister and I do not know anyone in Turnham Green, so there is absolutely no cause to worry.'

Ivo reminded himself that, until a few weeks past, he had been an officer in his Majesty's army, had been wounded far more severely than this in the past, did not appear to be concussed and therefore he was more than capable of summoning the authoritative manner necessary to detach this female. Only, if he did, then she would be alone and unescorted. *Damn.*

'This sounds like the doctor arriving,' Miss Newnham said brightly. 'You are being positively heroic about your wounds, but I am sure he will have you feeling better soon.'

There was a tap at the door and a redheaded, be-freckled man in his late twenties came in and smiled at them. 'I believe the gentleman has been attacked? I am glad to see you conscious, sir. My name is Jamieson.' He appeared to be expecting some reaction because he added, 'I know I do not look old enough, but I assure you that I am a fully qualified graduate of the medical school of Edinburgh University. Now, sir, let us remove your upper garments. I imagine it will require some care.' He advanced purposefully on Ivo.

'Doctor Jamieson, there is a lady in the room.'

'That is quite all right, dear,' his rescuer said soothingly.

Dear?

'My brother is being unduly shy. I am sure that

between us we can remove his coat and shirt and so forth with less pain to him than if you attempt it alone.'

So forth?

'Of course, ma'am. It is hardly as though we need to remove your brother's nether garments, now is it? Ha-ha! At least, not yet.'

Over my dead body are my breeches coming off with this female in the room, Ivo thought grimly.

On the other hand, his shoulder appeared to be infested by devils wielding tiny pitchforks and his ribs were aching as though he had been kicked by a horse, not merely by four brainless louts. He knew from past experience that this process was easier if the patient was relaxed, so he nodded. 'As you think best, Doctor.'

Miss Newnham was, to do her justice, both gentle and deft and did not fuss about, which usually ended up causing more pain. His coat came off eventually, his waistcoat was simple by comparison, his neckcloth was already untied and after five minutes he was down to his shirt. The makeshift pad that Miss Newnham had applied to his shoulder fell away and he saw she had used something with good lace on it. He would have to replace that, it was clearly beyond repair.

Miss Newnham, who appeared to have no inhibitions whatsoever, was pulling the shirt out of the back of his breeches, the doctor, thank goodness, was tackling the front. He dragged it over Ivo's head and stepped back.

'A military man, I assume,' Jamieson remarked after half a minute's steady scrutiny from narrowed eyes. 'You will have a matching pair of shoulders now, sir. What was this one?' He touched cold fingertips to the old scar above Ivo's right collarbone.

'Splinter from a gun carriage that was hit by shot,' he said tersely and glanced down to the left as a line of blood tickled, creeping down his chest. He could almost feel Miss Newnham's gaze on his back. The effort not to move made sore muscles tense painfully.

'If you could arrange for some warm water to be brought, ma'am?' Jamieson asked.

That, thankfully, sent the woman out of the room. A maid came in with the water a few minutes later and Ivo closed his eyes, sent his consciousness as far away as he could and submitted to the doctor's probing.

'Nothing broken,' Jamieson said eventually. 'I've cleaned out that shoulder wound—not deep, nothing critical hit—and put two stitches in it. The ribs are badly bruised, but I am not a believer in tight bandaging so I've not strapped them. Your back will be black and blue before much longer, but there are no serious marks in the kidney region. Everything all right down below?'

Ivo had done what he could to protect *down below*. There would be bruises across his thighs and shins, but that was all.

'Perfectly,' he managed to say. Reaction was beginning to set in now, he could feel his over-stretched muscles and nerves quivering with the need to tremble.

'Here is a clean shirt. Let me help you into it.'

That was almost too much, but he hung on and the doctor did not attempt to tuck it in. Somewhere there was that strange *scratch-scritch* sound he had noticed in the chaise. His ears must be ringing from a blow at some point in the fight.

'Now, time we got you into a bed, I believe,' Jamieson said.

'My wallet. Should be in my inside coat pocket.'

The other man held up the coat, searched the pockets. 'Nothing here, I'm afraid. They must have got it when they attacked you.'

'I have taken rooms for us,' Miss Newnham said from behind him. The scritching sound had stopped. 'Do not worry, brother dear, my reticule was quite safe, so we have no cause to worry about funds.'

Uno, dos, tres... Eyes closed, Ivo counted to ten in Spanish in his head. 'Have you been in this room throughout?'

'Of course, dear. Now, what do we owe you, Doctor?'

He told her, Ivo made a mental note, there was the clink of coins and then, oddly, the sound of tearing paper.

'You might like that,' she said.

'Why, that is... Marvellous! Thank you, ma'am. What talent. Good day to you, sir. Rest and remain in bed for a day or so if you become at all feverish. You've got enough scars on you to know by now how to treat wounds sensibly, I imagine.'

The door closed behind Jamieson as Miss

Newnham came around to face Ivo. 'Your room is just at the head of the stairs on the right. Shall I get one of the grooms to help you?'

'What were you doing in here?' he snapped. 'And what did you give the doctor besides money? And, yes, I can manage a flight of stairs by myself.' He hoped. 'Better than being dropped down it by that clumsy lump of a groom.'

Miss Newnham walked away behind him, then came back with a slim, flat book in her hand and flipped it open, holding it for him to see. There was a pencil sketch of the room, of his naked back, of Jamieson bending over him. It was rapid, vivid and anatomically accurate. Shocking, in fact, for a young woman to have produced. 'I did a quick portrait of him, as well. That is what I gave him.'

'Was that your pencil I could hear? Were you drawing in the carriage?'

In answer she turned back a page in the sketch-book. There he was, slumped in the corner of the chaise, eyes closed, hair in a mess, clothing disordered. She turned back another page to a portrait of a discontented female, tight-lipped and sour. 'That is Billing. You can see why I sent her home. She was sending me into a decline, so goodness knows what effect she would have had on you in your weakened condition.'

Chapter Two

The man she had rescued looked at the portrait, then at Jane. 'She was your *chaperon*,' he said, in accents at odds with his battered, disreputable, appearance.

'She was my gaoler. Never tell me you are shocked? You do not look like someone who would be scandalised by such a thing as a perfectly competent woman travelling alone.'

'You are not alone,' he pointed out. 'And I must look like a complete thatch-gallows.' He pushed himself to his feet and stood, swaying slightly.

'I am not certain why anyone would want to thatch a gallows, but I can assure you that I can tell from your voice and your clothing—to say nothing of your concern for the proprieties— that you are a gentleman,' Jane reassured him.

It was not a lie, he did make her feel safe for

some reason. She put one hand on his arm. Even through the coarse linen of the shirt she had borrowed from one of the waiters, he felt cold. *And hard*—although she could feel the faintest tremor beneath her palm. He was exhausted, she guessed, and in pain, and the loss of blood cannot have helped. 'You should go up to bed and rest now.'

He seemed to consider it, then nodded. At least she was dealing with a reasonable man and not a foolish one who felt he had to pretend to be invincible in front of a female. She gathered up his discarded clothing and opened the door. 'Just one flight of stairs to manage. The door is open. If you drop all your clothes but that shirt outside, I will have them cleaned and repaired.'

He nodded again and made his way out. She left him to it, conscious of his pride, but watched from the foot of the stairs. 'What is your name?'

'Ivo,' he said, then stopped on the next step up without looking back at her. 'Major Lord Merton.' He took two more dogged steps up, then stopped again, one big, scarred hand on the rail. 'Or, no, I keep forgetting: Lord Kendall.'

'But the Earl of Kendall died just a few months

ago…' Her brain caught up with her tongue. 'I do beg your pardon—that was your father?'

'Yes.' He kept climbing.

Jane opened her mouth, then closed it firmly. The Earl would not want to stand there discussing his titles on the stairs or satisfying her curiosity about what the grandson, and now heir, of a marquess was doing fighting ridiculous odds in an alehouse.

She waited until the door closed behind him, then climbed the stairs and sat three steps down from the top, waiting for there to either be the sound of about six foot of man hitting the floor or for the door to open and the rest of his clothes to appear.

There was some thumping, but no thudding, and then a pair of boots and a heap of clothing were put outside and it was closed again, very firmly. Jane scooped up everything and carried the bundle down. Out of habit she shook each item out and checked the pockets and found only a handkerchief of plain, good linen and a crumpled bill from an inn dated a week before. She set that aside. Then, as she folded the coat, something crackled. Inside the breast pocket was a folded paper, creased and marked with dirty finger marks. It was unsealed. She smoothed it out and tucked it, along with the inn account, into the pocket in the front of the sketchbook that she used to keep notes and spare pieces of paper flat. Neither looked important and she could replace them in his pocket when the maid had finished setting the clothes to rights.

She found a chambermaid and arranged for whatever washing, pressing and brushing could be managed, then ordered herself a pot of tea in the tiny private parlour.

She was not going to fuss over Lord Kendall, she decided as she sipped. Nor, unusually in her experience, did he appear to expect her to do so. Her father and brother always wanted to be made much of when they were ill. Even a mild cold in the head was grounds for medicines, stream infusions, large fires in the bedchamber and much gruel.

In this case she had organised a hot brick for the bed, a jug of water and some willow bark powder for the bedside and His Lordship's clothes would be returned to proper order—that, surely, was all that would be required of her.

If he was prepared—and able—to escort her to Batheaston in return for his rescue, then she would be happy to accept, because he was certain to be more entertaining than Billing and he would save her from any male annoyances on the journey.

Unless Lord Kendall proved to be a male annoyance himself… She pondered the question, adding sugar to her tea as she did so, aware that her own immediate instincts might not be reliable. But his manner had held nothing of either the predator, or the rake, and she was quite well aware that, although she was perfectly presentable, she was no beauty to tempt a man to try unwelcome flirting.

Goodness, but Melissa would be delighted with news of this accidental meeting, although Jane rather suspected that Lord Kendall was not good-looking enough to satisfy her fantasies. There was nothing wrong with his height or figure; his hair—and he had all of it—was thick and dark and his teeth seemed good. But he was not what one would consider a handsome man, exactly. He was too…too *male* for elegance. His brows were too heavy, his mouth set too hard, his jaw looked stubborn and his nose was not straight. The heroes of Melissa's novels tended to be elegant, blond and modelled on Grecian statues—with the addition of clothing, of course.

Jane picked up her sketchbook and studied her drawings. He did have admirably defined muscles which would be both educational, and a pleasure, to draw in more detail. Although that pursuit of accurate detail was what had landed her in trouble in the first place…

I am an artist, I must not be hidebound by convention, I must be prepared to suffer for my art, she told herself. If drawing Lord Kendall naked could be defined as *suffering,* exactly. *As if I could ever pluck up the courage to ask him to pose in any degree of undress.*

When the clock struck six Jane decided to order her dinner and to send one of the waiters up to see whether Lord Kendall was awake and, if so, whether he wanted anything to eat. The parlour appeared to have no bell, so she opened the door. 'Oh!'

'I beg your pardon, Miss Newnham.' The Earl stepped back so that her nose was no longer virtually in his neckcloth. 'I was about to knock.'

'You have your clothes back,' she said.

Idiot, of course he has!

'As you see.' A fastidious valet would probably shudder, but the inn staff had done an excellent job and had even managed to iron the neckcloth into some semblance of crispness.

'Would you like to come in and sit down? I was just about to find someone and order dinner. It is early, I know, but I have to confess to feeling decidedly hungry.'

'Thank you.' He stepped into the room just as a maid appeared behind him, looking harassed and wiping her hands on her apron.

'The missus says, sorry the bell isn't there, but a gentleman in his cups fell over and pulled it out of the ceiling last week and would you and the gentleman be wanting anything in the way of dinner, miss? Only the London stage is due in about ten minutes and the Mail half an hour after that and the kitchen will be in a right bustle when they get in.'

'We were just about to order. Do you have an appetite, my… Ivo dear?'

He gave her a *look* down that not-straight nose. 'I do indeed, Jane *dear.*'

'Well, we've got game pie or a roast fowl or there's some collops of veal in a cream sauce.

And oxtail soup to start and an apple pie and cream.'

'Everything, if you please,' said His Lordship. 'And send in the cellar man.'

'Should you be drinking wine or spirits if you have had a blow to the head?' Jane enquired. 'I am not nagging,' she said hastily when she got The Look again. 'Merely concerned that you do not throw a fever, because that would hold us up.' She sat down at the table to demonstrate her lack of desire to fuss over him.

'Us? I was not aware that there was an *us*.' Lord Kendall drew out a chair and sat opposite, both hands flat on the table like a man ready to jump up and leave at any moment.

Jane found herself studying the grazes across the knuckles, the neatly trimmed nails, the tendons and veins, the plain gold signet ring, and jerked her attention away. This was no time to wonder about making a series of studies of hands.

'You have no money, I do. If I had not rescued you, goodness knows what would have happened to you. As a result of that rescue I am without my maid. You could escort me to Batheaston.'

'It would be scandalous for you to travel with

an unrelated man. If I had any confidence that I could ride that distance just now, then I would offer to escort you on horseback and you could hire a maid to travel with you in the carriage. As it is, the option of staying here together until I am strong enough to ride is an even more outrageous proposition.'

'You are very honest about your strength,' she remarked, intrigued. 'Most men would pretend they were perfectly capable, whatever the truth of the matter.'

'If we encounter trouble and my right arm is not strong enough to use a pistol—not that we have one—or otherwise deal with an attacker, then I would have put my self-esteem above your safety.' He studied her for a long moment. 'Are you acquainted with many gentlemen?'

'My father, my brother, the local gentry and their sons. Oh, and the Bishop of Elmham—the retired one—and his secretary and the Duke of Aylsham. I was a bridesmaid at his recent wedding.'

'You move in very respectable circles, Miss Newnham.'

'You mean the Duke being such a pattern card of perfection? I can assure you, marriage to my good friend Verity, who is the Bishop's daughter, has changed him considerably.'

'Why am I not surprised by that?'

Jane felt the sudden heat in her cheeks. 'Might I suggest that we do not quarrel, Lord Kendall? Otherwise I might be inclined to take myself—and my money—elsewhere.'

'I meant,' he said, with only the faintest twitch of bruised lips, 'that Aylsham doubtless required enlivening.'

Hmm, Jane thought. *That was as neat a piece of foot-removal from mouth as I have ever heard.*

'Of course you did,' she said cordially. He stared back, his expression blandly innocent. 'You are not at all what I expected an earl to be like.'

'No? I have spent the last nine years in the army, perhaps that accounts for it. I have had only three months' practice at being an earl and only two weeks of that in this country.'

'Nine? My goodness. How old are you?'

'Twenty-seven. I joined as an ensign.'

He looked older, she would have guessed at thirty, but perhaps that was the bruises and cuts and general air of hard-won experience. 'I am twenty-two,' she offered in an attempt to elicit more confidences.

'And fresh from the Season, I presume?'

'I have not had a London Season. Papa considered that local society would be quite sufficient, although Mama disagrees.'

And I have an expensive older brother, she could have added, but did not.

'And *was* it sufficient? There is no fiancé or a string of beaux left behind in London?'

'They would be in Dorset if I had any, which I do not. We were only in London visiting Aunt Hermione for a month because she has been unwell. Not that I want a beau, let alone a betrothal.'

Lord Kendall stopped tracing a crack in the planked table top with his index finger and looked up sharply. 'Why ever not?'

'Marriage and husbands seem to complicate life so much. They restrict it. I am an artist. Matrimony and art are not compatible—unless one is a man, of course.'

It was the first time she had said it out loud, the thing she had been thinking secretly. It felt momentous, just to say the words, *I am an artist*, and to mean them, not as a description of what she enjoyed doing as a pastime, but as something that defined her, Jane Newnham. Artist.

'Surely that is not what you should expect of marriage. You certainly draw with great proficiency and insight, but what has a husband to do with that? Most ladies sketch and paint in watercolour and I assume you all have drawing masters or governesses to teach you.'

'I am not interested in a mere genteel pastime,' Jane explained. The strange sense of recklessness her declaration had produced seemed to sweep through her, take over her voice. 'I want—I *need*—to improve, to paint in oils to be as good as I want, to be able to paint portraits to a professional standard.'

'You mean, earn your living as a portrait painter? Impossible,' Lord Kendall said flatly.

Is that what I meant? Could I do that?

It was a terrifying prospect, something that had never occurred to her. Then his look of disapproving incredulity struck home.

Anyone would think it was the equivalent of earning a living on my back.

Jane almost said so, swallowed, and recited, 'Artemisia Gentileschi, Elisabeth Vigée le Brun, Angelica Kauffman, Mary Beale, Sofonisba Anguissola—' She wished she could think of more female artists, especially modern English ones.

'Exceptions that prove the rule. I refuse to believe in that last one and, besides, you are an English gentlewoman of tender years. You must have a husband.' There was an edge to that statement, some hint of scorn, almost. Whatever it was, it made her bristle. If he had not thought it a possibility, why had he suggested it? And the thought was tantalising, alluring and dangerous. Could she?

'I *must* have a husband?' Jane snorted inelegantly, almost drunk on the terror of her own rebellion, on the possibilities his careless, scornful suggestion had thrown up. 'I shall be an independent artist and I neither need nor *want* a husband. Men are dull or unsuitable or untrustworthy. Or lacking in originality and imagination.'

'Thank you.' This time his lips showed no sign of that amused twitch.

'There is no need to take it personally. You are an earl and heir to a marquess,' she said with a dismissive wave of her hand. 'You are certainly more than suitable. For all I know you might be exciting and faithful. But it is academic, I am not talking about *you.*'

'We might be if your family discovers that we are spending the night here.' That was said without the hint of scorn.

Aha, there was definitely an amused twinkle in his eyes just now.

And they were rather nice eyes, dark blue, long-lashed. His best feature, in fact, although there were those shoulders… It was gratifying to make the blue sparkle and it would be a challenge to catch that in oils. But one battered earl was not the problem.

How much could I charge for a portrait? Could I really make my living?

He was still regarding her quizzically.

'They will not discover it,' she assured him. 'Why ever should they?'

'Miss Newnham—'

'Call me Jane, then we do not risk tripping up in our pretence of being brother and sister,' she suggested. Wrestling with the practicalities of their present situation was at least calming.

'Very practical, Jane. And I am Ivo, although I think you may forgo the frequent *dears*. Siblings are rarely so affectionate from what I have observed.'

That was true, in her experience at least. She and Hubert, her brother, had quarrelled their way through childhood and had nothing in common as adults.

The maid came in, unfurled a large white cloth across the table, replaced the tea things when Jane clutched at the tea pot, produced cutlery from her apron pocket and bustled out again.

'Ivo is a nice name. An unusual name. Mine is so dull—Plain Jane.' She poured herself more tea. 'Shall I ring for another cup? No? If I am to succeed as an artist, I think I should change it.' Already in her imagination a picture was forming of a studio, an easel, a chair and a *chaise longue* for her subjects, a scattering of tasteful props and drapes, herself in a flowing smock, paintbrushes stuck in her elegant but artistic coiffure. The dream of achieving elegance with her mousy, rather fine and wayward hair was perhaps the most improbable element of that vision.

'Like a *nom de plume*?' Ivo queried. 'That would be *nom de pinceau*, I think.'

'Paintbrush name?' She found herself smiling

at him. 'I should have to find something, certainly. Bath would be an excellent place to set up a studio, don't you think?'

'No, I do not. How much money do you have, Miss Newnham?' The sudden switch to seriousness wiped the delightful imaginings from her mind and, with them, the flutter of happiness.

She did not want to be serious. Laughter kept the nerves about what she had just discovered about herself from tying her stomach in knots. Jane raised her eyebrows with mock *hauteur*. 'It is surely somewhat early in our acquaintance for you to be considering dowries, Lord Kendall.'

He did not rise to her teasing, the irritating man. 'I could not agree more,' he said with unflattering emphasis. 'I meant, how much money do you have at your immediate disposal?'

'Thirty pounds. Sufficient for the journey and contingencies.'

'That is ample to hire a respectable maid for the remainder of your journey—and to sleep in your bedchamber tonight. I am sure this inn could supply you with a suitable young woman for a few days.'

It was what she had told Billing to do, not what she wanted to hear herself. 'We have already established that there is not room for three in that chaise. Not in any comfort.'

'I remain here, of course.' The bruises, which were beginning to colour up nicely, did nothing to make his expression any more amiable.

'With no money, no means of identification, a wound in your shoulder and the visage of a not very successful pugilist, my lord?' He was unsettling her and it helped to hit back. 'Unless you have an acquaintance living nearby, I suggest that it might be a long walk to wherever you might be known.'

'I am aware of that. I am also aware that I have placed a lady in a compromising position. What becomes of me need not concern you.'

'Oh, for goodness sake.' Jane jumped up. The tea things rattled and she just managed to stop the milk jug from tipping over. Lord Kendall got to his feet, but she flapped one hand at him, irritated. 'Sit, do. I want to pace up and down so as not to throw the sugar bowl at you. I did not haul you into my chaise and prepare to fend off ruffians with my parasol to leave you battered and destitute here. Those louts may have followed us for all you know.'

'Indeed. Another excellent reason why I want

you to go. It is not too late now for us to find you a maid and for you to drive to the next inn for the night.'

'I am not leaving you like this. You are patronising, irritating and, just at the moment, a thorough nuisance, but I refuse to have you on my conscience.'

'And I will not have your ruined reputation on mine.' He stood up again, clearly furious at having to grab at the back of a chair for balance.

'Poppycock,' Jane pronounced inelegantly. 'I will feel much safer with a gentleman's escort than with an unknown maidservant. And do sit down, you are swaying. No one knows me and, with you having been abroad until recently and with your face like that, I doubt anyone would recognise you either.' A fleeting memory of something Cousin Violet had been gossiping about when she had last seen her came to mind. 'And your grandfather has an estate close to Bath, does he not? Exactly where you need to be.'

Chapter Three

There was a pain in his hand and Ivo looked down to see his knuckles white on the back rail of the chair. He unclenched his fingers. His grandfather's house: exactly where he did not want to be and precisely where he should have gone on arriving back in England instead of haring off on that wild goose chase after Daphne Parris. Charles Parris's wilful little sister. The girl he had grown up with, seen transform from a plain, sulky child into an exquisite young woman in front of his bedazzled eyes.

He had fallen in love, had proposed on the eve of his departure with Charles to join their regiment in France. She would wait, she had promised, if he would promise to come back to her. He was her hero, so gallant, so fine in his scarlet regimentals. She had been enchanting, that evening, so lovely in her wide-eyed admiration of him and he had felt like a demi-god, believing he could defeat Napoleon single-handed if she only wished it.

He had known her parents would think her too young for a formal betrothal and she had, too, but they could keep it a secret, she had agreed as they exchanged tokens—an enamelled heart on a chain for her, a lock of her hair for him. That white-blonde curl had been in the wallet he had lost in Knightsbridge.

Had he been arrogant to believe the love she had professed so ardently would last and that she would wait until the fighting ended? Deluded, perhaps. It seemed that he had misunderstood the depths of her feelings, but not his own, not as the war had dragged on across Spain.

His promise to Daphne had brought him through times when it would have been easier just to give in and die. And then Charles, dying of one enemy neither of them could defeat, had told him that news had reached him that Daphne intended to marry a rakehell baronet. Ivo must promise to stop her, Charles had pleaded. He was the only one who had known of the secret betrothal and he could not seem to grasp that his sister might actually jilt his best friend.

And Ivo did swear to it, reassuring Charles that it would all be well, even as he fought back the pain at Daphne's betrayal, his mind reeling with the shock that she had changed so much and he had not been able, somehow, to sense it. He had promised Charles and he had failed.

He had told himself that it must be a misunderstanding, that she had lost faith in him somehow and that it could all be set right if only they could talk. That had kept him together, right up until the moment that they were face to face. After that… How were you supposed to feel when the woman you loved rejected you, sent men after you to beat that rejection into your thick skull? Did she hate him so much—or was this how a woman who married in defiance of friends and family and sacred promises reacted to defend that decision?

'Why were you in that alehouse?' Jane asked abruptly, jerking him out of the dark downward spiral of his thoughts. 'Are you avoiding your grandfather?'

That is usually the most restful option…

'I had made a promise to a friend. A dead friend.'

'Oh. I am so sorry.' She sat down again. 'And

that deathbed promise was what sent you into danger?'

'Charles—that was my friend's name—was worried about his younger sister. It seems he had every reason to be anxious, although at first I thought he was exaggerating because he was in a fever. I could not believe that Daphne would be so...foolish.' *So disloyal.* 'I tried to tell him he was worrying about nothing, tried to keep him calm but, when the story became clearer, I realised it was serious. She was being courted by a baronet with a wild reputation. I won't name him, but Charles was convinced that he had no good intentions towards Daphne, who is well dowered and fatherless into the bargain. Besides, she was already promised to someone else.' Someone who was not in England to protect her. Someone who had thought that a love could be kept alive for years on hasty, irregular letters scrawled by campfires.

'Once news reached England of Charles's death there would be no one to stop her or to warn off her seducer.' Except the man who had blithely gone off to fight the French in the happy certainty that Miss Parris would sit at home patiently waiting for him.

'And she would not heed her brother? Had he managed to write to her?'

'He did—and received a letter in reply. She was certain it was love. The man to whom she had had an understanding was not there, she had grown tired of waiting for him because he would surely have come for her if his feelings were true. She felt neglected, I am certain.'

And I should have thought more about how young she was, how much she would need the reassurance of constant letters, not my scribbled notes when I had the time and the energy to think of that other world apart from the battlefield.

He tried to keep those betraying emotions from his face and from Jane's bright, interested gaze, and was fairly certain he succeeded. But *was* the fault his neglect of her—or a fundamental misunderstanding of Daphne's character? Or had he mistaken the depth of her feelings for him in the first place?

'Charles declared that he would ask for leave, just as soon as he could haul himself out of bed. He had no idea just how sick he was, I realised. He told me that he would go home, forbid the match. He was his sister's guardian, after all, and he could not sit by and let her fall into the hands of a confirmed rakehell, even if she was prepared to break her engagement to the man he had expected her to marry.

'Charles had tossed and turned, distressed that his sister could have betrayed his best friend, tormented by his inability to imagine why she had done so. "I must stop her," he'd said, just before he sank into the final delirium. I promised to do what I could. I would have done so even without that promise. I had known her all the years she was growing up.'

I loved her. Despite everything I still...

'But you were in the army—how could you get away?' Jane leant forward, both elbows on the table among the cups and saucers. Her eyes were fixed on his face. She caught her lower lip between her teeth as though she was listening to some gripping tale of derring-do. Clearly she had no idea that this was even more personal than he was admitting.

'I would have asked for leave, of course, but, in the event, the news of my father's death reached me on the day we buried Charles. I had every good reason to hasten home to England and sell out and my colonel sent me on my way with his blessing. The Treaty of Fontainebleau had been signed, Napoleon was defeated, I could easily be spared.

'I was too late: Daphne had already eloped from home with her dubious baronet. Her aunts were distraught, but finally received a letter from her four days ago. She was back from Scotland where they had married and had been for weeks. I found her in her new home, a crumbling old house just outside Kensington. Sir Clement was away from home and I thought that being abandoned with cobwebs and surly, unpaid servants while he dealt with unspecified *business* would be enough to bring her to her senses. I suggested that he was paying off his most pressing creditors with promises of Daphne's money, but that got me a vase thrown at my head.' He did not repeat to Jane the angry, defiant words she had thrown first. It was foolish of him to believe that such beauty was incapable of venting such spite and anger. He was shocked as well as hurt. What had happened to the laughing, clinging girl he had left behind?

'Ouch,' Jane sympathised.

'I ducked,' he said with a shrug, pride making him hide the personal hurt from her. 'It hardly touched me. She was defiant and determined and she refused my offer to take her back to her aunts while the problem could be settled of how legal the marriage was. I told her that the courts might be able set aside the union, although it would take some time and money. I pointed out that she was still just under age, was abducted from her home and married without her brother's permission.' And he had managed it calmly, somehow hanging on to his temper, somehow refusing to let Daphne see how deeply this affected him. All he had achieved was to salvage a little empty pride.

'How did she respond?' Jane asked. 'With another vase?'

'No,' he said wryly. 'She laughed in my face and told me that she loved her husband, that she knew perfectly well he was a rakehell and that was what she wanted, not·a dull husband like all her friends had married.'

Like me, the man she was promised to, the man who had dared put duty before her.

'She wanted adventure, freedom—'

He sought for the least shocking way of translating Daphne's frank admissions. 'She had come to appreciate the joys of the marriage bed, she told me as she tugged on the bell pull and demanded that I leave. I could hardly abduct her myself, so I left to think over my tactics. I was aware that I was being followed, but thought no more of it than that she did not want to risk my return. An hour later, I was nursing a pint of ale and facing the fact that there was probably nothing I could do other than to report back to her aunts that she was not being held against her will and wanted to remain in the marriage. Then I was facing four large louts with clubs and brass knuckles.

'It seems she felt that, to ensure I left her alone, I needed more convincing than her words could achieve. Or perhaps she feared that I would confront her husband. Whichever it was, she had sent her grooms to deal with me. You arrived in the midst of their very persuasive arguments for forgetting the whole thing and going away.'

So, yes, he did want to go down to Merton Tower because he wanted to lay his hands on the best legal advice. And the man who would know how to find it—if he was not already employing it—was his famously litigious grandfather. He could go back to London and waste time trying to find the right lawyers to help the aunts with what was, almost certainly, a hopeless cause or he could swallow his pride and ask the Marquess. And, faced with Daphne Parris's welfare, his pride was unimportant. She was in the hands not just of a rakehell, but, it now seemed, one who employed violent brutes as his grooms.

'If she has lain with him, then she may be with child already,' Jane pointed out, with far less embarrassment than a single lady should be showing when discussing such a thing. 'And even if she is not, then surely the fact that the marriage has been consummated will make any kind of annulment very difficult, especially as she would probably protest that she was entirely willing to go with him. And if it was possible to separate them despite that, her reputation would be in tatters.' Her brow was creased with thought as she concentrated on the problem. If she was shocked by Daphne's story, then she was hiding the fact.

'Quite,' he agreed. 'But I promised Charles I would try.'

And I owe that laughing, reckless, charming friend of my childhood something. If only I could believe that some trace of her remains.

'And you *have* tried and she now knows of

someone who will help her if she does repent of the match,' Jane said.

'True.' That had not occurred to him and it was some small consolation. Daphne had shown the spirit and determination to do what she had wanted and, surely, if she came to regret her actions she would show as much determination in escaping. 'I do need to get to Bath,' he admitted finally as he sat down. 'If we are careful, then we should escape detection and a scandal of our own.'

To her credit, Jane Newnham showed neither disappointment in him for failing to extricate the deluded bride nor triumph at getting her own way and his escort. He was coming, reluctantly, to like his improbable rescuer.

'That is a relief,' she said. 'I will feel so much more comfortable with your company on the road and I will not have to worry about you.'

It was a novelty, to have anyone to worry about him. His mother had died when he was five, he had no siblings and his father had appeared to believe that no Merton might be vulgar enough to be shot, skewered or blown up on a battlefield and, therefore, there was no cause for concern when his only son joined the army. Ivo wondered sometimes if the late Earl had ever seen him as anything other than the fulfilment of his duty. The title had been secured, tutors and instructors would look after the boy, there was nothing for him to trouble himself about.

As for his grandfather's emotions, they had always been a mystery to him.

'We will have our dinner soon. If we retire immediately after it, then we will be able to make an early start.' Jane finished her tea and carried the tray to the sideboard.

'It seems I have acquired a very managing sister,' he said. He meant it for a joke and wondered at the shadow that seemed to cross her face.

'It is about time I learned to manage and not be a mouse,' she said, with no amusement in her voice at all. 'I have accepted too much and not thought of alternatives.' The alternatives she appeared to be thinking about did not seem to be making her very happy, judging by her frown.

That sudden seriousness was a pity, Ivo thought, leaning back in the chair and trying to find a position where his bruised ribs would allow him to breathe in comfort. Jane's voice was pleasant, but nothing out of the ordinary until she was amused, when he found it made him want to smile, even when he did not know what the joke was.

There was clearly some difficult history behind that bitter remark, just as there was behind her quite impossible implication that she intended to earn her living from her art. He was curious, but he did not know her well enough to probe—she would, very rightly, snub curious questions. Still, pondering someone else's concerns was a pleasant distraction from considerations of either his own future or the futility of attempting to save Daphne, the stubborn Lady Meredith, from herself. He flatly refused to let himself think any more tonight about his own feelings for Daphne.

The maid came in with a laden tray and began to set food out on the table. She was followed by the cellarman, cobwebs in his hair and on the vast baize apron he wore, and Ivo discussed what he recommended, received a frown from Jane when he ordered ratafia for her and added a light hock to his own order of claret.

'I am resolved to ask for what I want and not meekly accept what is considered *appropriate*,' she said a few minutes later, wrinkling her nose in distaste over the word as she ladled out steaming oxtail soup.

'Are you used to drinking wine?' he asked, suddenly wary. Jane was a handful sober, he winced inwardly at the thought of her a trifle high-flown.

'An occasional glass with meals,' she said demurely. 'Ratafia makes my teeth ache, it is so sweet.'

She caught her lower lip between her teeth as she concentrated on passing him his bowl of soup and Ivo watched her, speculating on just why she was so set against marriage. This business about setting up as an artist was obviously so much fantasy. His immediate reaction was to wonder if she had become tired of being a wallflower, but he could not believe that the gentlemen of her acquaintance would be so unappreciative of such an interesting young lady. No great beauty, of course, but perfectly passable and clearly equipped with the correct social graces when she chose to utilise them.

'Your parents cannot approve of your desire to paint professionally,' Ivo remarked when the business of passing bread rolls and butter was dealt with. 'But they must be aware of your considerable talent.'

'Young ladies learn to sketch and to paint in watercolour. Approved themes are landscape, children and rural scenes—provided the rustics inhabiting the landscape are picturesque and not squalidly poor. Serious figure painting or the use of oils is not considered suitable,' she informed him. 'Besides, they do not know of my ambitions.'

'So how did you learn?'

'I had a watercolour and drawing tutor. Then my friend Verity, the one who has married the Duke of Aylsham, held regular meetings for her friends at her home. Our parents believed we were gathering to read worthy texts. Instead we had an entire turret in the Bishop's Palace to ourselves and our work.' He must have shown his surprise at the word because she put down her spoon with some emphasis. 'Female occupations may be *work* and just as serious as men's interests. Verity is an antiquarian. I paint. Lucy is a pianist, Melissa is a novelist and Prudence is a Classical scholar. None of us has parents who approve of our passions except for Verity.

The Bishop is also a scholar and encourages her work.'

'I gather that not a great deal of reading was done in your reading circle.'

'On occasion Melissa reads novels, Prudence reads Greek and Latin texts, Lucy reads music, Verity studies learned journals and I dip into the lives of painters. As far as our parents are concerned we study sermons and tracts together. Although the Bishop has retired—he had a stroke, poor man—he is still sent any manner of spiritual publications. Our parents are most impressed by the tone of the pamphlets we bring home.'

'And the Bishop connives in this?'

'He has no idea we are doing anything of which our parents would not approve and so he has been very generous in continuing to allow us to use Verity's tower, even though she has married and left home. He can hear the pianoforte, of course, and he would admire my sketches of the garden. He knew Lucy borrows books from his library and that Melissa writes, but then, all young ladies do these things. As amateurs. Dabbling,' she said with a suggestion of gritted teeth, 'is encouraged, but Heaven forfend that we become *serious*.'

'But you have left your remaining friends, and your tower of sanctuary, and are travelling to stay with a relative.'

'Yes.' She tore the bread roll in half with a vicious twist that made Ivo wince. 'In disgrace.'

'Might I ask for what reason? Not, I assume because of an unwise…er…friendship with a man, from what you have said about your views on marriage.'

'Oh, it was a man,' Jane said blithely. 'Arnold the under-footman.'

Ivo froze, soup spoon halfway to his lips. 'A *footman*?'

'He has quite remarkable muscular development—apparently he boxes in his own time—and I wanted to draw him and he was perfectly willing to strip off for half a guinea.'

'You were drawing him in the nu—? Nak—? *Without clothes*?'

'Of course. That is, *he* was without clothes, I was not. But how else am I going to learn about male anatomy?' she asked with sweet reasonableness.

Ivo dropped his spoon. Regrettably there was

still soup in the bowl and the result was not helpful to his general appearance. 'From books?' he suggested, attempting to remedy matters with his napkin. 'Prints of art works? Statues?'

'It is not the same as real flesh and blood,' Jane pointed out. 'It was remarkably useful to see your back under tension, for example.' His expression must have finally registered because she added, 'Naturally, I will give you the drawing if you wish. I am aware that I was carried away by the opportunity and should have asked your permission first. But it was so useful to see your spine close to,' she said wistfully.

Ivo reflected—inappropriately, given present company—that women had expressed appreciation of his body before now, but never in quite those terms and none of them had seemed remotely interested in his vertebrae. 'Please, keep it,' he said, dropping the napkin back into his lap. 'Feel free.'

Jane looked up with such eagerness on her face that he was irrationally glad of the napkin's coverage, even though there was the table between them. 'I *meant*,' he said repressively, as much for himself as for her, 'feel free to keep the picture. Although not to draw any more of me.'

Her face fell. 'Not in any absence of clothes, at any rate.'

The room was becoming remarkably hot and he wished he could mop his brow.

'Thank you.' Her smile was sudden, sunny, and he found himself smiling back despite the fact that she was going to prove a confounded nuisance and a worry he could well do without.

But she saved you from a much worse beating, his conscience reminded him.

The maid came in to clear the soup and Ivo changed the subject abruptly. Things were bad enough without informing the inn's staff that his 'sister' drew men in the nude. 'I suggest we stop at Newbury tomorrow night. That is about fifty miles. I imagine that you will not want to travel further in one day.'

A roast fowl and a carving knife were set in front of him along with a pie with a flaking golden crust. A dish with the rich aroma of cream and onions was placed in front of Jane. The maid deposited a bowl of vegetables in the middle of the table and made way for the cellarman with his bottles.

'Fifty miles sounds quite far enough,' Jane agreed. 'We will be lucky to do it in six hours,

I imagine, and with your injuries that is quite long enough to be bounced about in a chaise. Game pie or veal? They both look very good.'

'Some of each, please. Would you care for some chicken?'

My goodness, we are both managing a very good appearance of gentility—me with my bruises and she with her scandalous intentions.

Jane cut into the pie, placed a generous portion on a plate, added a slice of veal and some sauce, leaving room for vegetables, and pushed the plate across the table, receiving a chicken wing and a slice of breast in return. She helped herself to peas and carrots, with a mental lecture on eating too much—there was apple pie still to come—and took a sustaining sip of wine, then another appreciative swallow.

'I beg your pardon? I am afraid I missed that.'

'I was merely moaning,' she confessed. 'With pleasure.'

Ivo narrowed his eyes at her. For some reason there was colour on his cheekbones. Perhaps the roast fowl had been very hot.

'The wine,' Jane explained. 'Delicious.' She waited while he added chicken and vegetables to his loaded plate—clearly the military habit of eating well when one had the opportunity had not left him. 'I had not expected such good food. And the Pelican at Speenhamland, just outside Newbury, has a very good reputation, I believe, so we should eat well again tomorrow night.'

'The *Pelican* is extortionately expensive.' Ivo poured red wine into his own glass. 'There is a rhyme that says it is called the Pelican because of its enormous bill.'

'We can afford it,' Jane said, with an airy wave of her wine glass. The hock was really exceedingly good and eating alone with a gentleman had all the pleasure of novelty.

'*You* should be saving your resources. Naturally, I will repay you as soon as possible, but splashing your blunt around at the Pelican, as though we were Admiral Nelson—'

'He is dead,' Jane pointed out. Perhaps she would try a little of the game pie as well, it did smell delicious, and the food was just slipping down with the aid of the wine. It was so pleasant not to have Mama sending her warning looks down the table.

'A lady eats like a dainty bird. A lady has the

most refined appetite. A lady drinks half a glass of wine at the most...'

'Do *you* think ladies should just peck at their food and not show an appetite?'

'No.' Ivo sounded definite. 'For a start it is a waste of the effort the cooks have put into preparing the food and food should not be wasted. Going hungry is no joke. Besides, a lady with a healthy appetite for food usually has a healthy appetite for—' He broke off, coughing. 'Sorry, a crumb in my throat. *For life*, I was going to say.'

'Are you all right? You have become quite pink.'

'I am perfectly well, thank you.' Ivo topped up his glass. 'To get back to what we were discussing: Nelson might be dead, but everyone who is anyone calls at the Pelican.'

Jane shrugged. 'But I am not *anyone*, I am merely an unknown lady from Dorset. And no one will recognise you with those bruises if they are not expecting to see you. We must think of a surname if we agree to continue as brother and sister.' She scanned the table for inspiration and fixed on the vegetable dish. 'Pease? Pomeroy? Pomfret? Poppinghall?'

'Preposterous. We are Mr and Miss Turnham

who will be taking a private parlour—and going off to find an inn in Newbury if there is no privacy to be had at the Pelican, believe me!'

'Yes, Ivo,' Jane agreed meekly, earning herself a suspicious look. It was a novelty to get her own way about anything, almost as much as this whole adventure was new and exciting. Mama and Papa were loving parents, but they were also exceedingly conventional ones, in her opinion. And Mama was ambitious. Jane would be a pattern book of good behaviour if constant nagging could achieve it—and as a consequence of this behaviour she was confident that Jane would find herself an eligible partner. Even a titled one might be possible because, as Mrs Newnham kept repeating *ad nauseum*, 'Look at what Verity Wingate has managed.'

Jane had pointed out that there were no eligible dukes presently available, but that had merely sent her mother back to the *Peerage* to check each ducal line for unmarried heirs, or sons of heirs. But none was in Dorset and it was too much for even the most optimistic mama to hope that any would stray into the path of Miss Newnham, so her parents, who had treated as mere politeness previous vague invitations from Aunt

Hermione in her letters, had decided to see what might be achieved.

'Poor dear Hermione has not been well, it seems. We really should make the effort to visit her now she has recovered. And she has such a generous nature,' Mama had murmured.

Jane had no trouble in translating that as, *If we play our cards right my wealthy sister-in-law will fund a come-out.*

Her father's younger sister was inclined to approve of her niece, it seemed, and the hoped-for invitation for Jane to make her somewhat belated London debut next Season was on the verge of being made, if the hints Aunt had dropped were to be believed. And then, one naked footman later, Jane was on her way to the sedate safe-keeping of Cousin Violet whose sole male indoor servant was sixty if he was a day.

Her wine glass was empty and both the bottles were nearer Ivo's side of the table. Jane pointed this out.

'You have had quite enough to drink.'

'Two glasses only.'

'Three and that is doubtless two too many.'

Perhaps it would not be as easy as she had thought, getting her own way with Lord Kendall. Jane reached for the bottle and he moved it out of reach, his expression suddenly reminding her that he had been an officer and was used to being obeyed.

'You, my lord, are no f…fun.' Although perhaps he was right after all, her tongue had almost got in a tangle and it was a most improper thing to say, mumbled or otherwise.

'I am delighted that you think so, because that is absolutely the impression I wish to give, Miss Newnham. This entire expedition should not be amusing, entertaining or, in any way, *fun*. If we are fortunate it will be routine, dull and uneventful. If not, it has the potential for scandal, disaster and extreme embarrassment—'

He broke off as they were interrupted once again with more food—the promised apple pie. The open door admitted the noise and bustle of stagecoach passengers, the sound of the guard blowing his horn, impatient to be off, the cries of, 'Here! Waiter!'

'Close the door firmly, please,' Ivo said to the maid as she carried out the remains of the main course. 'You see—anyone could blunder in at any time. I must be mad. We should return you to your parents, not be planning to set out towards Bath.'

'Absolutely not. Oh, bother, she has forgotten the cream.' Jane looked round, then remembered that the bell was not functioning.

'I should not have even contemplated going to Batheaston with you,' Ivo said, ignoring the cream shortage completely. 'I cannot imagine what I was thinking. I will take you back to your parents in London first thing tomorrow morning.'

'No! I will not go and you cannot make me.'

'I most certainly can.' Ivo got to his feet and circled the table to her side.

He's in pain, she realised, even as she pushed her chair back. *Tired and in pain.*

He was white under the tan his army life had given him and he could not quite hide the wince as he moved his arm incautiously. It was an effort to feel sympathetic with a large male looming over her, but she made the attempt.

'Shall we sleep on it? In the morn—'

There was a sudden increase in noise behind her, the door swung open. 'I quite forgot the cream, miss. We're that busy—'

The maid broke off with a little shriek as

Ivo moved and the door hit him square on the wounded shoulder. With a gasp he spun round under a shower of something white, thick and sticky.

'Oh, lawks, miss.'

Chapter Four

'Lawks' struck Jane as somewhat inadequate under the circumstances. If Ivo had opened the wound up again infection could set in at the worst, or they would be delayed at the best. 'Go and fetch hot water and cloths immediately—and close the door after you!' She went to his side and found, to her relief, that he was muttering curses. If he could swear, then he couldn't be in too much pain.

When she touched him, he straightened up and let go of his shoulder.

'No, stay there, wait a moment before you try and move.' She rested one hand on his unhurt shoulder, but it was shrugged off.

'Don't fuss, the stiches are intact. But after ten years fighting, I could swear I am more battered after less than a day in your company than I ever was on the battlefield, Jane.'

'Of all the unfair—' She broke off, conscious of the maid ineffectually dabbing at the spilled cream with her apron. 'Please fetch some hot water and towels as I asked. That is making things worse, not better.'

'What the devil *is* this mess?' he demanded, mopping his face with his handkerchief.

'Cream, I am sorry to say. Very thick cream in copious amounts. I only hope they have someone able to clean your coat. I fear you will have to wash your hair to get it all out.'

The maid came back with a bowl of steaming water and some cloths as Ivo struggled out of his coat. 'Here.' He thrust it at the flustered girl as Jane took the bowl. 'Kindly do what you can to restore that.' As she fled with it he turned, took the bowl, put it on the table and plunged his head into it, scrubbing at his hair and face. 'This is the final straw,' he said grimly as Jane handed him a cloth. 'I am going to bed and so are you. You will lock the door and you will not emerge until I call you in the morning. Is that clear?'

'Perfectly.' She bit her lip as he took a final exasperated swipe at his dripping hair. 'But might we eat the apple pie first?' She tried an encouraging smile.

'I find nothing amusing about this situation, Miss Newnham. If we are fortunate, I may be able to appear tomorrow morning as your escort looking merely as though I buy my clothes at a down-at-heel second-hand stall. If we are not, then you will be accompanied by someone closely resembling the local rat catcher. Neither are suitable escorts for a young lady, especially one who should not be drawing attention to herself, given the irregular nature of this enterprise.'

Jane managed to choke back the laughter. 'Quite. Absolutely. I was not laughing at you. It was, um, hysteria, I think.' Somehow she did not think that Ivo would appreciate the true explanation, that heroes in Melissa's novels were not sent reeling by careless maids and showered with cream. One of *her* heroes would have avoided the door with a graceful swerve, typical of an accomplished fencer. Real life was clearly far removed from fiction.

The damp, battered, irritable man in front of her frowned, then blinked as the water on his lashes ran into his eyes. 'Confound it, Jane. I can organise a baggage train, lead a cavalry charge and deal with an ambush by snipers—I do not appreciate being thwarted at every turn by a chit of a girl who appears to attract chaos like iron filings to a magnet.'

Chaos? Chit?

'Might I remind you that I had nothing to do with your wounds? Perhaps you should retire to bed as you suggest if you find my company so tiresome.'

'And miss this apple pie, Sister dear?' He made his way, jaw set, back to his seat and waited while Jane, shaking her head, served pie—without cream. 'And perhaps you should return to London,' he added darkly.

'I am going on to Batheaston, whatever you say. You can hardly make me go back by force and I am the one paying the postilion,' she pointed out.

'I could wish I had you under my command for twenty-four hours, Miss Newnham,' Ivo said grimly. 'But you are quite correct, you are not responsible for the pathetic state that I am in.'

'Pathetic? What nonsense,' she said briskly. 'You were fighting back against ridiculous odds at the alehouse—and those louts were armed. And that door opening just then was a complete accident, anyone might have been struck by it. You are not going to make me feel sorry for you with such tactics, Ivo.'

'*Sorry* for me?' Ivo demanded, indignant. The little witch! And then he closed his mouth with a snap. It was true, he had been within inches of feeling very hard done by. Not that he would ever want Jane Newnham, or anyone else, to pity him.

Not that I haven't got good reason for being in a foul temper, he thought.

He missed his regiment; he hurt all over, including in places he'd hardly been aware of before, even after battle; he had failed to carry out Charles's dying wish; the girl he loved and had expected to marry had run off with a rakehell in preference to him and had ordered him to be beaten for objecting. On top of that, a new life he did not relish was waiting for him in Somerset and he had his hands full with an argumentative, awkward female.

So far, so bad. Now pull yourself together, Major, you have been in worse fixes. You've got food, shelter and no one is shooting at you. Yet.

For all he knew Jane's father, armed with a

shotgun, would be setting out from London when that sour-faced maid returned.

'If you have finished your dinner, I suggest we retire to our rooms as I proposed fifteen minutes ago,' he said with what dignity he could muster in the face of Jane cheerfully scraping the last drop of apple sauce out of her bowl. She knew she had the upper hand—and the money tightly clenched in it. If she would not see reason then his duty was clear—he must escort her safely to her relative in Batheaston and do his best to discourage her from this insane scheme of earning her own living.

Goodness knew, he was grateful for her help back in Kensington, but if she went around helping complete strangers on an impulse like that, he shuddered to think who or what she might pick up next.

'Very well, I confess to feeling quite weary. I cannot imagine why—I am usually wide awake after dinner,' she admitted.

'That,' Ivo said grimly, 'is the wine.' Which was yet another thing to keep in mind on the journey. By the time they arrived he was going to be fully qualified to write a handbook: *The Care and Safeguarding of Wilful Young Ladies.*

In two volumes, price three shillings each, to be had of any reputable stationers... The country must be full of fathers who would pay good money for that.

'What are you smiling about?' she asked as she got to her feet. 'Not plotting to kidnap me and return me to my parents, I trust?'

'No, I admit defeat on that head. I was merely recovering my sense of humour from the dark corner where it was cowering, whimpering.'

Jane laughed. 'I must be a sad trial to you, Ivo. Never mind, the day after tomorrow you can be rid of me.'

'A cause for cheerfulness indeed,' he said, answering her smile as he held the door for her. 'The rooms have keys, I believe. Please lock your door and wedge a chair under the handle as well.'

'That seems a little dramatic,' Jane protested as they reached the landing.

'Humour me. I have no wish to have to leap out of bed in the small hours to rescue you from some drunken buck who has discovered by chance that every key in this place fits all the doors.'

He was still smiling at her wicked chuckle as

he stripped off his clothes and climbed between the sheets to lay his throbbing head on the pillow.

Jane had a headache. To be more accurate, as she was informed by Ivo, she was suffering from a well-deserved hangover.

'You are a novice drinker, no wonder it has affected you. I would advise one glass in future and plenty of water with it,' he added with a marked lack of sympathy as they climbed into the post chaise at eight the next morning.

He was clearly stiff and sore to the point of gritted teeth and she had a thick enough head to resolve never to touch another drop of alcohol again, so they were silent for the first few miles as the coach travelled towards Brentford. She tried to find enthusiasm for the view of Kew Bridge, then closed her eyes in silent anguish as they were jolted over the town's notoriously stony main street.

'This is Hounslow,' Ivo said, waking her from an uneasy doze some time later.

Jane roused herself to peer out of the window at the bustling street. 'Is it the Heath next?' She squinted at the road book, half expecting to see *Here Be Highwaymen* inscribed along the edges of the strip map in the manner of ancient charts with their dragons and strange sea monsters.

'It is.' Ivo was looking out on to Hounslow High Street as they rattled through without stopping, passing a London-bound stage drawn up outside the George Inn. 'We will change horses at Colnbrook on the far side. You sound apprehensive—there are very few highwaymen to worry about nowadays.'

'That is like saying that there are very few crocodiles in a stretch of river—it only takes one to eat you,' Jane said. 'And I do not believe any of those tales about gallant gentlemen of the road like Claude du Val offering to dance with the ladies he held up.'

'I am sure all of them are nasty, dirty, uncivilised louts,' Ivo agreed. 'And I am equally certain that our postilion will be able to outdrive them, even if one did appear.'

'A pity.' Jane scrabbled in the depths of her reticule and produced the little muff pistol that was stretching the fabric. 'I was rather hoping to try this out. I quite failed to disentangle it in Kensington in the heat of the moment, which was very remiss of me. It would surely have given those bullies pause when they saw it.'

'Indeed. Is it loaded?' Ivo said calmly. He sounded like a man attempting to talk someone down off a high ledge.

'Of course it is. I think. But, naturally it is not cocked.' She studied it, lower lip caught between her teeth. 'At least, now I come to look at it, I am not certain.'

'If you were to remove your finger from the trigger, turn it away from its current aim at the middle of my chest and hand it to me, I will check.'

She surrendered the little weapon into Ivo's large hand where it looked even more like a toy.

'Not cocked and unloaded, praise be to whatever guardian angel looks after rackety young women. Do you have powder and bullets for it?'

'No.'

Rackety young women indeed! On consideration she rather liked the sound of it. *It sounds positively dashing...*

'Then what was the point of bringing it?'

Ivo did not quite say, *Foolish chit*, but, judging by his expression, it was a near run thing.

'It made you wary enough,' she retorted. 'I

should have thought it would make a highway-man think twice about attacking me.'

'Certainly it would. He would hesitate long enough to decide whether to club you over the head as a nuisance or break your wrist to make you drop it. Where the devil did you get such a thing?'

'My Uncle Giles gave it to Mama one Christmas. I think it was a joke and she would not dream of using it, but I knew where it was and thought it might be useful. And do not roll your eyes at me! What was I supposed to do if we were waylaid? Have Billing glare at them?'

'That would probably have been more effective, especially as you were unable to produce it in Kensington.'

That was unfortunately true. Perhaps a rackety lifestyle would not suit her after all.

'And what will you do if we *are* waylaid, might I ask?' she asked.

'It is highly unlikely to occur. If someone did attempt it and the postilion was unable to outrun them, then I imagine there are slim pickings here.'

'There is my jewellery in my dressing case and

more than twenty pounds in my reticule. You might consider that slim pickings, but I do not.'

'I agree, losing the money would be exceedingly inconvenient and I suggest that you hide fifteen pounds under one of the seat squabs immediately. But a young lady's trinkets are hardly likely—'

'Um...'

'Um? Why does that fill me with foreboding? What have you stolen from your unfortunate parents?'

'Nothing whatsoever.' Jane was indignant. 'The diamond parure *and* the pearl set are both mine, left to me by Great-Grandmama. I took them up to London because I wanted to have them valued. When I had asked Papa he said I should not worry my head about them and that, even you must agree, was an infuriating thing to say.'

'Must I? And why should you need them valued?'

'I was not certain, then,' she admitted. 'The idea of living independently and painting was just wishful thinking because I never expected that I would have the opportunity, not for years until Mama accepted that I was completely on the shelf and despaired of me. But now I know I want to sell the jewellery in order to set up my studio. It was only yesterday, talking to you, that I realised that going to Bath was the perfect opportunity to make what had been a daydream into reality.'

She rather thought she heard an ironic mutter of, *'Despair? The very word.'*

'Anyway, it was only a dream and a plan for the future, but then here I am, being sent off to Batheaston—which is right on the doorstep of Bath which must be an excellent place to obtain commissions, even if it is not the height of fashion any longer. Just think of all those moneyed people who retire there, all wanting elegant trifles to spend their money on.'

'Have you considered precisely how you, an unknown female, are to attract the attention of these eager, wealthy clients?'

'I thought about it last night.' The details were somewhat cloudy this morning and she had to concentrate hard to present her plan concisely. 'I intend to rent a *very* small shop in a select street and create a tasteful window display—just one portrait on an easel with artistic draperies and a notice—in gilt, I thought, in a flowing script—

Portraits by X. Enquire within. And I will have my studio inside. I will have to have my new name decided before then, of course.' She smiled at him, warmed by the happy vision. 'All I need are one or two commissions to start with and then word of mouth will do the rest.'

Ivo did not smile back. 'That is insanity.'

'No, it is not. Why are you being so discouraging?'

'Because you have no idea what it will cost for the rent, let alone the quantity of materials you will need. You could lose every penny you can raise from those gems and it is quite certain that you will lose your reputation. You must employ a maid to lend you countenance—which is more expense—and even then, you will be seen as little better than a…than an actress.'

'And I know just what you mean by that! Why a lady employed in a respectable artistic career should be considered in the same light as a street walker, I cannot imagine.'

'Because she cannot be thought to be supporting herself and it would therefore be concluded that she has a male protector,' Ivo said.

'But do consider, Ivo.' She twisted round on the seat to face him and make her point more strongly. 'There are so few female portraitists at work that the profession cannot have acquired the stigma that acting has. I would have thought that ladies might feel more comfortable sitting for a female artist and they must surely think one safer than a man if it is a picture of their daughters in question.'

'Tell me, Jane—are your parents white of hair and addicted to drink?'

'Certainly not. Neither drinks to excess and Mama is only forty-six and hardly uses any... I mean she has no grey hair and Papa is forty-eight and has just the slightest touch of silver at the temples. Why ever should you suppose—? Oh, unkind! You think I have made them go grey with anxiety.' She would have added more, but the carriage made a sharp left and right turn and came to a halt. 'We are stopping.' She peered through the glass and fanned herself with her hand, laughing at her own idiotically racing pulse. 'I thought we had been waylaid for a moment. Where is the Heath?'

'We have crossed it, bickering. The sound of our acrimony must have scared away the hordes of skulking ne'er-do-wells who might suppose the chaise contained a bear with a sore head and a cockatrice. This is Colnbrook and the George Inn. Do you wish to enter?'

Jane studied the façade of the inn. It looked respectable and Mama always maintained that on a journey one should take advantage of whatever decent amenities came one's way. 'I think so.'

She came back into the yard to find Ivo leaning against the chaise while the postilion argued with the ostler over the proposed horses for the change. A be-whiskered ancient had hobbled up and was clearly in the throes of a long and gruesome story.

'...and down they'd go into the boiling vat beneath. Ah, famous for its meat stews was the Ostrich,' he was saying with a cackle as she reached Ivo's side. 'And the landlord made himself rich on all the possessions he found in their bedchamber.'

'And what happened to this villain of a landlord?' Ivo enquired.

'’Twas in ancient times, so they say. Before King Henry's day, even. Hanged, drawn and quartered he was, his guts wound out on a windlass before his very eyes, his todger cut—'

'Yes, thank you. Have a pint of the best, that

must have made you thirsty.' There was a clink of coin and the ancient tottered off, his thanks floating back to them.

'What on earth was that all about?' Jane demanded as the postilion finally agreed on a new pair and Ivo helped her into the chaise.

'A murderous innkeeper at the Ostrich, opposite. The bed was part of a mechanism that tipped the sleeper into a vat in the cellars, so the story goes.'

'No! How terrifying. I shall have to check every inn bed in future or I will have dreadful nightmares.'

'Ridiculous,' Ivo said briskly. 'No one could get away with that for long in this modern age.'

'But what if one was the first victim? Goodness, but it would make a dramatic painting, would it not? The poor sleeper half-awake, clutching at the sheets in terror as he slid inexorably to his doom… The evil landlord stirring his bubbling cauldron below. But perhaps too gruesome to be commercial. I shall have to tell my friend Melissa about it—I am sure she can incorporate it into one of her novels.'

'Hardly a very suitable pastime for a lady, writing about such things.'

'You sound like my father when he found me reading a novel. And it is not a pastime: Melissa intends finding a publisher for her work.'

Ivo's silence was more stinging than words would have been. Jane turned a shoulder on him and stared out of the window.

'If you are going to sulk all the way to Newbury...' he said after they had passed through two villages.

'I am not sulking. I am refraining from conversation with someone who is prejudiced and antiquated in his views.'

'You, Miss Newnham, are a severe trial to my patience.'

'Then please feel free to descend at the next change of horses and make your own way to Bath. As a soldier I imagine you are used to marching.'

'I am—*was*—a cavalry man.'

'How dashing.' She turned to look at him. 'Oh, do not look like that! I was not being sarcastic. The cavalry has such glamour. I would love to have painted you in your uniform astride your mount. What colour was it?'

'Percy is black with one white foot, sixteen

point three hands tall and is in livery stables in London until I can retrieve him.'

Jane relaxed a little. Ivo sounded warm and human when he described his horse, perhaps she was misjudging him.

'Can you draw horses with any degree of competence?' he asked.

That truce lasted all of ten seconds!

'Competently,' she admitted. 'Not as well as I draw people.'

'Then I fear you will receive no commission from me. Percy has been through too much on my behalf to have to make do with mere competence.' The twist of his mouth was mocking when he added, 'And you are attracted to painting solely what is glamorous or flashy? Will your subjects only be beautiful women and handsome men? I note you did not wish to paint my portrait until you heard about the uniform.'

'That is unfair.' Jane tipped her head to one side and studied him. When she met his quizzical gaze she realised it was the first time she had done so while he was aware of it. 'You cannot be described as handsome,' she said, as dispassionately as she was able. 'Your features are irregular. However, your figure is good, if not elegant, your hair is thick and dark, which lends an air of drama... One would need to pose you against some rugged outdoor scene, I believe.'

'Do you intend to be as ruthlessly frank with all your intended sitters?'

It was attractive that Ivo did not appear to be personally wounded by her assessment. 'Of course not,' Jane said.

And then he smiled and something inside her seemed to take a sudden sharp breath. Not handsome, but when his face was lit up with genuine amusement and that smile was directed at her, he was...

Oh, my goodness.

He made her want to smile in return. He made her want to touch him. He made her feel... female.

'Why am I different, then?'

'You are a friend.' *Is he?* The word had come to her lips without any thought—she knew next to nothing about Ivo's character, he spent most of his time disapproving of her and yet *friend* did not seem inappropriate. It was considerably safer than the purely factual description.

Large, male creature with decided animal magnetism who is sitting so close to me in a confined space that I can feel the heat of his thigh through my skirts.

'I am flattered.' It was impossible to tell whether he was laughing at her. 'And we are past Slough and this is the famous Salt Hill where the Four Horse Club gathers on its excursions. Did you know they drive out from London at a sedate trot all the way? They stop at various hostelries for food and drink, arrive at Salt Hill, spend the night and trot back the next morning.'

'Every time the same route? How boring. I would want to explore—and at faster than a trot if I had a team of four in hand. How thrilling to drive,' she added wistfully. 'Where will we change next?' She found the road book and opened up the strip map. Geography seemed a much safer topic than Ivo's looks.

'Maidenhead, so we have fresh horses before we tackle the infamous Maidenhead Thicket, although its highwaymen may be as thin on the ground as Hounslow Heath's these days. Even so, I think we had best tuck your jewels and money under the seat.'

'I see the place, it is marked on the map. You know, I have always thought that Maidenhead is a most improbable name for a town—I mean, maidenheads and virginity are not a topic for polite society, yet here is a place actually referring to the matter.'

Ivo made a sound somewhere between a choke and a laugh. 'I suspect it is a corruption of some Middle English words that have nothing to do with, er, virginity.'

'That is disappointing—I had imagined it as an exotic place of dissipation. Oh, stop laughing at me, Ivo, it is not my fault that young ladies are kept so sheltered that one cannot even ask a question about a place name.'

'No, it is not, but the longer I associate with you, Miss Jane Newnham, the more I am convinced that actually locking up all young ladies before marriage would be an excellent plan.'

Chapter Five

They arrived at the Pelican in Speenhamland, near Newbury, at six o'clock without any excitements along the road and certainly without an encounter with a highwayman, romantic or otherwise.

The yard was bustling and their postilion drew up in one corner, giving Ivo space to hand Jane out into a gap between chaise and wall and away from disembarking passengers and the flurry of boys leading out changes of horse.

He held the door for her, at the same time looking around to scan the yard. 'I cannot see anyone I know.'

'Is it likely that you would, if you have been out of the country?' Jane asked, giving him her hand and stooping to keep her bonnet brim from touching the top of the door. 'Oh, we forgot the valuables.'

She twisted round, lifted the seat, extracted the bag and turned back, off balance, missing the top step.

The fall was inevitable, but as she tumbled, the bag gripped hard in one hand, she knew Ivo would catch her and he did, holding her secure with both hands around her waist, even as he gave an involuntary grunt of pain as she hit his injured shoulder.

'I am sorry!' She looked up as he bent his head and their lips brushed, a fleeting sensation of warmth and the alien flavour of another person. Back on her feet, she found she was staring up at him, panting slightly.

'Are you hurt? Have you twisted your ankle?'

'No,' she managed to gasp.

'Then what is wrong?'

'I have never been kissed before.'

'That was not a kiss.' His eyes seemed very dark, his voice deep.

'No?' Somehow she could not make herself let go of his lapels. 'Oh. How disappointing, I have always wondered what it was like.'

'This is a kiss.' Ivo bent his head, pressed his lips to hers and pulled her in close to him.

It was almost as quick as that fleeting, accidental brush, but it sent tingles down to her knees and into parts that no young lady should experience tingling in an inn yard. Ivo let her go abruptly, leaving her with an impression of strength, a clean spicy scent in her nostrils and the taste of him on her lips.

He licked my lips. Is he supposed to do that?

'I trust that has satisfied your curiosity?' Clearly, whatever it had done for her, it had not given Ivo any pleasure, judging by his exceedingly starchy tone.

'Quite. Thank you. I must say, I cannot imagine what all the fuss is about.' With a dismissive sniff Jane made a little show out of checking the bag of valuables and straightening her bonnet, and was fairly confident that she was not bright pink when they emerged from the shelter of the chaise to make their way to the inn door.

Ivo was clearly not in a mood to take any nonsense from the innkeeper who began by informing them that he had no private suites, then that he might possibly find one, but at a price that made Jane blink.

'We are here for one night only,' Ivo said crisply. 'My sister is tired, we require a small, quiet, private sitting room and two adjacent bed-chambers at a price that would not pay for their entire refitting in Bond Street style. I had heard that the Pelican was a superior establishment, but if mine is an unreasonable request, doubt-less we can find adequate accommodation else-where.'

It was a tone Jane had not heard from him before. There was definitely an officer's air of command in it, but there was also a quiet con-fidence that he had only to state a reasonable desire for it to be gratified. Given that his cloth-ing was disreputable, his face was discoloured with multiple bruises and he had not given name, rank or title, the confidence seemed to her to be misplaced. It appeared she was wrong.

'Just let me check, sir. The girl may have made an error...' The innkeeper vanished into the Peli-can and Ivo turned to glance back at Jane.

'No wonder,' she said as she saw his face.

'No wonder, what?'

'That he fled to check. You look so grim he must have thought you would sack and pillage his fine establishment if he did not accommo-date us.'

Ivo grunted and turned back. Probably his shoulder was hurting him, Jane thought. She could not imagine what else could have put him in such a bad mood.

'Fortunately we appear to have had a cancellation, sir.' The innkeeper re-emerged, clicking his fingers for the boy to carry Jane's luggage. 'Exactly the arrangement of rooms you requested.'

'Good.' Ivo checked and found that Jane was waiting meekly by his side. Doubtless she was plotting some new devilry. 'Come along, Sister.'

What had possessed him to kiss her, even fleetingly? He could tell himself that it was the painful blow to his shoulder that had momentarily disordered his senses, but he knew perfectly well that the feel of a trim, curvaceous feminine waist under his hands, the ingenuous invitation in those wide eyes and parted lips, the disappointment when he told her that her first kiss had been no kiss at all—those had all been enough to overset his common sense.

He had never met a female so straightforward in what she wanted. There had been no flirtation, no hints and subtle encouragement. Their lips had met by accident, so her thoughts had turned to kisses—and, being Jane, she had not hidden her curiosity. This was a dangerous woman, he thought grimly as they followed on the innkeeper's heels, up a flight of stairs and along a corridor. And an outspoken one.

'I cannot imagine what all the fuss is about', indeed! Women did not normally complain about the quality of his kisses, even such fleeting ones...

At which point his sense of humour caught up with him.

Your nose is out of joint, that's what's the matter with you, Ivo Merton. She did not swoon on to the cobbles in ecstasy and so you are offended.

And a good thing, too—what would he have done with a swooning female?

'I think this will do excellently, provided the beds are aired.'

Ivo jerked his attention back to find Jane surveying a small parlour with a housewifely air while the innkeeper bristled defensively.

'Damp beds at the Pelican? I can assure you, ma'am, no such thing has ever occurred!'

'In that case, please have hot water sent up. At what hour do you wish to dine, Brother?'

'In an hour,' Ivo said, conscious of a decided sensation of inner emptiness. That was what he needed: a good dinner, some decent wine and a solid night's sleep. After that he would be able to cope with anything, including one innocent young lady who apparently had been born with as much sense of self-preservation as a kitten— and just as much inclination to chase whatever caught her eye or her fancy.

By eight o'clock, with a succulent beefsteak and the best part of a bottle of claret inside him, he made a determined effort to bring Miss Newnham to a better understanding of the realities of life for a well-bred young lady of marriageable age.

'You cannot go about kissing men in inn yards.'

'*You* kissed *me*,' she pointed out calmly without a hint of accusation.

'Only because you wanted me to,' Ivo protested, feeling any authority he had slithering away beneath his feet.

'I did not. I merely said... Oh, I expect you are right, I must have appeared to have been asking.

I admit I was curious. Do you kiss any woman who asks you?'

'No.' He was feeling hunted now. 'And a gentleman's life is not strewn with such offers either. Leaving that aside, you cannot be too careful. Reputation is a fragile thing and impossible to restore once blemished.' He was quite pleased with that pronouncement—it sounded like something the starchiest matron would say.

'Fiddlesticks.' Jane waved a well-nibbled chicken leg at him. 'My friend Verity, the one who married the Duke, was quite ruined because she spent the night on a tiny island with him— *and* they were discovered by the current Bishop and his entire entourage. Now she is completely respectable again.'

'Virtually anything may be forgiven by marriage to a duke,' Ivo said acidly. 'Unfortunately, there are none spare to come to your rescue in this case.'

'Mama was only complaining about that recently,' Jane said. 'She has been scouring the *Peerage* in the hope of finding me one. An heir would do, but she is discovering that is a problem as well. But as I told you, I have no desire to be married to anyone and I will be carrying out my business under my new name, so Jane Newnham can be as ruined as she likes and it will not matter.'

Ivo wondered if it would be completely unmanly to bury his face in his hands and give way to sobs and decided it would be. 'You would refuse a *duke*?'

'Not if I was madly in love with him as Verity is with Will. But it is highly unlikely, don't you think? To discover an unknown duke on the marriage mart and one with whom I shared a deep love?'

'Indeed it would be.' He imagined that Mr and Mrs Newnham, who by now would surely have received a distraught ladies' maid confessing that she had lost Jane, would settle for *any* respectable, solvent, gentleman under the age of seventy who could remove their errant daughter to a life of safe domesticity. 'There are another fifty miles to cover tomorrow. Somehow we are going to have to deliver you to your cousin without her realising that you have travelled from the outskirts of London with a strange gentleman and not even a maid as a chaperon.'

'That seems simple enough, surely? I can tell the postilion to drop you off at the gates of your grandfather's estate and then I continue on to Batheaston.'

'That would take you almost fifteen miles out of your way, diverting off the route and back again, and I cannot like leaving you to finish the journey alone.' He thought while he waited for her to serve him from a dish of Rhenish cream. 'I could get down at the entrance to the village, I suppose. I am concerned that you might be seen with a man in the chaise with you.'

'That would be compromising,' Jane agreed after a moment. A dab of cream fell from the spoon she held suspended over the dish and the *plop* made her jump. 'Yes, I can see your concern. How would you travel to Merton Tower, though?'

'I can walk. Despite what I said about the cavalry, I am capable of walking the distance on a fine day.'

'Yes, of course you are.' She passed him a bowl that appeared to have received an absent-minded double helping of dessert.

Ivo eyed her suspiciously. No reference to his injured shoulder, no arguments? No protests that he was being over-sensitive about guarding her reputation? 'Have the fairies spirited Jane Newnham away, leaving you in her place?' he asked.

'Whatever can you mean?' she asked with a twinkle that told him she knew exactly what he meant. 'I am tired, that is all. I do not wish to quarrel, or argue. Could we not make a later start tomorrow? Perhaps order breakfast for nine?'

Ivo was tempted. His bruises ached like the devil, his shoulder throbbed and the thought of a decent night's sleep on a good mattress was powerfully tempting. 'I would say, *yes*, but I fear your papa may be on our heels by now, breathing fire and brimstone. The sooner you are safe with your cousin, the better.'

'It is not very likely that he will catch up with us,' Jane said. She put down her spoon, apparently requiring both sets of fingers for calculation. 'Billing would have spent an hour fussing and haranguing the innocent inn staff, then she would have had to catch the first coach into London that had room for her. Let us suppose that it was three hours after we left her that she found a seat. Then an hour, perhaps more, to get to central London, then she would need to find a hackney carriage to take her to Aunt Hermione's house. She might, at the earliest, be back there five hours after we left her.

'She would not find anyone at home except the staff because Mama and Papa and Aunt were going to an exhibition at a gallery in Piccadilly and then visiting Aunt's elderly godmother in Hampstead where they were expecting to stay for dinner. Which means that by the time they had returned to Hill Street and Billing had told them what had happened and Mama had had the vapours it would be far too late to set out. Especially as they could not be certain where I was going,' she added, a look of dawning apprehension wiping all amusement from her face. 'Even Billing could not be foolish, or suspicious enough, to think that we met by arrangement, but I am sure they would all ascribe the worst possible motives to you—kidnap, or seduction or some such dastardly thing.'

'So, you believe they would expect me to be heading for the Border with you? Or to some den of iniquity?'

'Papa is probably expecting a ransom note. Oh, dear, I had not thought of it like that, but why *would* they think that I would pick up a strange gentleman and then continue on to Cousin Violet as though nothing had happened?'

'I cannot imagine.' It should have been the first thing he thought about, not how much his wounds hurt, not how bad he felt about his failure to fulfil his promise to Charles, not his own bruised heart or even how to stop this infuriating female careering around the countryside like a loose cannon with a sketchbook. 'Do you think they will call upon Bow Street?'

'That is *exactly* what Papa would do. He is not at all the kind of gentleman who would rush off in pursuit armed to the teeth. He is exceedingly conventional.' She regarded him across the remains of their dinner. 'You look very thoughtful.'

'I am considering how to raise bail when I am arrested, without involving my grandfather,' Ivo said, only half joking.

She bit her lower lip, clearly taking him seriously, and the memory of her mouth under his, of the sweet taste of her and the light floral scent that she wore, made his breath catch. The last thing that he needed was an inconvenient physical attraction to an innocent who was under his protection, he told himself. Perhaps the attraction was that she was so unlike Daphne. 'There is no need to worry, I was teasing you.'

'Even so, perhaps we had best not linger too long. If we set out at, say eight, that would be safe, I think.'

He had to agree. Given that Jane was going to exactly where she was supposed to go would probably be the least likely scenario that her parents might imagine so an eight o'clock departure should see them safely in Batheaston by one o'clock.

'I suggest that you write to your parents and tell them you are on your way to your cousin, quite safe and sound. They should receive the letter by late tomorrow afternoon, I imagine. Then write again with some kind of explanation when you reach Batheaston.'

'Without naming you, naturally. Let me think—I took you to an inn and called a doctor. When I was satisfied you were not in danger, I continued on my way. I simply do not mention that I continued with you, so it is not exactly an untruth.' She beamed at him, pleased with her solution, and Ivo felt an unexpected jolt of sympathy for her father. For any parent of a daughter, for that matter, he concluded.

'I suggest we have an early night and tell the staff that we require waking with breakfast and hot water at seven.'

'Perfect,' Jane said and tugged the bell pull.

Ivo slept like the proverbial log, only stirring when the faint light of dawn struggled between the gap in the curtains. He lay, half-awake, wondering what had woken him. A scuffling sound in the corner of his chamber? He came up on his elbows and peered into the shadows. Nothing stirred and he could just make out the shape of his clothes draped and piled on the chair. Mice, that was all. He punched the pillow into a more comfortable shape and closed his eyes again. This was an efficient inn, they would be woken up in plenty of time. He could relax again and get perhaps another hour's sleep.

The sun streaming through the gap in the curtains woke him eventually. That and the noise from the inn yard. Ivo sat bolt upright in bed and grabbed for his pocket watch. The hands stood exactly at the right angle. Nine.

'*Nine?*'

He flung back the covers, pulled on his clothes

and tugged on the bell pull. He was wrestling with his boots when a pert maid in a large white cap and crisp apron came in.

'What kind of hour do you call this? I left orders to be woken at seven.'

'Yes, sir. But the lady, your sister, said to let you sleep. She came down at half past six, sir, and said she'd break her fast at the first change and to leave you to your rest, sir. She ordered you a very good breakfast and she has paid the shot. Said something about needing to reach a relative urgently and that you would understand. There's a note on the dresser, she said.'

The little witch.

Ivo grabbed the note and coins fell out as he opened it.

Dear Ivo,

I realised last night that just as I might be compromised, then so might you, and really the last thing you need is some kind of misunderstood entanglement with a country gentleman's daughter! It was foolish of me not to realise the delicacy of your position.

So, here is enough money to take the stage

and then hire a gig or a horse when you are nearer home.

Please do not worry about paying me back until a convenient time for you—it will be some weeks before I need money for a lease on a shop and studio, I am sure, and in any case I have the jewellery to sell.

Thank you so much for your company on the road. I do hope your shoulder is much better soon and that you find your grandfather in the very best of health.

With kind regards,
Your friend,
J.N.

Ivo swore. The maid squeaked.

He had no hope of catching Jane now. He had best go to the Tower. Go *home*, as Jane put it. Go home and face the future.

Chapter Six

'Jane, dearest girl!' Cousin Violet surged down the path leading to her front gate, arms flung wide, bosom breasting the breeze, like a ship running before a high wind. She was a lady designed on generous lines by nature, with a personality that matched her figure.

Jane was enveloped in an enthusiastic embrace and breathed in the familiar Violet scent of chocolate, jasmine and face powder.

'You have been a very naughty girl and I am selfishly delighted, because it means I will have your company. Your mama wrote that I should chastise you, so consider yourself thoroughly scolded and then we can forget all about it and enjoy ourselves.' Violet turned to lead Jane back down the garden path between rose bushes and mounds of lavender as generously proportioned as she was. Billows of scent rose around them.

'Do mind the bees. I should have Tomlin cut it all back, but I do not have the heart.'

'I should think not, it is wonderful.'

Violet always referred to her house as a cottage. In fact, it was a late seventeenth-century house of three storeys built of mellow Bath stone and set back from the High Street behind the front garden. There was a walled back garden and a yard behind that with stables, reached by circuitous lanes.

'Where is your maid? Has she gone around to the back with the post chaise? Your mama wrote that she was sending her woman with you. Trilling, was it? It cannot be Cooing, I refuse to believe that.'

'Billing—and she neither trills nor coos. I sent her back shortly after Kensington. I have to confess to an adventure, Cousin Violet. A very small one,' she added hastily as Violet turned to regard her with wide brown eyes full of speculation.

'A man?'

'Er…yes. A gentleman, of course.'

'My dear! Tell me all. Are you in love with him?' Violet swept on through the front door, Jane behind her like a skiff towed by a galleon, she thought wildly.

'No! Not at all. He is infuriating, not at all handsome and far above my touch. I have to confess to missing him already, though. Much as one does a tooth after it has been pulled,' she added after a moment's thought.

And she was faintly worried as well. Ivo had seemed strong and fit and able to cope with the after-effects of the beating and stabbing, but men were proud, devious creatures and more than capable of lying about their health. He would not be pleased to discover that she had tricked him, but she hoped he had slept long enough for him to realise that pursuit was futile and would take himself home at a steady pace.

'Come and sit down and we will take tea.' Violet ushered her into the front parlour. 'The girls put the kettle to the fire the moment we saw your chaise. Now, sit there, take off that bonnet and tell me *everything.*'

Jane did as she asked, around mouthfuls of tea and delicious cakes. *Almost* everything: she omitted the arguments about her proposed career as a portraitist—she would have to decide what to tell Violet about that and when—and for some reason she did not feel able to talk about that kiss.

'So, you have travelled all the way from Newbury today? Alone?'

'Yes. I have to confess I would not wish to stay at an inn by myself, because I did receive some impudent stares from a few men when I went into places to take refreshment or use the necessary along the way. But I gave them a very haughty look and they did not trouble me further.'

'And so your mystery man does not know where you have vanished to? It sounds as though you were exceedingly fortunate in the person you chose to rescue so recklessly, for his behaviour seems most gentlemanly.'

'I told him I was coming to you so that he would not worry. He is an aristocrat and an army officer. Or he was,' Jane confessed. 'But even if he had proved to be a street sweeper, I could not have left him to be beaten to death, now could I?'

'Your parents would doubtless say that you should have fetched a constable.'

'By which time he could have been dreadfully injured!'

'I agree,' Violet said warmly. 'There are times

when a lady must act. But you spent two nights with him…'

'I spent two nights in the same inn as he did,' Jane corrected. 'Not *with* him. And no one but the three of us knows. I wrote to Mama and Papa explaining that I was not kidnapped or eloping or in any danger and I gave them the impression that after I rescued Iv…the gentleman, I continued on my way alone having left him at an inn in the care of a doctor. I must write now and tell them I am safely arrived with you.'

'No, I will write,' Violet declared. 'Then they will be certain you are not being constrained to write by your dastardly kidnapper.' She selected a small biscuit and nibbled it daintily, watching Jane as she did so. 'Are you quite certain you have not fallen for this man? You would tell me if he did anything for which he should be called to account, I hope.'

'I am positive I have not fallen for him.' Wanting him to kiss her again and feeling a strange little ache inside when she remembered the smile in those deep blue eyes did not amount to *falling*, she was sure. 'And he most certainly did nothing to make me feel at all uneasy in his presence. I confess to feeling a strong desire to box his ears on occasion, I must admit, but that was because of his stuffy attitudes.'

Which makes it all the stranger that I wish he was here to talk to.

'Excellent. Then I can write with a clear conscience to set Cousin Mildred's mind at rest. I will do that now and then the letter will be ready for the evening Mail.' She reached out and tugged the bell pull. 'Dorothy will show you your room and unpack for you and you can rest after your journey. Then we can make our plans.' She beamed at Jane. 'Mildred said you can stay for weeks—I am so looking forward to it.'

Jane smiled back. Cousin Violet was a dear and she felt like a sister because she was so warm and understanding. The youngest daughter of Mama's youngest sister, she was only fifteen years older than Jane. The temptation to tell her everything—the sudden revelation that she could create a studio and shop in Bath and paint professionally, the unsettling effect Ivo had on her—was powerful and she hated to deceive Violet. But she resisted the urge to unburden herself. She had done nothing yet, so she was not deceiving her cousin. Time to worry about it when she found her shop.

* * *

'What the devil do you mean by presenting yourself here ten days late and looking like the riff and raff of an alehouse brawl?' the Marquess of Westhaven demanded. He was seventy years old, as upright and belligerent as he had been in his forties. He was used to having his wishes obeyed instantly, to receiving all the deference he felt he was owed—which was considerable—and, Ivo guessed, no one had said him nay for years.

'I look as I do because my luggage is in London and I have, indeed, been in an alehouse brawl. I am later than you requested because I had an obligation to a friend of mine who asked me on his deathbed to try and detach his sister from an unwise alliance. I was too late. She is married and took exception to my interference to the extent of setting her grooms on me.' Ivo took the seat on the other side of the vast oak desk, noting that the Marquess still had no time for this modern fashion for furniture that did not look as though it had been hewn from a warship. He had not been invited to sit, but he was not going to stand there like a naughty schoolboy summoned for a caning.

His grandfather, eyes narrowed in thought, appeared not to notice this disrespect. Ivo wondered if that was tactical and the old man suspected he would not win every round against his grandson nowadays.

'That will be the Parris chit, I imagine. I recall you were friendly with her brother when you were growing up. They had a family place near Longfield, had they not?' he said, mentioning the estate Ivo's father had used most. 'Her aunts are raising a merry storm in London, so my correspondents tell me. Foolish creatures. Nothing to be done about it now. Clement Meredith seduced her, bedded her and wedded her, they say. Probably got a child in her belly by now if he's got any sense. Is she of age?' He pulled a wry expression when Ivo shook his head. 'They'd do better to put a good face on it and spend their energies on making sure he cannot get his hands on her money.'

He focused suddenly on Ivo's face. 'I recall you and she had some boy-and-girl fancy for one another at one time.'

Ivo shrugged, apparently not nonchalantly enough to fool his grandfather.

'Ah, so it was more than that. April and May

foolishness. You are well out of it if she is capable of such behaviour. Are you telling me that she ordered her men to do you that much damage? Don't pretend your ribs aren't cracked—and what's wrong with your shoulder?'

'We had an understanding, but that's all in the past,' Ivo said, slouching back as casually as he could in the chair and ignoring the twinges in his ribs and shoulder. 'But she was unhappy with me interfering and there were four of them. Nothing's cracked, just bruised, and I got a knife in the shoulder. It has been stitched.' He shrugged to demonstrate it was not too bad.

'Pshaw.' The older man made a disgusted face. 'And Meredith let her do it? That is not the action of a gentleman. He should have called you out, not set his bullies on you.'

'He was not there. This was all Daphne's idea, it seems. Do you think I should now challenge him so I could kill him and fulfil my promise to Charles?' he suggested wryly. 'I do not think that he would expect me to go to the lengths of becoming an exile on his behalf.'

'No, I do not suggest you fight him. The man's a bounder, not a gentleman. And don't you waste any more effort on the foolish chit, you've done all her brother could have expected of you.'

'I promised I would do what I could,' Ivo said. 'I would have tried anyway. Even if she no longer feels anything for me, there is an obligation. Once I realised that they were wed I suspected that nothing was possible, but I hoped one of your squadron of high-flown lawyers might be able to advise her aunts on possibilities.'

'Fulfil your promise at the expense of my purse, eh?' His grandfather did not look displeased.

'I will pay, but I need your advice on the best men to consult.'

The Marquess waved that away. 'I almost married the silly girl's grandmother. Fond of her—she had more brains than her granddaughter, it would seem! I'll pay the lawyers for her sake. But do you have any money?' he asked abruptly.

'I have savings, my arrears of pay and whatever my father left me.'

'That will not keep you as my heir should be kept. Here.' The Marquess tossed a thin folder across the desk. 'I have made these estates over to you. You'll have the income from them—and the management, too. There's too much for me to be worrying about these days. Your father had no head for business, not a lot in his cockloft, if we're to be frank. Took after his mother.' There was a faraway look in his eye for a moment. 'Pretty thing, your grandmother, but I should have married Amelia Thistleton.'

Ivo didn't feel there was much he could usefully add to that remark, but he had the feeling that something was still to come. He picked up the folder and leafed through, suppressing a whistle of surprise as he did so. His grandfather had handed over control of a good third of his substantial estates to him. Not the most valuable, of course—he knew enough about the family holdings to judge that, despite having spent his adult life in the army.

'Which brings me to the crux of the matter,' the Marquess said abruptly.

Ivo put down the folder and had no trouble looking attentive. *What matter?*

'Not entangled with anyone else other than that foolish Parris chit, are you? You young officers seem to attract silly girls like a candle does moths. No harm in it, unless you don't keep your wits about you and have to marry one of them, eh?'

'I am not married, sir. I would, naturally, have informed you should I have taken such a step. My understanding with Daphne Parris was, I admit, not known to anyone but her brother, but I regarded it as binding.'

'So you are not promised? No understanding with anyone?'

Ivo had experienced the sensation of being in the sights of a French sniper often enough to be familiar with the prickling sensation down his spine, the lifting of the hair on his nape. It was not amusing, being the hunted and not the hunter.

The old man appeared to think that Daphne had been a youthful fancy, that the engagement had been a mere boy-and-girl infatuation that would not have lasted. He was certainly not going to tell his grandfather about that moonlit evening when he and Daphne had kissed on the terrace and he had asked her to wait for him and she had said that she would, for ever, because she loved him.

'What exactly is the point of these questions, sir?'

Find cover...

'The point? Are you as dense as your father?

Heirs, that's the point. Why Matthew didn't marry again when your mother passed away, I will never know. We would have had some spares if he had. I pushed enough chits with plenty of brothers and good wide hips in front of him, but, no. Too lazy or preferred his mistress. Found her less trouble than a wife, I imagine. But now there's just you and the next in line is your cousin Alfred and he is... Well, let's just say he's not the marrying kind, damn it. And then it's your Uncle Horace and I'll not rest easy if I'm to be succeeded by that mealy-mouthed bishop of a son of mine.'

'Uncle Horace does have six sons,' Ivo pointed out. His youngest, and only surviving, uncle was, indeed, a prosy old bore. His sons, in reaction, it seemed, were a pack of hellions. 'I am only twenty-seven, Grandfather. Plenty of time.'

'Not when you're throwing yourself at French siege works or getting beaten up by packs of hired bully boys, there isn't,' the Marquess growled. 'Or your horse puts its foot in a rabbit hole or you have some other damn fool accident or another and then where are we?' His son Matthew, Ivo's father, had died in just such a random riding disaster.

From the expression on the old man's face he was not interested in hearing expressions of sympathy—or of making any, come to that, Ivo thought. His grandfather had offered him no words of consolation on the loss of his father, but then he was probably all too aware that there had been a yawning gap of mutual indifference between the two of them.

'I see your point. But I am not in the army now, sir.' Ivo still thought his grandfather was being pessimistic, but the loss of his elder son, however much the pair of them fought, must have been a shock to the old man. He wondered if he should say something, however unwelcome, then told himself it would be hypocritical. His father had been a distant figure, almost a stranger, and he had no idea what words might help the Marquess.

'So, are you?'

'What?'

'Betrothed! Or promised or entangled? Because if you are not, then I've just the girl for you. Tredlestone's middle girl. Fine healthy stock, good bloodlines, sisters married well and they have all got boys. She'll have an excellent dowry. I've not sounded out Tredlestone—nothing said, you know, just hints and nudges, but he'll be a happy man if you offer for her, I can tell you.'

And what will Miss Tredlestone be? Happy to be married off to a man she has never met? I have only to show the slightest interest, pay a visit and that will be that, thanks to the old devil's hints and nudges. *I'll chose my own bride, thank you very much, sir.*

He just had to put his grandfather off for a while, gain some breathing space. He must marry, he knew that, but it was too soon, he felt too raw and, even after what she had done, some foolish part of him wanted Daphne. Still loved her, however impossible that seemed. It would not be fair to another woman to begin a courtship, even if he could find the heart for it.

'No... Not exactly betrothed, no,' Ivo said slowly, pushing all thoughts of Daphne away as he searched for a delaying tactic. 'There's a young lady I met very recently for whom I have, I suppose, developed feelings.'

Very simple feelings—mainly a desire to box

her ears or have her locked up for her own good.
Or kiss her until her toes curl.

'We have spent some little time getting to know each other. Nothing has been said, there is no commitment, but I find I cannot forget her. I certainly do not feel it would be honourable to pay court to Miss Tredlestone with my feelings for another lady so…unresolved.'

What was largely unresolved was whether he should go to Batheaston, locate Cousin Violet and make sure Jane had arrived safely. And then decide what to do about her hare-brained scheme to set herself up as a portrait painter in Bath. What he should do, he was well aware, was to put a stop to that. That was what her parents would want.

'Who is this young woman? Good family?'

'Not as good as Miss Tredlestone. Gentry. Respectable, prosperous.' At least, he supposed so. Jane's travelling dress had been well made and was in the current fashion, her luggage was of excellent quality and her parents could afford a post chaise. 'But intelligent, lively, pretty enough. Firm-minded,' he added. *Stubborn as a mule.* 'Artistic.' *Eccentric.*

'Hmm. Perhaps an injection of solid gentry

blood would do no harm. Look at my other grandsons: good breeding hasn't done much for them. What's this girl think of you, though? Interested, is she? She would be a fool not to be.'

Ivo did not take that as a personal compliment. Any young woman would be expected to look more than favourably on the heir to a marquessate who was under seventy, had his own teeth and was not noticeably debauched. Her mama, having failed to identify an available duke or ducal heir, would be in ecstasies—which was dangerous. He would have to tread very carefully so as not to raise expectations in either breast—Jane's or Mrs Newnham's.

'She considers me to be too staid.' He ignored the old man's rasp of amusement. 'I have reason to believe that she does not find me actively displeasing.'

She wanted me to kiss her, after all.

'But I am not at all certain she wishes to settle down at present. As I said, I have not resolved in my mind what action I wish to take in respect of her.'

All I do know is that I would have to be all about in the head to fall for such a difficult female in reality.

'You had better make up your mind, then, hadn't you? Miss Tredlestone will not be sitting on a shelf waiting for you.'

'Quite.' *Thank goodness.*

'Where does this young lady live?'

'Not far from Bath. I may call in a day or so when I have settled in,' Ivo said casually, waiting for an interrogation about any other plans, aspirations or interests he might have.

Instead he got a dismissive wave of the hand. 'I have got papers to attend to. I will see you at dinner. The entire East Wing's yours, I've had them move the clothes you left behind in your old rooms into the dressing room there. Do what you like with it—just don't hold rackety parties that keep me awake half the night.'

'No, sir. I can undertake not to do that,' Ivo said to the top of his grandfather's bent head. The once thick dark hair was all white now and there were glimpses of pink scalp beneath. He swallowed his irritation. This was an ageing man who had received a hard blow with the loss of his son, however he might pretend otherwise. He would do what he could to make life easier for the Marquess—provided that did not involve having his marriage arranged for him.

* * *

'The village is as charming as I remember it.' In the early afternoon, two days after her arrival, Jane strolled along the High Street, arm in arm with her cousin. 'But it seems very small.'

'We have scarcely two hundred inhabitants,' Violet said with a chuckle 'So you soon learn to recognise everyone. I cannot pretend that it has the most varied and stimulating society—there is the church, of course, and the Ladies' Gardening Gathering and there are perhaps fifteen families with whom one might dine. But there is always Bath. As you can imagine, a new face is always welcome and I am sure your arrival will stimulate a positive flood of invitations.'

They walked on a few yards and Jane admired some of the gardens—clearly the Ladies' Gardening Gathering had enthusiastic members.

'My goodness, speaking of new faces—' Violet gave her arm a little tug. 'I do not recognise that gentleman. Just ahead of us, speaking to the Vicar.' She stopped and pretended to admire the pink blossoms of a late-blooming rose that tumbled over the wall. 'A very well-set-up man, I must say. I wonder if he is staying locally.'

Jane pulled a flower down to her nose as

though to smell it and peered through the foliage. The man talking to the Vicar was partially obscured by the leaves, but she could tell that he was tall, broad-shouldered and well dressed. He had a pair of very fine boots, she noted, following the line of his legs down. He would be a pleasure to draw, Jane thought as he raised his hat to the Vicar and the two stepped apart.

Then the Vicar must have seen them. He raised a hand in greeting to Violet and said something to the stranger who turned.

'Oh.' It was not a stranger and Jane had had the pleasure of drawing him already.

'What is it, dear?' Violet looked at her, clearly puzzled.

'Miss Lowry?' The stranger was upon them. He raised his hat politely. 'I hope you will excuse me accosting you without an introduction, but the Vicar pointed you out to me.' He turned and smiled at Jane. 'I had the pleasure of making Miss Newnham's acquaintance in Kensington and I was calling to enquire if you had a safe journey, ma'am.' He turned back to Violet. 'I am Kendall.'

Chapter Seven

Cousin Violet might not mix in aristocratic circles, but she certainly knew the names of the families from the great houses that ringed Bath and she was not intimidated by meeting a representative of one of them. 'Lord Kendall.' Her slight curtsy was perfectly judged, too.

She and the Earl made a striking, if improbable, couple, Jane thought, mentally composing a picture of the encounter. Violet did not have a figure perfectly suited to the styles of the day, but she had good taste and the independence of thought to adapt the mode to suit herself and she did not look out of place alongside Ivo's unfamiliar elegance. Studying them served to calm her jittering nerves a little. What on earth was Ivo doing here in Batheaston? At least now she knew he had reached Merton Tower safely.

'How fortunate that you encountered us, Lord

Kendall,' she said, recovering enough from the surprise to be puzzled. 'Quite a coincidence as I do not believe you had either my cousin's direction or her surname.'

'I realised that your Cousin Violet would be among the gentry listed in the *Bath Directory* and there is only the one lady in Batheaston with such a charming forename. Then I was fortunate enough to encounter your Vicar as I was searching for the address.'

Ivo seemed to have acquired a particularly smooth manner along with his smart wardrobe, Jane thought, watching him suspiciously.

'And we are just on our way home,' Violet said. 'We came out so that I could show Miss Newnham Mrs Broughton's spectacular rose. We ladies are very enthusiastic about gardening in Batheaston.'

You cunning thing! Jane thought admiringly. They had been heading in the opposite direction to Violet's house with no intention of turning back for at least another twenty minutes or so. Admiration gave way to mild panic as Ivo took his place between them, offered each an arm and proceeded to stroll back along the High Street.

What does he want?

Not to betray their unconventional journey, it seemed, not with that reference to Kensington, as though their meeting had been on some social occasion.

Ivo kept up a stream of polite talk all the way back. He encouraged Violet to hold forth on the Ladies' Gardening Gathering, admired the architecture and enquired about the flood risk with the Avon, it being so close to the main street.

Jane, her hand tucked into his left elbow, tried a warning squeeze, hoping he would take the hint to be tactful. Under her fingers his arm felt very solid. Then she recalled that this was his injured side. 'Sorry,' she whispered.

Not quietly enough, it seemed. 'I beg your pardon, Jane dear,' Violet said, leaning forward a little to see around Ivo.

'I was just… I was concerned that I might be hurting Lord Kendall's arm. I heard he had sustained an injury to his shoulder.'

'It is healing well now, thank you, Miss Newnham.'

The wretched man sounded as though he was smiling. She kept her gaze firmly forward, blinkered by the sides of her bonnet.

'A war wound, Lord Kendall?' Violet asked. 'I

believe I am correct in thinking you have been serving in the army?'

'I have been, but I am in the process of selling out now in order to support my grandfather. And it was not a battle injury, merely an accident, Miss Lowry.'

Jane restrained herself from leaning heavily on his arm.

'Even so, your grandfather must be so relieved that you are home safely from the wars. Now, here we are, my cottage.'

'Delightful.' Ivo stopped at the gate and admired the mellow stone and the bountiful garden. 'I can understand why Miss Newnham was so happy to be leaving the dirt and smoke of London for this.'

Violet, leading the way down the front path, might be flattered, but she was no fool. 'Your acquaintance with my cousin is a recent one, I gather.'

'Fairly recent, yes. We were introduced by some acquaintances of the sister of one of my late army friends.'

They were inside the hallway now and the maid came to meet them, taking bonnets and reticules and Ivo's hat and cane. Jane caught him glancing at her and rolled her eyes. She was not certain whether she was more relieved at his smooth answers or annoyed at how easily he could turn awkward truth into acceptable fiction. There was a twitch of his lips, but whether it was a smile or a rueful acknowledgement of her unspoken reproof, she was not certain.

'And how will you be entertaining yourself in this lovely part of the world, Miss Newnham?' he asked when they were settled in the parlour and tea had been sent for. 'You paint a little, I think I recall. There must be delightful landscapes to tempt your brush.'

'I paint a great deal, mainly portraits. Surely you remember, Lord Kendall? We discussed the subject at some length.'

'It had slipped my mind, I'm afraid. I am not at all artistic myself. And have you visited Bath yet?'

'No.'

Violet raised her eyebrows, clearly confused at Jane's abruptness. 'We will do so presently. Bath is not what it was, of course, but I am sure my cousin will enjoy browsing among the shops. I take little interest in them myself, but most of the ladies of my acquaintance find them satisfactory. I imagine you will not be wanting to sample the waters, will you, dear?'

'No, indeed.' Jane repressed a shudder at the thought. 'I confess that I would enjoy visiting the city. Perhaps you can spare a maid to accompany me, Cousin—then I will not need to trouble you, given that you do not find window shopping entertaining.'

'Bath is certainly very respectable,' Violet said thoughtfully. 'I am sure you would be quite safe with Charity. She knows the city well.'

'Perhaps I might offer my escort if Miss Lowry will entrust you to my care?' Ivo said as he got to his feet to shift a side table for the maid carrying the tea tray. 'It would be a pleasure to rediscover Bath.'

'You know it well?' Jane could not fathom Ivo's motive for making such an offer. He was surely not intending to help her find suitable premises?

'I did once.' He was smiling blandly back at her, his expression quite unreadable. 'The family home is not so very far.'

Whatever Cousin Violet saw there, she was clearly disposed to trust him. 'So kind, Lord Kendall. I am certain dear Jane would enjoy exploring with you far more than she would with me or a maid.'

'Cousin—'

'I find the hills exhausting and I have the greatest sympathy for the poor chairmen when I am forced to use their services,' Violet said with a rich chuckle. 'We will go to the Assemblies and concerts, of course.' She favoured Ivo with her warm smile and Jane could almost see him hit by the force of it. Her cousin was a lovely woman.

If the gentlemen could only stop thinking that willowy females in fashionable gowns were the sole image of perfection, Violet would have an abundance of suitors, she thought.

Ivo put down his cup, refused more tea and turned to Jane as he stood. 'Would tomorrow afternoon be convenient? You have no objection to a phaeton with a groom in attendance, Miss Lowry?'

'That would be perfect,' Violet replied before Jane could say anything. 'About two o'clock? Delightful. Do allow me to show you out, Lord Kendall.'

She swept back in a few moments later. 'Well!'

'Well indeed! Whatever were you thinking of, Violet?'

'Thinking of? Why, your parents will be in ecstasies if you can attach Lord Kendall—you will be quite forgiven.'

'The man is an earl. He is the heir to a marquess. Whatever the reason for his call, it is certainly *not* to court me. Besides, I have no desire to find a husband, even if Ivo Merton were not quite impossible anyway.'

'Ivo, is it?' Violet, normally the most sensible of women, produced something perilously close to a simper. 'And I cannot believe you do not want a husband.'

'You seem to do excellently well without one,' Jane said, goaded into frankness.

'I have money,' Violet said simply. 'An independence.' When Jane did not respond, she added, 'Even if he has no intentions of that sort, it can only do your standing good to be seen escorted by Lord Kendall. It will mean you have more partners at the Assemblies and we will receive more invitations if you are seen about Bath in his company.'

'I am sure you are right, Cousin, but please—

no matchmaking. We are the merest acquaintances.'

I just happen to have seen him with his shirt off and he has kissed me...

'Besides, I find him annoyingly self-assured.'

Violet's response was a most unladylike snort.

Ivo returned to Merton Tower and sought out his grandfather whom he found still in the study, surrounded by piles of paperwork.

'Is there nothing I can do to help, sir? Surely your man of business and your solicitor and your steward should all be assisting you.'

'They are. They assist me by endlessly wanting decisions, raising problems, quibbling over detail.' The Marquess pushed his wire-framed spectacles to the top of his head, making him look like a somewhat less amiable version of Benjamin Franklin. 'This lot...' he swept a hand around at the piles '...is what they want decisions on today.'

'Then tell me when something arises with which I can assist.' Encouraged, or at least not dismissed, by a grunt, Ivo sat down. 'It is four months since my father's death. I note you have not ordered mourning for the household.'

'Or myself. The older I get, the less I hold with it. All that money going to pay for yard upon yard of black cloth, everyone looking like crows, people whispering disapproval behind their hands if you turn up at a party—what good does it do the deceased, I ask you? Matthew is not sitting on some celestial cloud tut-tutting at us. The sticklers soon forget to be shocked if you aren't wearing black to remind them.' He shot Ivo a sharp look. 'I see you are not wearing it either.'

'I was in uniform when the news reached me. Then, when I got back to England, I was in too much of a hurry to try and catch Miss Parris before it was too late to bother with tailors. I think I agree with you, now I consider it.' It would be an empty conventional gesture, but that was all. He wished suddenly that he could feel some pain, some deep sense of loss, but there was just regret for a life lost needlessly.

'Excellent. If we are not officially in mourning, then there is nothing to hinder your courting, either.'

'No, sir.'

Ivo beat a hasty retreat to his own wing. What had come over him, offering to take Jane to

Bath? The call had been to set his mind at rest that she had reached Batheaston safely and also, if he was honest with himself, to tease her a little. That was all that was necessary. He could have honestly told his grandfather that he had called on the young lady who had been causing his uncertainty and leave him to stew for a week or so while Ivo looked around, put thoughts of Daphne in the past where they belonged and found the will to consider seeking a suitable wife.

Now he was committed to escorting a young lady who was going to want to explore not the contents of Bath's shops, but to search for empty ones. And what was he going to do if she found something? Tell her formidable cousin, he supposed, although that would feel like a betrayal. Which it should not because it would be for Jane's own good.

Jane Newnham was a distraction. She was difficult, provoking but, unfortunately, interesting. Interesting in much the same way as one was interested in why a particular piece of music stuck in your head in a maddening manner or why Byron's writing was so compelling when he was such an infuriating individual.

An afternoon in her company should be enough to quell that particular irritation, he decided. And, if he saw a shop with a *To Let* sign in the window, he would simply steer her in the opposite direction.

Most young ladies would take infinite pains before being taken for a ride by an eligible earl. Ivo knew that and knew perfectly well that such efforts would not be due to his own personal charms. However, he was ready to be suitably admiring of the result, as was expected of him. He left Robert, his groom, with the reins of the fine pair of bays he had chosen from the Tower stables and strolled down the footpath between Miss Lowry's admirable rose beds.

He was also prepared to be kept waiting so that the lady in question could make an entrance. In consequence it was difficult to keep the surprise off his face when the front door opened and Jane stepped out when he was halfway down the garden path. She was wearing a neat but perfectly ordinary walking dress—one he recognised from their journey from London. Her bonnet was familiar, too, as were the sensible walking shoes that kicked the single flounce on the gown as she walked briskly towards him. No flirty little parasol either, he noticed. Only the reticule was different. Hopefully she had left the pocket pistol behind.

'Good afternoon, Miss Newnham,' he said, raising his hat and conscious of the ears on the phaeton and, probably, those behind the front door. 'No sketch pad today?'

'Notebook,' she said, all brisk efficiency. 'And good afternoon to you, Lord Kendall.'

He handed her up on to the seat where she made herself comfortable with a little wriggle and one, unfussy, twitch at her skirts.

'What a handsome pair,' she observed. Clearly his horses were of more interest than he was, he thought, amused at the fact he felt faintly piqued.

'My grandfather bred them. I have to confess to finding it hard to drag myself away from the stables.'

'Then I am to be congratulated on giving you a pretext to try these beauties,' she said.

'Come now, Miss Newnham, how can you believe I had any other motive than the pleasure of your company?' He clicked his tongue at the bays and they walked on, ears pricked. They were eager, but well mannered, and with a flick of the reins he sent them into a brisk trot past the lane leading to the ferry to Bath Hampton and on towards Bathwick.

Jane laughed. 'You, my lord, were set on teasing me by inviting me and we both know it.' She lowered her voice, clearly conscious of Robert perched up behind. 'But you may certainly pay for your mischief by being useful today.'

The day was fine and the road, which was the stage and Mail route, was well maintained, so they bowled along at a good pace, making suitably banal conversation. Jane admired the view of the canal, Ivo remarked on the likely problems of flooding, both agreed that the view of Bath ahead of them, spilling down the hillside, golden in the sunshine, was very fine.

They rattled over the cobbles of Walcott Parade, swept past St Swithin's Church and then up steep, narrow, Guinea Lane into Bennett Street. Ivo drew up in front of the Assembly Rooms and turned in the seat. 'We will meet you here at four thirty, Robert. I will drive us down to the head of Milsom Street now and you can take them to the livery stables from there.'

'Aye, my lord.'

'Milsom Street? But I do not—' Jane subsided,

but as soon as they were on the pavement and Robert was driving away, she turned to Ivo, indignant. 'You know I do not want to go shopping. Or window shopping, for that matter. And I know perfectly well that shop rents in Milsom Street will be far too expensive for me.'

'Are you really determined on this mad scheme?' Ivo demanded. He tucked her right hand firmly under his arm and began to stroll downhill. 'You know perfectly well it is too much of a risk both to your reputation and to your resources.'

There was the faintest of hesitations. 'If I can find the right premises, yes, I am determined.'

'And what of your cousin? What are her views on the matter?' Silence. He glanced down at an uncommunicative hat brim. 'Have you discussed it with her?'

'No, not yet. There is time enough when I find a suitable shop and studio.'

'You *are* going to tell her, then?' Ivo spotted a hat shop and veered towards it.

'Of course.' There was that hesitation again, then she rallied and found a response. 'I can hardly catch the local stage into Bath and disappear for hours every day, can I?'

'Quite.' Ivo stopped in front of the shop window. He must try and reinforce the doubts he could hear in her voice. 'That is a very handsome pink bonnet.'

'The one with the exaggerated poke and the feather? It is rather fine.'

'Why not go in and try it on?' he suggested.

'Ivo, are you trying to distract me?'

'Just a little. It would suit you.' And that was no lie. He found he had a desire to see that feather lying alongside her cheek.

She tipped her head to one side, studying the hat. 'It is certain to be too expensive. Shall we explore the side streets? I do not want to be too far from Milsom Street because it is the most fashionable, so I need to find something close, but inexpensive.'

Short of throwing her over his shoulder and carrying her back to the Assembly Rooms, Ivo found he was helpless. Jane dived down every turning, then turnings off turnings, questing like a hound on the scent.

He put up a spirited rearguard action, taking her into parfumiers, glove shops, an establishment selling nothing but ribbons and even a coffee merchant's, but, however diverted by pretty things, Jane was soon back on the trail.

'Are you not becoming weary?' Ivo asked when she paused at the bottom of Milsom Street, then plunged on towards the Abbey.

'Not at all.' She stopped, swung round and laughed up at him. 'I am enjoying this.' Worryingly, all trace of her earlier hesitation had vanished. 'Oh, are your feet aching, my lord?'

'No, they are not.' Although to be honest he was thinking longingly of his oldest pair of boots and not the smart new Hessians he had ordered months ago and picked up on his way through London. They had seemed right for this expedition and now he chided himself for thinking like a park saunterer and not a practical man.

'Fibber. Never mind, you can take a chair back up to the Assembly Rooms.' She danced off in a flutter of hat ribbons, reticule swinging.

With a grin, Ivo followed, caught up and secured her hand again. He tucked it under his elbow in the hope of tethering her to him. 'Be carried like a gouty old colonel? I will do no such thing.'

But Jane was not attending to him. They had

emerged on to Westgate Street and she was staring at the shops opposite with rapt attention.

'A shoe shop? We haven't looked in any of those yet,' he said, steering her across the road, avoiding two burly chairmen trotting towards the Abbey and a Dennett gig being driven over the cobbles with more speed than flair by a very young man.

'No, next to it.' Jane tugged at his arm. 'Look.'

Beside the shoe shop was a dirty green door and a shop window perhaps ten feet in width, equally begrimed and festooned with cobwebs. A new-looking sign propped up inside read:

Premises to Let
Apply Pertwee and Forster,
4a Milk Street, Bath

Jane rattled the door handle. 'Locked.' On the other side was an agency for domestic servants. She hesitated, then marched into the shoe shop.

'May I be of service, madam?' The assistant was about thirty with very white hands, pomaded hair and improbably tight trousers. Ivo wondered how he ever managed to bend down to fit shoes.

'The premises next door, the shop for rent. Do you know how large it is?'

'Oh, the old snuff shop? Minute, madam. Positively Lilliputian. Just the width of the front and, as you can see from the angle of our wall, it hardly comes any further back.'

Both Jane and Ivo turned to see what he meant. Once inside the shoe shop the space opened up and it looked as though the old snuff shop had either been there first and been built around or had taken a bite out of the larger establishment.

'Old Mr Flowers owned both. When he died one nephew got these premises and several more in the street and the other, who was out of favour, only got the snuff shop. And he will not sell to us out of spite.' The assistant made a complicated sound of disapproval.

'Thank you so much.' Jane smiled at the man and Ivo held the door for her. 'Oh, dear. It sounds as though the owner may be a difficult person to deal with,' she said as they regained the pavement.

'Absolutely,' Ivo agreed. 'He probably enjoys having it empty and blighting the other properties to spite his relative. Come and have a Sally

Lunn,' he suggested. 'The bakery is just across there by the Abbey, as I recall.'

Jane did not appear to have heard him, or perhaps the idea of a hot buttery treat did not appeal. 'The front is perfect,' she said, as though to herself. 'The location is excellent and the rent must be cheap, surely. It would not be advertised if the owner would refuse *all* offers.' She opened her reticule and noted down the agent's address.

'No,' Ivo said with all the authority he could muster. 'Absolutely not.'

'But...' Jane turned and looked up at him, those hazel eyes wide within their sweep of lashes, and something inside him seemed to contract sharply.

Her eyes were her best feature and well she would know it, he told himself firmly. She probably practised that appealing look in front of the mirror every morning. Then he realised he was swaying towards her, mesmerised. 'And stop gazing at me with those stricken eyes. I know you well enough not to be beguiled by you fluttering your lashes at me.'

'Fluttering my lashes?' The appealingly puzzled expression vanished to be replaced with indignation. 'You think that I am trying to flirt

with you to make you do what I want? You…
You *beast*.' She gave his arm a slap with her reticule. 'And I hope that hurt!'

Behind Ivo a deep voice growled, 'This cove
bothering you, young lady?'

Chapter Eight

Ivo swung round and behind him Jane saw that two burly chairmen had stopped and were frowning at them.

For some reason she had never understood, Bath chairmen tended to be Irish. By virtue of their occupation they were large, strong and well-muscled and by temperament they must be respectfully attentive to ladies or they would soon be out of business.

This pair seemed to be chivalrous into the bargain. They grounded their chair and shrugged out of the carrying straps, clearly preparing to rescue her.

'Bothering me? I—' She had no chance to explain that she was perfectly safe, simply frustrated by her escort's attitude, because Ivo squared his shoulders and stepped between her and her would-be rescuers.

'My sister is upset because I will not allow her to waste her money on expensive fripperies. There is no cause for you to concern yourselves. She is perfectly all right. Thank you for your concern.'

'I am not his sister.' She side-stepped around Ivo and smiled at the chairmen. Their frowns deepened into scowls directed at Ivo and she realised that she had made everything much, much worse. 'But—'

'You heard what the lady said,' the larger of the two men said, shifting closer to Ivo. 'Sister, is it? You move along and stop troubling her. We'll take you where you want to go and see you safe inside, miss, never you fear. And no charge neither. Don't hold with these bucks harassing nice young ladies, we don't.'

'I am not a *buck* and I am not harassing her.'

All three men seemed to grow in size as they squared their shoulders and drew themselves up. Any moment now Ivo was going to lose his temper and fists would fly. The odds against him were not as bad as the last time, but really, she could not allow him to get into another fight—this time on her account.

'Ivo, dear.' He turned and looked at her as

though she had burst into song or was speaking Russian. Jane ignored him and smiled sweetly at the chairmen. 'He is not my brother, he is my…' What would be less inflammatory? 'He is my intended. He was being discreet because it is a secret, you see. And I fear I *am* very expensive in my tastes and I was trying to wheedle such a pretty pair of shoes from him. Those blue ones on the left, you see? Irresistible.' She managed a giggle as she slipped her hand under Ivo's arm, feeling the tense, bunched muscles relax slightly. 'Thank you so much, gentlemen, for your concern, but—'

'I say, Merton! No, I mean Kendall!' A chubby blond gentleman was hailing Ivo from across the street. 'Didn't know you were back down here,' he added as he strode over to join them, dodging around the sedan chair. 'Should have thought, what with your father, of course you'd be at the Tower.'

By his side was a tall, thin saturnine man who raised one hand in greeting to Ivo, then turned the gesture into a polite lift of his hat to Jane. 'Good day, ma'am. Problem, Kendall?'

'You gents know this man?' the more belligerent chairman demanded. 'He says he ain't troubling this young lady and she says she's his intended, but *he* said she was his sister and we're worried about the young lady.'

'Didn't know you had a sister, Kendall,' the chubby man said, peering at Jane. He, too, lifted his hat. 'Don't think I've had the pleasure, ma'am.'

'I do not have a sister,' Ivo said between audibly gritted teeth.

'Clearly, our friend was merely exercising some discretion,' the dark man said, rather too obviously kicking his companion lightly on the ankle. 'This is a most respectable gentleman, I can assure you.'

'He is, truly,' Jane interjected before Ivo reached boiling point. 'Thank you so much for your concern, it is most gallant of you.' She smiled at the chairmen and gave Ivo a little nudge.

He dug out something from his pocket and passed it to the two men. 'Thank you for your concern. It is most encouraging that ladies in Bath can rely on such protection,' he said tightly. There was a clink and they visibly relaxed as Ivo handed them the tip.

Jane stood with the three men on the pavement

and watched as they shouldered their carrying harness again and jogged off to answer the summons of an elderly lady who had just emerged from the direction of the Abbey.

When she turned back Ivo was looking blank, the chubby man was clearly agog with curiosity and his companion was regarding Ivo with the air of a man waiting to be entertained.

'Do allow me to present my friends,' Ivo said. Jane was convinced she could still hear the gritted teeth. 'Colonel Marcus Bailey.' He nodded towards the thin man. 'Captain Lord George Merrydew. Bailey, Merrydew, Miss Newnham.'

'Gentlemen.' Jane smiled and they bowed.

'So!' Lord George was almost bouncing on the balls of his feet. 'Congratulations are in order, it seems. When is the happy day?'

'It was just a mis—' Jane said and clashed with Ivo.

'It is not what—'

At which point the two men waved at another who was balancing several brown paper bags in his arms. 'I say, Pennington!' Lord George hailed him as he crossed to their side, limping heavily. 'Come and meet Miss Newnham who is about to make Kendall a far happier man than he deserves! Miss Newnham, ma'am, this is Captain Henry Pennington.'

They were attracting attention now and Jane realised that a service must have just finished at the Abbey, for a stream of ladies was emerging from that direction, some with gentlemen by their side, some with maids in attendance.

'Oh, Lord, there's Mama with Lady Tredwick,' Lord George muttered as two fashionably dressed matrons crossed to join them. 'Never mind, Kendall, she'll hear sooner or later, can't keep news of nuptials from her for long. Mama! Lady Tredwick, ma'am. We were just congratulating Kendall here. This is Miss Newnham, his intended, the lucky dog.'

He continued to prattle on, introducing Jane to the ladies, reminding them—quite unnecessarily, it seemed—that they'd known Ivo since his cradle and commenting happily on what a lark it was that he and Bailey and Pennington should encounter their old comrade in arms in Bath of all places.

'Sold out, the lot of us,' he finished by way of explanation to Ivo. 'Pennington's leg's not up to it any longer, Mama wants me home now Papa isn't so hale and hearty and Bailey's inherited that pile in Northumberland from his great-uncle.'

The ladies ignored him; both had their attention on another victim entirely. Jane swallowed and managed a polite bob of a curtsy, realising what a field mouse watched by an owl must feel like.

'Miss Newnham?' Lady Tredwick said. 'One of the Norfolk Newnhams?'

'Of Dorset, ma'am.'

'Oh. Felicitations.' Her smile was frigid. 'This is a surprise. I had thought Kendall… But never mind that,' she added hastily.

'Er… That is… We are…' She caught Ivo's gaze, saw the almost imperceptible shrug of his shoulders. This was all too public. 'Thank you, ma'am.'

'Indeed, thank you for your good wishes, Lady Tredwick,' Ivo said. 'We are intending to keep it private at present. My father, you understand.'

'You are not in mourning, however, Kendall,' the other matron observed. She lifted her eyeglass, quite unnecessarily in Jane's opinion— however short-sighted she was, she could not fail to see that Ivo was wearing buff breeches, white linen and a deep blue coat.

Jane decided that she really must learn how to do that with her eyebrows. Lady Merrydew managed to combine disbelief, disapproval and reproof all in one elegant arch.

'My grandfather's wishes, Lady Merrydew.'

'No doubt we will have the opportunity to see more of Miss Newnham in due course. You are staying in Bath?' Lady Merrydew's gaze seemed to assess, price and judge everything from the crown of her bonnet to the tips of her practical boots.

The owl was about to swoop. Jane swallowed. 'No, ma'am. With my cousin, Miss Lowry, in Batheaston.'

Why couldn't I think of some convincing lie? Too late now.

'Miss Lowry? I do not think that I have the pleasure of her acquaintance. I regret that we are due elsewhere and cannot continue this enlightening discussion. George, you will accompany us.'

'Mama.' With a jaunty wave Lord George followed his mother, his friends at his heels.

Jane looked around and found they were alone again outside the shoe shop. 'Oh, dear.'

'That hardly begins to cover it,' Ivo said

grimly. 'We need to talk and the urge to dive into the nearest inn and drown myself in gin is too strong. Respectable tea will have to do.'

He raised his cane and gestured to a pair of chairmen. 'The Assembly Rooms.' He handed Jane into the chair and the door was closed before she had the opportunity to say more. Jane sank back against the rather lumpy upholstery as the chair lurched and then settled and the men set off on the long uphill climb.

This was a hideous situation, there was no pretending otherwise. No gentleman could have stood there in public, in the presence of the lady concerned, and announced that he was not betrothed to her—it was up to the lady to laugh lightly and explain that it was all a foolish misunderstanding or a joke. If she'd had rather more social experience, she could probably have pulled it off, Jane knew. As it was, she had hesitated and stammered and had presumably looked the picture of a lovelorn young woman whose secret had been discovered.

The ladies would probably not waste an instant in finding a copy of the *Landed Gentry* and scouring it to see just who this Miss Newnham of Dorset was, she who had so improbably captured the heir to a marquess.

It was her fault that Ivo was in such a fix and it was up to her to repair the damage, because the thought that he might find himself honourbound to make the betrothal real made her feel quite ill with embarrassment. He must despise her and she could not blame him. In fact, she decided, plunging into total gloom as the chairmen paused to cross George Street and tackle the final climb up Bartlett Street, Ivo probably suspected she had been planning something like this from the moment she discovered who he was.

Jane virtually tumbled out of the chair when it halted in front of the Rooms. She had no idea whether the tea rooms were open when there was no Assembly in progress, but Ivo seemed confident enough when he paid the chairmen and turned to the open front door.

'Hopefully it will be quiet at this hour.'

'I will write to them, all of them,' she gabbled as he swept her inside without a pause. 'I will explain that it was just to reassure the chairmen and get us out of an awkward situation. I know

I should have said something at once and that you could not, but I—'

'Shh,' Ivo said. 'Take a deep breath, sit down here.' He glanced around the tea room. Only three other tables were occupied, all by parties of ladies deep in conversation and none of them close enough to overhear. A maid arrived before they could even take their chairs. 'Tea for two and cake. A selection,' he added with a glance at Jane.

'I panicked,' Jane admitted the moment the girl had gone. 'I should have explained the moment I realised they had overheard. I will write to the ladies,' she repeated. 'Tell them all about the chairmen.'

'It was not your fault.' For a man who had found himself accidentally betrothed in the middle of Bath, Ivo was looking remarkably calm, if serious. Perhaps it was shock. 'I should have squashed George the moment he bounced up.'

'If you had not been so cross with me about the shop then we would not have been arguing and the chairmen would not have thought I needed rescuing and none of it would have happened,' Jane said, determined to accept her full blame.

'And if we could all foretell the consequences

of every action nothing would ever be done,' Ivo retorted.

'Yes, but usually one's actions do not lead to anything so ghastly happening.' She broke off to smile her thanks to the maid who set the tea tray on the table and walked away slowly, clearly agog to hear more about the *'ghastly happenings'*.

'I am sorry if the prospect of marriage to me is so distasteful.' Ivo disposed of a blameless jam tart with a snap of white teeth.

'*If* I were not resolved to remain unwed and *if* our ranks were not so disparate that I would spend my entire marriage trying not to disgrace you and *if* we did not spend so much time arguing, then I am sure that marriage to you, my lord, would be delightful,' Jane said crossly as she pushed a cup of tea across the marble table top without too much care not to slop any into the saucer.

Ivo's lips twitched into his almost-smile and he licked a crumb of pastry from the lower one.

He does have very good teeth, Jane mused. *And a well-formed mouth.*

She was thinking as an artist, of course she was, she told herself. But the sight of those lips brought back the memory of that fleeting kiss, of the taste of him, and she felt herself blushing.

'The matter would be dealt with perfectly simply, as you say, with notes from you to the ladies and by me having a word with my erstwhile comrades in arms.' Ivo was looking at her face, which did nothing to help the blush subside.

'But? There is a *but*, isn't there?' Jane eyed the cakes and decided that she had no appetite.

'Eat,' Ivo said, correctly interpreting the glance. 'You need sugar. Lady Tredwick is an old friend of my grandfather. A very close friend. Apparently, they still meet weekly to play cards and assassinate the reputations of all their acquaintance, or so Partridge, our butler, informs me. Not quite in those words, but you get the gist. I imagine the first thing she will do when she arrives home is to pen a note demanding to know why he has not informed her of my betrothal.'

'Then you need to reach him first and explain,' Jane said. 'What is the time? Is there long before your groom brings the phaeton around?'

'Ten minutes,' Ivo said, with a glance up at the clock at one end of the long room. 'Unfortunately, it is not quite that simple. My grandfather is, understandably, anxious about the succession and he is urgent in his desire to see me married. In fact, he has as good as arranged a match, although fortunately I was able to stop him before matters progressed too far. I have not met the lady concerned and I most certainly do not want to find myself committed before I have any idea whether we may suit.'

'Goodness, how awkward for you. The Marquess seems to be a very, um, commanding figure.'

'He's an old tyrant who has had no one to say him nay for decades,' Ivo said ruefully. 'He and I will lock horns sooner or later, but I'm conscious that he has had a difficult time lately with my father's death, not that he'll admit to it. I do not want to make things worse just now.'

'Therefore the sooner you explain about me, the better.'

'Yes. However, when he first raised the matter of Miss—of the bride he had selected for me—I told him that I had met a young lady, was uncertain of the nature of my feelings for her and needed time to decide whether to propose to her or not. I told him, when he probed, not your name, but that you were from a gentry family.'

'You were uncertain of your feelings for *me*?' Jane stared at him, teacup halfway to her lips. 'Me?' It came out as a squeak.

'The feelings I was unclear about, as I am sure you realise, were a choice between amusement, exasperation or panic,' Ivo said. 'But it was all I could think of on the spur of the moment and had the virtue of being true, even if my grandfather chose to read more into it than I actually said.'

Jane put down her teacup with a rattle and stared at him. It was not often that she found herself speechless, but this... The shock of thinking, even for a few seconds, that Ivo meant he was falling for her, was considering proposing, was literally breathtaking. Not that she wanted him to, of course not, but even so... And then he had tossed out words that were as bracing as a bucket of cold water over her. She amused him and exasperated him.

Not as much as you exasperate me, my lord.

Now her brain was working again she could see why Ivo was so concerned. 'Lady Tredwick meets your apparent betrothed, who, she quickly realises, is no member of the aristocracy. We are both flustered, you say we had not intended to announce the betrothal yet. When your grandfather hears that, then he is either going to assume that I am the lady you told him about and will take a poor view of you changing your mind virtually the moment you propose or he will conclude that you have two young gentlewomen dangling and that you are not behaving in a gentlemanly fashion.'

'Or he will realise that I was inventing a story to thwart his well-meant plans for my future. Oh, and dangling after innocent young women in the process,' Ivo said leaning back in the spindly chair and gazing at the ceiling as though expecting celestial guidance. 'Ah well, nothing for it but to make a clean breast of matters. I will go and confess all, with your permission. I shall have to tell him the entire story of our journey together, but you may trust him entirely to be discreet about your identity.'

'I had better come with you,' Jane said. 'He is not going to be very trusting if you produce an even more unbelievable tale than the first one about your confused feelings for some country gentleman's daughter.'

'It would make you far too late returning to

Batheaston,' Ivo protested. 'Besides, this is entirely my problem.'

'Aargh!' Jane threw up her hands, making the maid, who was approaching with a fresh jug of hot water, shy away. 'This is exactly what I meant about not wanting to marry. Men are so unreasonable when you get a notion into your heads. This is *our* problem, not yours alone. It was my decision to pull you into the chaise, my misjudgement when I said to the chairmen that we were betrothed instead of supporting you and pretending to be your sister. My fault that I did not immediately correct the impression that the ladies and your friends formed.'

Ivo had that stubborn expression again—he certainly had the jaw for it. He was not going to allow her equal blame in this, or an equal part in setting it to rights. She tried another tack. 'Besides, when Lady Tredwick looks up my family, as she surely will, she cannot fail to find the Dorset Newnhams with a daughter of my age called Jane. We, together, must tell your grandfather everything and then he, surely, can control Lady Tredwick's propensity for gossip?'

'But not today,' Ivo said. 'I will take you back to your cousin, then attempt to convince Grandfather that this is all a complete misunderstanding by telling him everything. If he still will not accept it, then I will come and collect you. He cannot fail to take a lady's word on the matter.' He gestured to the maid for the reckoning. 'What will you tell your cousin?'

'Everything,' Jane said with a sinking heart. 'Everything except my plan to be a painter.'

Ivo made a sound suspiciously like a growl.

Chapter Nine

First thing the next morning Jane asked permission to drive into Bath again with Charity the maid as chaperon. She would confess the previous day's dramas when she had the facts about the painting scheme. Violet, frowning over a letter from her sister, nodded vague agreement. 'Match me some of the lilac embroidery silk would you, dear? Hopkin's Haberdashery just off Milsom Street, Charity knows it.'

Hopkin's shop proved to be next to an elegant jewellers. Jane sent the maid in to buy the silk and announced airily that she would enquire about having a loose clasp repaired. Ten minutes later she emerged from the shop, clutching her reticule and decidedly shaken. The diamond set was, the jeweller said, not diamonds at all, but a very nice example of paste and would deceive anyone without a loupe to their eye. The pearls were just the thing for a young lady, but worth perhaps twenty guineas. Her nest egg was nothing of the kind.

Perhaps the shop rent would be very cheap, given its condition, she told herself, bundling a surprised Charity into the carriage and telling the driver to take her to Milk Street. It was certainly very low, the agent informed her, given the small size and poor condition. A positive bargain, in fact, he said, quoting an amount that made her gasp.

'This is Bath, madam,' he said reproachfully as she stared at him. 'A bargain, I assure you.'

Jane did her calculations in the carriage driving back. Rent, repairs, redecoration, equipment, advertising, a maid, her own maintenance. It was impossible. Ivo had been right and thank heavens she had thought to check before she did anything irrevocable like sign a lease. She sat in the corner, staring at the figures until they blurred, gloom creeping over her, yet, strangely, she did not feel as disappointed as she would have expected. In fact, it was almost a relief.

Telling Cousin Violet about the argument with Ivo and the subsequent misunderstandings plunged her from gloom into misery. Violet was a tolerant woman and, in many ways, an unconventional one, but it seemed to Jane that morning that she had reached the boundaries of her independence from convention.

'What your parents are going to say I cannot imagine,' she said, tossing aside her embroidery after a luncheon they had both picked at.

'They need never know, surely?' Jane eyed her cooling cup of tea with distaste.

'From the sound of it, letters full of gossip from Lady Tredwick and Lady Merrydew—most of it distorted—will be fluttering on to the tables of every one of their doubtless extensive Dorset acquaintance by the first post. Your mama will be receiving visits of congratulation from half the county within days.'

'Lord Westhaven will stop them writing. He is a friend of Lady Tredwick and she and Lady Merrydew will hardly wish to displease him.'

Perhaps a biscuit? No.

Jane sipped tea instead. 'Ivo—'

'Ivo is an earl. He is going to emerge from this smelling of roses,' Violet said, her voice bleak. 'You will appear as the ambitious young miss scheming to ensnare a lord and he will seem to have been too chivalrous to have contradicted you in the middle of the street when you seized the opportunity to ensnare an exceptionally eligible husband.'

'Oh.' That was one hideous scenario that Jane had not managed to conjure up in the long watches of the night.

The afternoon dragged on. Surely Ivo would either send a note to say all was well or dispatch a carriage to take her to explain herself to the Marquess? Violet sat down to read a large pile of horticultural journals, apparently as a means of soothing herself, and Jane attempted two sketches, tore them both up and instead tried to write to her friend Verity, the new Duchess of Aylsham.

It took some effort to reduce the events of the past few days into any sort of coherent narrative, but finally she managed it. Then there was the more difficult part, admitting that she had been dazzled by the daydream of herself as a society portraitist, her work admired, people flocking to her studio in such numbers that she could support herself.

But I am not that good—not yet, she wrote,

wondering if that was boastful, the assumption that she might, one day, achieve that standard. No, it was not, she decided. She was honest enough to know she could improve and ambitious enough to work to do so.

And I do not want to starve in a garret for the sake of my art while I learn and improve—not that I think I would improve, not under those circumstances.

How would I even buy materials?

Violet appears to enjoy my company—perhaps, if I was certain that it would not be an imposition, I could remain here as her companion, although Mama is set on me making my come-out next Season.

Do you think that if I do not 'take' she might agree—?

Violet looked up. 'Is that a carriage stopping?'

Jane covered her letter with a clean sheet of paper and went to the window. 'Yes, I cannot see properly, it is behind the wall. Strange, it looks like—Violet! It is Papa and Mama.'

Violet put down her journal, took off her spectacles and stood up. 'Oh, rats,' she said, with what Jane considered considerable restraint until she saw how pale her cousin had become. 'It would seem that our joint letter writing has not been as reassuring as we thought.'

'At least they do not appear to have brought Billing. Nor can they have heard about yesterday. Oh, no, there *is* Billing and Papa's valet, Simpkins.' Jane took a deep breath, smoothed down her skirts and went out to the hall. 'We must overwhelm them with the warmth of our welcome—and somehow keep them away from Ivo.'

She threw open the door and ran down the two steps to the garden path. 'Mama! Papa! What a lovely surprise.'

Violet came down to stand beside her. 'Cousin Mildred, Cousin Arthur, how delightful to see you. I do hope you had an uneventful journey.' She turned and called back into the hall, 'Dorothy—prepare the Blue Bedchamber and the one next to it for Mrs and Mrs Newnham and tell Cook to send in tea and cakes.'

'Just some thin bread and butter,' Mama said faintly. 'You know that I cannot eat anything rich after the exertions of a journey. Oh, *Jane.*' She shook her head reproachfully, but allowed her daughter to kiss her cheek.

'Come inside,' Violet urged. 'My footman will help your people with the luggage.' To Jane she sounded perfectly at ease and delighted with her new guests, but the colour was rising and ebbing in her cheeks and her smile looked forced.

Her parents settled in the parlour with the air of explorers who had braved storm-tossed oceans and snow-blocked Alpine passes to reach their daughter, not undertaken a straightforward journey over good roads in the comfort of their own travelling carriage.

'Jane,' her father said, fixing her with a stern gaze. 'Your mother and I have endured the most distressing anxiety.'

'Papa.' She sat down to keep her quivering knees under control. 'I do hope you received our letters.'

'Of course we did. And naturally we set out immediately. Where is *that man*?' Mama demanded.

'What—oh, you mean the unfortunate person I assisted? I have no idea.'

Which is true. Ivo might be doing almost anything at the moment.

'I took him to the first respectable inn and summoned a doctor, as I told you in my letter.

I am sorry about Billing, but I had no idea how badly he was hurt and she was being so obstructive that I feared she would delay me getting him to medical aid. Imagine how dreadful if he had died as a result.' Jane managed a look of surprised innocence. 'You surely do not think that I brought him *here*? That would be shocking.'

'Violet?' Mama turned to her cousin. 'Tell me this is so!'

'I told you in my letter, Mildred,' Violet said. 'I had thought I had made it quite clear. I cannot imagine why you felt it necessary to rush here in such haste. Not that you are unwelcome,' she added with a tight smile. 'But really, Cousin, I cannot help but feel that you are overreacting to the actions of a young lady who showed both courage and a truly noble concern for a person in trouble. One could say that Jane was a perfect Good Samaritan.'

'You have been gravely deceived,' her father said. 'Billing, loyal servant that she is, set out the next day once she had recovered herself and learned that Jane spent the night at Turnham Green in company with *that man* and then set out in the morning with him.'

'I told her to go home and gave her the money

to do so,' Jane said indignantly. 'Of all the sneaking… I did not spend the night in his company, merely in the same building—'

Jane was interrupted in mid-flow by the sound of the knocker. All four of them looked towards the door as the sound of Violet's footman speaking to the new arrivals came indistinctly through the panelling.

'I shall tell Albert that I am not receiving visitors,' Violet said as the door opened and the footman stepped inside.

'The Marquess of Westhaven and the Earl of Kendall, Miss Lowry.' He shot a nervous glance at his mistress, clearly trying to convey that he had not felt brave enough to ask a marquess to wait on the doorstep.

'My lords.' Violet shot to her feet. 'Good morning.'

'Miss Lowry, I presume? My apologies for calling unannounced,' the Marquess said with great amiability and a smile that could have cut teak. 'I did not feel, under the circumstances, that this was a matter that could wait.'

'Circumstances?' Violet said faintly. 'Er… My lords, may I present my cousin Mrs Newnham, her husband Mr Newnham and her daughter Miss Newnham.'

Jane found she was being assessed through rather faded blue eyes by a man who, quite clearly, was what Ivo would look like in fifty years' time. The Marquess nodded sharply. 'Miss Newnham. Ma'am, sir.' He sat down when Violet made a vague gesture towards the best armchair.

Ivo, meanwhile, was shaking hands. 'Mrs Newnham, Miss Newnham, Mr Newnham.' His fingers tightened on hers, whether in warning or apology she could not guess.

Violet jerked the bell pull, but Albert was already bringing in fresh tea and more cups and saucers, followed by Charity with a plate of biscuits.

'Tea?' Violet asked and began to pour before anyone answered. Her hand shook and she put the teapot down for a moment, then resumed filling cups more steadily.

Jane's parents were staring as though mesmerised by the sight of a marquess in Violet's front parlour. Neither spoke. Perhaps, Jane thought, they were working on the principal that a marquess was like royalty and one had to wait to be addressed. Jane, who at least had had the benefit of a duke to practice on recently, took the plunge. Someone had to.

'My parents have arrived from London within the hour, my lord.'

'Excellent timing,' he said drily. 'A smooth journey, Mrs Newnham?'

'Very, my lord, thank you, although, like all travel, exhausting. We used our own carriage, naturally.'

'I find it best,' the Marquess, presumably owner of an entire carriage house full of the things, agreed gravely.

What are you doing here?

Jane tried to catch Ivo's eye, but he was looking at her mother, politely attentive as she chattered on, apparently in the grip of nerves. Once started she did not seem able to stop.

'Your family are clearly intrepid travellers, ma'am,' the Marquess remarked, stopping her mother in her tracks. 'I have to offer my most sincere thanks to Miss Newnham for her courageous efforts on behalf of my grandson.'

He might as well have dropped a bomb, fuse fizzing, into the middle of the room. Ivo, who had been so expressionless as to appear carved from wood, visibly winced. Violet let a low moan escape her and Jane's parents stared at Lord Westhaven and then at Ivo and then at her and then back to the Marquess. Her father's jaw had dropped, her mother gave a faint shriek.

'*He* is the man? This is the...*person* you removed from a common alehouse?'

At which point there was another knock on the front door, followed moments later by Albert, wide-eyed with nerves at this apparently unstoppable deluge of aristocrats. 'Lady Tredwick, Lady Merrydew and Lord George Merrydew, Miss Lowry.'

Jane wondered if she had fainted without anyone noticing, because she was aware of nothing until she heard her name and, blinking, found the new arrivals seated. The room was becoming exceedingly cramped, but the ladies settled themselves on to the sofa with the air of two large chickens making themselves comfortable on their nests with much fluffing of feathers and gentle clucking.

And the clucking was, presumably, the sound of two gossips looking forward to a truly wonderful session, full of delicious revelations.

Ivo stood up abruptly. 'Mr Newnham. I wonder if I might have a word with you in private, sir?'

Her father, still looking faintly stunned, got to his feet. Her mother fanned herself vigorously with one of the tiny embroidered napkins and Violet gave herself a visible shake.

'Please, use my little library. It is just across the hall, Cousin Arthur.'

Presumably Ivo, with great good sense, was removing her father from the crowd to explain the situation in a more tranquil setting, Jane thought. She could only hope that Papa would be sufficiently soothed by Ivo's status. She realised that everyone else in the room was staring at her and felt the colour rising in her cheeks.

'My goodness, Miss Newnham, never tell me that the news we learned yesterday was in advance of your parents' approval?' Lady Tredwick said coyly as the door closed behind the two men.

Her mother gave an audible gasp. 'News?' she murmured faintly.

'Honoria, dear friend.' The Marquess fixed Lady Tredwick with a look that made Jane, on the periphery of it, gulp. 'I never took you for a gossip.'

Her Ladyship bridled. 'Certainly not. I was merely—'

He turned to Jane. 'I understand that you are a considerable artist, Miss Newnham.'

She found her voice from somewhere and, by some miracle, did not babble. 'Lord Kendall is too kind. I do find it very satisfying to attempt to master the skill.'

'Portraits are your *forte*, he tells me. In oils.'

And what else has he told you? Not, surely, that I talked of painting professionally or you would be shocked. Even more shocked than you must be already.

'That is my favourite subject and medium, my lord.'

'And Jane does such lovely little watercolour sketches,' her mother interrupted. 'Landscapes, posies of flowers, kittens…'

'How delightful,' Lady Merrydew cooed. 'Such a charming pastime for a young lady.'

Jane forced a smile and tried to look like a young lady who painted kittens and posies in watercolour. There had been no sound from beyond the door since it had closed. Perhaps Papa was believing every word Ivo said and was perfectly happy and reassured as a result. It did seem unlikely, knowing Papa...

The door opened again and her father stood on the threshold. 'Jane, could you join us, please.' He looked as though he had received a shock, not necessarily an unpleasant one, but something that had rocked his certainties. Surely after realising that his daughter was capable of painting footmen in the nude—she mentally rearranged that sentence to *painting nude footmen*—the discovery that she had spent some time in the company of a respectable earl was not so very earthshattering?

She followed him into Violet's book room. Ivo was standing in front of the little fireplace, looking even more than usually aloof. When she closed the door he gave her the ghost of a smile.

Her father cleared his throat. 'Lord Kendall has done us the great honour of requesting my permission to address you,' he said. His voice cracked halfway through the sentence.

'Permission to address me? Lord Kendall has no need of permission to speak to me, surely?' And then, as her father made a choking sound and Ivo looked at her quizzically, she realised what he meant. 'I—He… *What?* Could I speak to Lord Kendall alone, Papa?'

'Of course.' Flustered, her father went out, closing the door with exaggerated care.

'Ivo? What on earth are you thinking? Papa has not tried to pressure you into this, has he? You *knew* what I will say.'

The smile was gone. Ivo raked his fingers though his hair. 'No. I asked his permission before he had the opportunity to express his outrage or to make demands. With your parents here already, knowing that we spent at least one night under the same roof, and those two scandal-mongering old hypocrites finding us all in a huddle, what else can we do? Either we are conspiring together to conceal a scandal or we are a happy family group planning a wedding— I cannot see any other explanation for how this looks, can you?'

'I can cope with a scandal,' Jane said.

Ivo made a move as though to reach for her and she took a couple of steps away from him, was brought up short by the desk, turned and paced back. She found she was wringing her hands and made herself stop.

'I am no one of any consequence and I told you

I do not want to marry, so it does not matter if other gentlemen look at me askance.'

Ivo, who had not moved from the fireplace, looked grim.

'Oh, of course—it will look as though you have ruined me and refused to do the right thing! Well, that is easy to deal with. You have asked Papa, he said *yes*. I have said *no*. So, there is no stain on your honour, is there? If anyone should ask me, I will say that I realised that I could never marry a man I did not love and that I am resigned to spinsterhood. Your grandfather will be relieved.' She frowned at him. 'Why has he come, anyway?'

'He came because he wanted to meet you, hardly expecting to find your parents here. I had told him the full story—it was the first time I can recall him laughing until the tears ran.'

'What is so amusing?' Jane demanded.

'The scene in Bath,' he admitted ruefully. 'But it seems that, on reflection, he was impressed by your actions and declared that he is coming to the conclusion that some sturdy gentry blood is just what the family line needs. Apparently a recent encounter with some of my cousins has rattled his belief that the more ancient the name, the better.' He shifted his position to watch her as she paced away. 'Your friend Verity married a duke.'

'Her father is a bishop and they have connections to any number of great families.' This room was too small. Jane felt trapped, as though at any moment she would be battering herself against bars like a goldfinch in a cage. 'They are in love,' she said. 'That is what matters.'

'We do not dislike each other, do we?' Ivo offered.

He did not make the error of declaring warmer feelings, for which she was exceedingly grateful. Nor did he try to touch her again and, strangely, she was sorry for that. Just now it would be nice to be held, to have a broad male chest to lay her head against, warm hands to... She straightened her back and looked him firmly in the eye.

'I dislike you intensely when you try to stop me doing what I want—what I *need* to do for my future.'

Ivo laughed. 'Other than that. We get on, do we not?'

'It is not the *point*.' She was not going to admit that she had thought better of her plan to set up as a portraitist. 'Nor is it amusing.'

'There are advantages to being married, you know.' His voice had dropped, making the words resonate with a meaning she realised she understood very well. 'I think we could improve on that kiss, for example.'

Jane was not aware that he had moved. Perhaps it was her restless pacing. Now they were very close indeed, close enough to see the grain of his skin, the precise, sharp groove between lip and nose, the thickness of his eyebrows. She could smell his cologne and the starch of his linen and a faint, tantalising hint of masculinity. *Hold me.*

Chapter Ten

Ivo took her right hand, his thumb tracing over the swelling at the base of her thumb. Shivers ran through her.

'Shall we see?'

'What…?'

Stop dithering, you ninny!

'If we can improve on our one kiss?'

'Why not? Since there will not be another one,' she said defiantly.

'Oh, Jane. Either you are the most artless girl I have ever met or you are the most cunning.' He took her other hand.

'What do you mean? Cunning?'

'If you hoped to provoke a man into giving a kiss his full attention and every ounce of skill in the matter that he can summon, you could not do better.'

They were standing toe to toe now. She found

she liked his teasing. She liked the sensation of being so close, of anticipation. She wanted him to kiss her.

'Excellent. But could you do it now, please, because Mama will be rushing in any moment now, you realise?'

Being kissed by a man who was smiling was really rather wonderful. It made her smile back against his lips, made it so easy for his tongue to slip in, teasing, stroking. That was such a surprise she almost jumped, almost bit him, then she found she could stroke back with hers and that when she did Ivo's arms tightened around her and he made a sound, almost a purr, deep in his throat. That gave her a strange feeling— almost tenderness, almost power, certainly a longing for more.

When he lifted his head and set her back a little, she blinked at him and found they were both still smiling. 'That was very... Verity said it was very...but I did not believe her.'

'Did she say anything more about the married state?'

'I did ask her,' Jane admitted. 'Mama would never explain. I mean, what on earth have bees and flowers to do with anything? Or closing one's eyes and fixing one's mind on duty and children? So, Verity told me and, I have to say, it does sound highly improbable that it is an enjoyable thing to do, but she assures me that it is. With the right person.'

Ivo was still smiling. She hoped he was not laughing at her. Or at her pink cheeks. It was surprising that they were not scarlet, because this was a very naughty conversation to be having.

'Perhaps I am the right person for you after all,' he said and there was a question in his eyes and something else, something unsettling.

Something very like pain? Surely not. And had she imagined the very lightest emphasis on *you*—as though *she* might not be right for *him*. But if that was the case Ivo could be proposing purely out of gallantry.

'I am not sure that nice kisses, or whatever happens in bed, are good enough reasons for risking marriage,' she said.

'I would encourage you to paint,' Ivo said. 'You could paint whoever you wanted—there would be no need to do it for money, so there would be no criticism of you.'

Jane studied his face, the line between his

brows as the smile faded and he watched her, studying her face in his turn as she thought it through.

This was what I want, surely? But I would be painting at his whim, with his permission...

'You wanted to be independent?' he said, clearly reading her doubts. 'I can see that would be a stumbling block. Would you accept my word that I will not stand in the way of your art? Would you be very kind and tolerate being a rich woman?'

'Yes, I could tolerate being a rich woman,' Jane agreed, not certain whether to laugh or cry. It all sounded so very tempting, so very easy. Approval from Mama and Papa, no need to fight to paint as she wished. No risk of finding herself starving in a garret, cast off by her family and failing to find any customers for her art.

Accepting Ivo's offer would mean life with this man who was having an unsettling, but very pleasant, effect on her equilibrium... She tried not to think about that or about the intimacies that marriage would bring. Those thoughts went far beyond unsettling if she let them. Her mind shied away and found something else to worry about. Marriage meant more than what happened beyond the bedchamber door. 'But I would acquire a great many duties, would I not? I have not been raised to be an aristocratic wife.'

'We have a very competent housekeeper, there is nothing for you to worry about.'

The word *yes* was on the tip of her tongue, then, for some reason, one of her friend Melissa's favourite sayings came to her. *If it is too good to be true, then it probably is.* Why she should choose that moment to recall it, she did not know, but it was certainly timely.

'But you do not *want* to marry me,' Jane said. 'This is pure gallantry. You would not have thought of it if we had just happened to meet socially. You would not have decided, *There's the lady I will court and wed*, now, would you?'

'I had intended to marry when I returned to England,' Ivo said, after a pause so short she might have imagined it. But she could not miss the fact that he had not answered her question. 'And this is clearly my duty—' He broke off, presumably realising that this was not a tactful approach. 'We find ourselves in a position where it would be most sensible to wed. We have rubbed along very well except when the question of you earning your living by your art came up, have we not?'

'Rub along? Is that really all you want from marriage?'

'It seems a perfectly reasonable proposition,' Ivo said. 'You were prepared to go to any amount of trouble and deceit to get what you want—the opportunity to paint as you desire. You were willing to accept the risk of social ostracism, a rift from your parents, difficulties for your cousin Miss Lowry, poverty and loneliness.'

She should tell him that she had changed her mind, that he had helped her see that it was not what she truly wanted after all. Pride stopped her.

'I am offering you social acceptance, wealth, access to subjects to paint you could not have dreamt of. Your parents would be delighted—'

'And what about love?' she broke in. 'What if I fall in love with someone else after we marry? What if you do?'

'It does not last, romantic love.' Ivo stepped back from her stabbing finger before she could make contact to emphasise her point. He turned away and it must have been that which made his voice seem less distinct, less assured.

'Ivo?'

He turned back to face her and she thought she saw that darkness shadowing those blue eyes again. 'There might be a fleeting attraction, but mature, sensible people can ignore it, turn from it until it fades, believe me.'

Was he speaking from experience? 'But Verity and Will—I cannot imagine their love fading.'

'The Duke and Duchess met when both were free to indulge their feelings, to build on that first attraction. If they had not been free, then it would all have been forgotten soon enough.'

'So cynical!' She could not believe it, not after seeing the look in Will's eyes when he watched Verity, not when she saw the bloom of happiness that love had brought to her friend.

'I am realistic,' Ivo said, his voice harsh. He raised one hand to touch cold fingertips to her cheek and his tone gentled. 'Jane, the situation we now find ourselves in makes your fantasy quite untenable.'

She opened her mouth to protest that if he meant her career in art, she knew that, but if he meant her dreams of true love, then he must be wrong.

The door creaked before she could speak. 'Jane

dear?' Her mother peeped around the edge with a coyness that made her toes curl. 'Now then, you two young people cannot be alone in here so long, you naughty things. You must come out and share your news.'

'Not quite yet, Mrs Newnham,' Ivo said with a smile that did not reach his eyes, Jane saw. 'We will go out into the garden.'

'The back garden,' Jane added. 'Then, Mama, you may watch us from this window if you fear for the proprieties. This way, Ivo.'

Ivo held the door open with the hint of a bow. 'Do come in, ma'am.'

Jane stood aside as her mother, smiling a little uncertainly at Ivo, allowed herself to be seated at the window. They escaped into the hall, out of the back door into the grassed area to the rear of the house. It was scattered with old fruit trees, apples and pears and cherries, lichen-covered and bent with age.

Ivo offered his arm and Jane took it. They could hardly stand in the middle of the grass glaring at each other.

'That…my painting…is nothing to do with this,' she said, picking up their argument as they began to pace away from the house.

'I wish I could believe that,' Ivo retorted. 'It is inconceivable that you could establish a business in Bath relying on the patronage of the middle and upper classes without Mesdames Tredwick and Merrydew discovering it. They know your true identity. Can you imagine the gossip? I guarantee that you would be characterised as my discarded mistress, or the hussy who jilted me *or* the poor creature that *I* jilted within days. No one of any respectability would dream of commissioning you to paint their family.'

'I know that,' she said at last, trying to ignore the sick feeling in the pit of her stomach. If he sneered, if he said, *I told you so*, she would not forgive him. 'I do not have enough money.'

'No, you do not,' Ivo agreed. 'I am sorry. If there was almost anything else that you wanted so badly, then I would give you the money and be happy to do so, but I am not going to pay for your ruin.'

'I could not take money from you anyway.' Jane saw the pale oval of her mother's face at the window of the book room. She walked further under the shelter of the trees. 'That would make me a kept woman, would it not?' She tried for a laugh and failed. 'You did warn me about that.'

'It would if I asked for anything in return,' Ivo said.

'Thank you, but I shall return home to Dorset, having made it clear that I have refused your most flattering offer. No doubt I will be in disgrace with my parents for months, but I will be no worse off than I was before.'

'You will be very much worse off when the gossip reaches the ladies of your neighbourhood—and it will—and they learn that you were declaring yourself betrothed to the Earl of Kendall in the street one day and jilting him the next, once your parents arrived. Goodness knows what the tale to explain that will be, but I have no doubt that it will be lurid enough to make you the talk of the county for months.'

'Oh, those wretched chairmen! Why did they have to take a fit of gallantry just then?' She glanced up and saw Ivo's mouth twist into a wry smile. 'And there is no need for you to look like that, I am quite well aware that it was all my fault. I thought that if I said I was your betrothed it would make the story of an argument more plausible.'

'Because betrothed couples will surely argue?' he asked with a flash of the old laughter back in his eyes. 'Jane, will you accept the inevitable? It is not only for your sake, you know—your parents and your cousin will be saved much distress and anxiety. My grandfather is ready to accept it now he realises that I am not going to dance to his tune and marry to order.'

'And it would be best for your reputation,' she said, making the argument that he would not.

Ivo made a dismissive gesture with his free hand.

'Tell me one thing, then.'

'Anything.'

'Is there anyone who has hopes of you? Are you in love with anyone?'

'I am not promised to anyone, you have my word on it.' Ivo gestured towards a seat against the wall. 'Shall we?' He stopped as she tugged on his arm and came to look up into his face. 'No, Jane, there is no one who has hopes of me, upon my honour.'

'In that case...' Jane swallowed, her mouth suddenly dry. There would be no going back from this and the implications were life-changing, whichever choice she made. On the one hand, scandal and disgrace, not just within her family, but within a wide social circle. She would be the girl who jilted the Earl of Kendall after she had done something so awful that he had felt bound to offer for her. On the other, to marry out of her world, to take on responsibilities she could hardly guess at, to risk never being able to practise her art as she so passionately wished to. And to be married to a man she did not love, who certainly did not love her, the two of them tied for ever.

But I like him. I think he finds me...interesting. I trust him. I will do my best to make sure he does not regret this and his grandfather seems disposed to approve of the match. I wonder why, when he had plans for another marriage altogether?

She had not so much hesitated as come to a complete stop. She glanced at Ivo who had abandoned trying to get her to sit and was leaning one shoulder against the down-bent branch of a gnarled apple tree. He did not look impatient, or bored, either of which would have been understandable, Jane thought. Instead he appeared interested, as though he was following her mental processes and found that a worthwhile exercise.

If he had merely been politely patient, that would have made her hesitate, but if Ivo was inclined to find her worthy of curiosity, then she would have some foundation to build a marriage with him. It would be like painting a portrait: they had a rough scribbled outline of a relationship and now she had to lay down a ground to support the picture as they built it up together— layers of colour, of light and shade or ambiguity and certainty.

'You are smiling,' Ivo said. 'Does that mean that you have made up your mind?' He straightened up from the tree, tall and strong in the dappled shade and her breath caught. Why had she not thought him handsome merely because his face had strength and character and power? She, an artist, should have known better: this was a masculine beauty all its own and she wanted it for herself.

'Yes, I have.' Jane took a step towards him, reached for him. 'And I accept, if you are quite certain. I will not hold it against you if you have changed your mind.'

'I was rather hoping to hold *you* against *me*,' Ivo said and took her hand, drawing her in close, then leaning back into the bough so she tipped forward against his chest with a squeak of alarm. 'I have you safe. And we have an audience. Shall we show them that they have something to celebrate?'

'Them? Where? Who? I thought we were out of sight now.' Jane tried to see but Ivo settled her more firmly in his embrace and bent his head.

'An entire flock of chaperons has decided to take the air and admire the orchard and is tactfully pretending they cannot see us,' he murmured against her hair. His breath was warm and it tickled a little, then his cheek was against hers, the faint grain of his beard, even after a close shave, a new sensation. His breath was teasing her ear now and he was murmuring soft words, too low for her to understand.

It seemed her body did know this whispered language because Jane found herself pressing closer against the intriguing layers of male clothing, the softness of broadcloth and the crispness of linen, the buttons in places ladies had no buttons, the faint discomfort of his watch chain against her ribs.

Her own mouth was moving, too, without her will. She kissed slowly across his cheek, tasting faint saltiness while her nostrils registered verbena and spice and shaving soap and an interesting muskiness. Then Ivo moved his head and their lips met.

They had not learned each other yet, she realised, surprised to find that learning was needed, that exploration would be pleasurable. Their noses bumped, she found the corner of his mouth…and then they had it, lips moving together, parting to share heat and moisture, ready for new discoveries.

'Hurrumph.'

Jane jumped. Against her lips Ivo sighed, then he straightened, setting her on her feet and steadying her with one hand under her elbow as he turned to face his grandfather, two trees away, apparently studying the graft on a pear.

'You startled me, sir. I had no idea anyone was in the garden.'

Fibber, Jane thought, embarrassed, but also amused.

'No time to be billing and cooing out here,' the Marquess said, still glowering at the lumpy bark. 'Plenty of time for that. Business to be completed, agreements to be made, dates to be set.' He looked at them then and Jane had the sudden thought that he had tears in his eyes, then she blinked and the fleeting impression was gone.

What would he have to be sad about? If he disliked the idea of this match, then he would make his feelings very plain.

'My grandfather is not of a romantic inclination, you note, Jane,' Ivo said drily. 'You will be glad to hear that Miss Newnham has accepted my offer, sir.'

'I should hope so after that exhibition. Come along in, the pair of you, and speak to Mrs Newnham. The poor lady has no idea whether she is on her head or her heels with you two and your harum-scarum idea of courtship. Wouldn't have done in my day, I can tell you.' He turned then looked back. 'I have got rid of their Ladyships, you'll be glad to hear. Told them in confidence that the reason your mama is in such a taking is that her sensibilities are shattered by an engagement when we're in mourning. They are in such awe of her putting such scruples before an advantageous match that they are quite prepared to overlook the disparity in rank that had been exercising them before and have rushed back to Bath to inform all their acquaintance of the fact.'

'And you, my lord?' Jane asked, finding herself suddenly bold enough to ask. 'Can you accept such a disparity?'

He looked at her from under thick grey brows. 'Frankly, Miss Newnham, I would overlook my grandson marrying any young lady of good upbringing if she keeps him in the present and not in the past.'

She felt Ivo stiffen, then he said, 'I do not think I need a wife to remind me that I am not in the army any longer, Grandfather. I suspect that the work you are heaping on me will serve that purpose well enough.'

Jane felt a pang of guilt. It had not occurred to her that Ivo might be mourning not only his father, but also the loss of his military career. She had been so tied up in her own hopes and dreams and frustrations that she had been selfish, she realised. She gave his arm a little squeeze. 'I am afraid that I will be adding to your burdens, because there must be a great deal for me to learn.'

Ivo felt the light pressure of Jane's fingers, the anxiety in her voice, and frowned at his grandfather's back as he led the way out of the orchard. Not only had the old man dropped a heavy hint that Ivo had some kind of past to be put behind him, but now Jane was worrying about her new life.

'It will not be a burden—I will be discovering a new life at the same time. Don't forget that I have to learn about the estates and become used to life as a civilian again. We can muddle along together.'

He was aware of her relaxing a little and she chuckled. 'I cannot imagine you *muddling* anything, Ivo.'

No? What have I just done if not landed us both in a muddle?

But what else could he have done but persuade her into marriage? It was not what he had hoped for, expected, but he was never going to have that and he refused to pine and turn himself into a recluse because he could not have Daphne. He had his duty to his name, to his grandfather, to the future.

And it might not be what Jane wanted, had dreamed of, but he would make certain she could paint what she wanted, how she wanted.

That gave him pause. No, possibly he would draw the line at naked footmen. The thought amused him, lightening his mood as they reached the back door into the house.

Then his grandfather turned. 'I clean forgot—I have spoken to Pettigrew and Arnold about that problem you mentioned. They are preparing an opinion for you, but I have to say, they are not optimistic.'

'Thank you, sir. I look forward to discussing it later,' Ivo said. He would have to make it clear to the old man that he did not want Daphne Parris discussed in Jane's hearing. As his physical wounds healed he found himself feeling more in sympathy with Daphne's rebellion. She had dreamt of romance, he supposed, and instead was left to twiddle her thumbs demurely while her husband-to-be was hundreds of miles away, communicating erratically as months turned into years, unable to say when—or if—he would return.

This young woman beside him had dreams, too. Unconventional ones, to be sure, but he could help her achieve them—or as much of them as was safe. If the legal experts told him the marriage was indissoluble, then all he could do for his lost love was to stay out of her way and try and find some satisfaction in helping another dreamer fulfil her hopes. It was that or mope about nursing his fading bruises and his broken heart, he thought grimly. Or set out cold-blood-edly to find a 'suitable' bride. The first tasted of self-pity, and he had no intention of throwing his life away by wallowing in that, and the second risked boredom or worse.

Ivo glanced down at Jane as he held the door for her. She seemed calm, although her colour was up and her eyes were bright. Was she fighting tears or was it the effects of that kiss under the apple tree? He hoped it was the kiss because he had enjoyed it more than he had expected.

He was conscious of a twinge of guilt for that. He loved Daphne and he should not be taking pleasure in kissing another woman. And yet, if he was to marry Jane, then he must make love to her and do so without ever letting her guess that she was not his first choice, that there was still another woman in his thoughts. For a second he wondered whether a marriage such as his grandfather had been plotting for him would not be more honest. The lady who accepted him then would have no illusions about the nature of the union, but Jane, he feared, was a romantic with her talk of love matches.

Then her parents and her cousin descended on them, driving away any second thoughts or introspection. Jane was hugged and kissed, Mr Newnham shook his hand, Cousin Violet kissed him on the cheek and went bright pink and, taking the plunge, he kissed Mrs Newnham, making her gasp and blush and stammer something that sounded suspiciously like, 'Dear boy!'

The die was cast and there was no going back now, Ivo thought as he smiled and laughed and generally exerted himself to be pleasant to his future in-laws. He must put all thoughts of Daphne behind him, except for offering the practical advice of his lawyers to her aunts. There was no reason why he should ever see her again, after all. Her husband had neither the money nor the reputation—nor, probably, the inclination—to mix with the same society that the heir to the Marquess of Westhaven would be keeping, so there was no danger of any accidental meetings. What was important now was to make this marriage work.

Chapter Eleven

Three days later

Jane took out the letter she had begun to Verity the afternoon that Ivo had proposed to her and started afresh, wondering if writing it all down would help her believe what was happening.

> *And so you see how it comes to pass that I am making almost as good marriage as you! Mama, you will hardly be surprised to hear, is beside herself and half convinced that she would have discovered Ivo herself, once she had exhausted her search for distant heirs to dukedoms. He is, of course, the pineapple of perfection in her eyes—and I have to admit he is proving to be a very satisfactory husband-to-be.*
>
> *Sometimes I have to stop and pinch my-*

self. I said I would never marry except for love. Then in a moment of madness I swore that I would be independent and paint for a living. And now I am doing neither.

But is this the right thing? I keep think-ing, What if? What if those two chairmen had not been passing just as we were argu-ing? What if Ivo's friends had not appeared at just the wrong moment?

But then I come back to worrying about what would have happened if we had not been held up at just the right point in Kens-ington. Then I would never have met Ivo and he might have been seriously injured. And that makes me feel quite sick.

From your letters, Verity darling, I know that you sometimes find it difficult, learn-ing to be a duchess. At least I will not have to be a marchioness immediately—not for a long time, I hope, because I am learning to love the Marquess despite all his growling.

Anyway, I hope you will able to give me some advice on how to go on—I am relying on you.

But I am not writing to bore you with all my dithering thoughts and three-in-the-

morning doubts. Will you lead my attendants at the wedding? I am writing to Lucy and Melissa and Prue to ask them to be bridesmaids, of course, but you would be matron of honour—although I find the idea of any of us being matrons so funny that I giggle every time I think of it.

You will receive a formal invitation, of course, for you and Will and all his brood of brothers and sisters. I am so looking forward to seeing them meet the Marquess!

It would mean so much if you can be there to watch over me.

Your ever-loving and quite distracted friend,
Jane

17th September—a week later

'Oh, thank goodness,' Jane said, looking up from the drift of letters that half covered the breakfast table. 'They can all be bridesmaids, even Verity who tells me she is expecting a little dukeling, which is wonderful news.'

'A duckling?' Startled, Cousin Violet looked up from her own correspondence.

'Dukeling. I suppose it might be a girl, of

course, but Verity seems convinced it is a boy. You appear to have a great deal of post.'

'Acceptances,' Violet said, rescuing one envelope from the butter dish. 'At least, most of them are, but there must be at least three letters from your mother, who no sooner seems to seal one missive than something else occurs to her and so she writes another. At this rate your father will be spending more on postage than on your wedding dress.'

After much debate it had been agreed that Jane would be married from Cousin Violet's house and that the ceremony would take place in Merton Tower's own chapel. Bath, although no longer at the pinnacle of fashion, still had enough excellent *modistes* to provide Jane's trousseau and far more shops for all the trifles she would need than could be found in rural Dorset.

Mrs Newnham had been only too delighted to pass on the organisation to Violet, reserving to herself the pleasant responsibility for thinking up endless tasks for other people to do and changing her mind three times a day about her own gowns. Jane suspected that she was also scouring the *Peerage* to trace every one of Ivo's illustrious connections so she could boast about them to her long-suffering acquaintance.

Jane had expected that the Marquess would want to keep the marriage in a very low key. He had recently lost a son and she would have thought that the new bride was far from being a trophy to be celebrated, but he had been quite clear about his wishes.

'It is not what people might expect, so we must avoid any suspicion I do not entirely approve. There will be no undue haste—six weeks will be adequate, I believe—and the guest list will be…comprehensive.'

'Comprehensive?' she had wavered.

'Very.' He had given her a stern look as though she might have been about to protest that two witnesses would be all she wanted. 'It will be spoken of far and wide and my approval will be clear to all. However, the fact that it will not be in London will limit the numbers, I fear. I trust you will not be disappointed at perhaps two hundred guests, Jane?'

'Oh, no,' she had managed to say. 'Two hundred? Goodness, no, not disappointed. Not at all.'

Terrified.

The acceptances had come flooding back. The Marquess had despatched a clerk to assist Violet while his own secretary dealt with the far greater number of responses to the Tower for the Mertons' family and acquaintances. Meanwhile Jane searched for a *modiste* who would provide her with the gown she wanted—simple, elegant and economical. She had the 'diamonds' that she had inherited and those, despite being merely paste, would distract from the fact that Papa simply could not afford the kind of trousseau Mama thought she should have.

Anxious, Jane had asked Ivo and to her relief he had been very understanding. 'We have time before you will be making your appearance in London society and I can buy you just what you need then—do not let your parents worry about it.'

So Jane had edited down the extensive lists her mother sent her—all but the nightgowns. Verity had emphasised the importance of elegant naughtiness in nightwear for married ladies and had sent a box of outrageously pretty garments as an engagement present. Jane had tried them on and had been startled and surprised at the effect. But men, Verity had explained, liked such nonsense. Jane reasoned that, as the man in question was not already blinded by love, every little effort would help in making the wedding night go well.

She hid her blushes at the thought of it by pouring herself another cup of coffee.

It is too late now. You cannot change your mind. Then, *Admit it—you do not want to change your mind.*

After her parents had returned to Dorset Jane went into Bath escorted by Charity, the maid, and had her jewellery cleaned. On the way back they had driven past the little shop near the Abbey and it made her think again about the choices she had made.

Ivo had not been patronising her when he had told her that her dream was impractical, he had been correct. It was a hard truth to swallow but it made her respect him more, both for caring that she should not suffer the consequences of her impetuosity and for taking her ambition seriously in the first place.

I can trust him, she thought as the carriage had rattled out of the City. Trust seemed a good basis for a marriage.

'Lord Kendall, Miss Violet,' Albert announced.

He had become almost blasé about the comings and goings of the aristocracy by now, even unconventional ones who arrived while his mistress was taking breakfast.

Ivo appeared, apologetic about disturbing them. Violet dimpled at him, Jane blushed, which was, disconcertingly, all she ever seemed to do these days when they met. She supposed it was a combination of the fact that she was beginning to find Ivo decidedly attractive and the realisation that the wedding day—and the wedding night—were coming rapidly closer.

'I am sorry to call at such an hour, but it occurred to me that you might wish to tour the house with Mrs French, our housekeeper,' he said to Jane once he had accepted a cup of coffee. 'If we leave it much longer, Mrs French will be wrestling with all the arrangements for the wedding and I thought you might feel more comfortable if you had a better idea of the place before you move in and take over.'

'Take over?' It came out as a squeak. 'But Mrs French—'

'As housekeeper she will be a great support, but you will be the mistress of the house.'

Jane swallowed a jagged piece of toast. Surely

she recalled him soothing her worries with the mention of the competent housekeeper? She had not questioned the arrangements at Merton Tower when she and her parents and Violet had paid a formal visit after the betrothal. Her mother had been in a tizzy because she had no clothes she considered adequate for a marquess's home and so they had made the excuse that they could not dine and stay because they had to travel back to Dorset to make arrangements there. But, of course, the Marquess was a widower and Ivo had no sisters or sisters-in-law who might take the place of the Marchioness.

Ivo had given them a brief tour and Jane had stared at the single central medieval tower that was all that remained of the castle, had blinked at the number of windows in the flanking wings, built in the early eighteenth century, and had brought away an impression of acres of gleaming wood and costly draperies formed through a haze of nerves. If she had been asked afterwards to describe the public rooms that they had seen—the entrance hall, the great hall in the tower, the drawing room and dining room—she doubted she could have done so. But she did recall the portraits, ranking from stiff Tudor panels to lush Georgian groups.

'Yes, of course,' she said now. 'How thoughtful of you, Ivo.' She owed it to him to make a good impression on the staff.

He gave her a sudden smile and she wondered if he guessed just how anxious she was. It was good to see him smile because she had seen little of that side of him lately, she thought as she went upstairs to put on her best spencer and bonnet and to find a respectable pair of gloves. Was that why he had appeared so serious, the last few times she had seen him? Concern that he had done the right thing in marrying the daughter of a country gentleman?

She had been raised as a lady, she knew she could hold her own in polite society, could dance and make conversation and display the proper manners in most formal situations, but she had never attended more than local dances and Assemblies, never been invited to a London party. She knew how to keep house, of course—provided the house had a mere six bedchambers and a handful of servants.

Jane came downstairs with the lowering feeling that the unknown Mrs French would despise her. The upper servants in great houses could be as snobbish as their employers, Verity had told her. She fixed a cheerful smile on her lips, waved Violet goodbye and let Ivo help her up into her seat in the phaeton.

'What is wrong?' he asked quietly, the moment they were in motion and the sound of the wheels on the road surface masked their conversation from the groom up behind.

Clearly her acting was worse than she imagined. 'Why, nothing at all. What a lovely morning it is!'

'Jane, I can read you like a book,' Ivo said.

That was depressing. No one liked to think they were transparent.

'Merely nerves—your housekeeper is going to despise my lack of knowledge and I cannot imagine that, after running matters in the absence of a lady of the house for years, she is going to look very kindly on my bumbling efforts.'

'She will be delighted, believe me. You have the sensitivity not to try and ride roughshod over her and she will enjoy showing you her kingdom. Day to day there is nothing for you to do but agree menus with Cook and make any decisions that, until now, Mrs French has had to lay before Grandfather. You may imagine how well they get along on matters such as deciding how to replace the hangings in the Blue Suite or whether we require another parlourmaid!'

He laughed and she found herself laughing with him. Yes, the crusty Marquess would give short shrift to choices of braid and tassels.

'Be yourself,' Ivo said. He shifted the reins into his whip hand and laid the left over hers where they lay clasped nervously on her lap. 'I have every confidence in you.'

'Which gives me a very poor opinion of your judgement,' Jane retorted, but she did not attempt to free her hands and he kept his, warm in his leather gloves, over them for a heartbeat longer.

To her relief Ivo did not try and lecture her on the house as they drove, but pointed out landmarks on the way.

By the time they turned in through the gates, their high pillars topped by rearing seahorses for some reason she must ask about, she felt more relaxed than she had done in days.

Then the drive went around a bend and she

could see, spread out in front of her, the park and the house at its heart. Arriving in a closed carriage, in the company of her parents who were even more nervous than she was, the impact had been far less and somehow she had not realised just how large her new home was.

'What is wrong?' Ivo asked, steadying the pair as a small herd of deer ran across the drive.

'Wrong?'

'You gulped.'

'No wonder! Just look at it. How many bedchambers are there?'

'I have no idea. Too many, no doubt. But Mrs French will be able to tell you.'

'It was a rhetorical question.' Surely he could comprehend what a shock this was, although, of course, she should have expected it. 'I will have to take a ball of twine with me everywhere, like Theseus in the Minotaur's labyrinth, or I will get hopelessly lost and my skeletal remains will be found in some distant corridor a hundred years hence.'

There was a suppressed snort from behind that reminded Jane that there was a groom with them and it behoved an almost-countess to be discreet in front of the servants.

'Take a footman with you everywhere at first,' Ivo suggested. 'But it is hard to get lost. We had an ancient relative staying when I was a child. She was confused, poor dear, but she would wander all over and then shout when she became too lost. Someone always heard her. You can work out roughly where you are by looking out of the window, after all. The park is littered with eye-catchers which make useful points of reference.'

Jane looked around and saw he was right. Even a quick glance revealed a little Grecian temple on one hill, a glimpse of a marble cupola through the woods on the other side and the glint of water curling around the side of the house.

'What is that down in that hollow? A little chapel? It looks charming.'

'An ice house with the entrance disguised as a hermit's cell,' Ivo said, not even glancing in that direction. 'It is disused now. Grandfather had one built closer to the kitchens.'

'It would make a very pleasant short walk, I imagine.'

'Not at all. The ground is boggy and there are biting insects,' Ivo said shortly, then seemed to realise how dismissive that sounded. 'The best walks are around the lake, or up to the temple, and the park has a great many rides.'

'I cannot ride,' Jane admitted cautiously, wary after his reaction to her desire to walk to the ice house.

'I will teach you. Are you nervous of horses?'

'Not at all, but then I have rarely encountered one at very close quarters. I should like to learn how to drive more than to ride. Just a pony cart, I think.'

'For rural expeditions with your easel and paints?'

'Exactly,' she said, relaxing. 'Or perhaps a donkey?'

'Countesses do not drive donkey carts,' Ivo said, making her nervous all over again with visions of smart little vehicles and showy ponies that she must learn to drive with a dash when all she wanted was something she could amble about the countryside in.

The groom jumped down when they arrived at the front of the house and Ivo came round and lifted her to the ground. He had done it before, but this time he seemed to linger, letting her slide down close to his body until they were standing toe to toe, his hands still on her waist.

'Welcome to the Tower. I do not think that you paid it very much attention on your first visit.'

'None at all,' Jane admitted.

At that moment her view consisted entirely of Ivo's neckcloth—spotless and crisp—his tie pin—a rather good oval sapphire—and his chin—firm, stubborn, smoothly shaved. If she came up on tiptoe she could press a kiss right in the middle, below the sensual line of his lower lip. It was a disconcerting and unexpected thought—most improper, of course, but surprisingly exciting. It was one thing to enjoy being kissed by an attractive man, quite another for a well-bred young lady to think about kissing *him* in broad daylight, virtually on the steps of a great house. Was she falling for her husband-to-be?

It was dangerous, instinct told her. This was to be a convenient marriage, one of liking, certainly, and perhaps some desire, but feeling anything more laid her open to heartache and worse.

She was just telling herself to step back when Ivo bent his head and kissed her lightly on the lips. Jane closed her eyes, then opened them again seconds later when he moved away from her. 'Now I have shocked Partridge,' he said with a huff of laughter. 'He is so starched up that nervous visitors have been known to assume he is the Marquess. Come and charm him.'

Jane realised that they had an audience. The front door was open and a black-clad figure stood there, a footman at his side. A flicker of movement, a flash of blue and white behind the short stone balustrade disguising the service area, made her suspect that several maids had been peeping at them and a bulky figure moved away from one of the long first-floor windows. The Marquess himself?

Was that why Ivo had held her for so long, had kissed her? Was he demonstrating something for the benefit of the household? Jane shivered, suddenly chilled by the thought that Ivo was play-acting an affection he did not feel.

The butler, for whom the word *cadaverous* could have been coined, greeted them with funereal solemnity. 'My lord. Miss Newnham.'

Jane repressed the urge to curtsy. Ivo merely grinned, 'Cheer up, Partridge, or Miss Newnham will decide to employ a young, jolly, butler for our half of the household.'

Partridge permitted himself a frigid smile. Jane imagined the sound of ice cracking. 'You will have your little joke, my lord. Lord West-haven is in the library.'

'No joke,' Ivo remarked as they made their way towards the staircase. It rose from the centre of the hall, then split into two sweeping arms. 'We have an entire wing to ourselves and we can set up an entirely separate household if you wish it.'

'Good heavens, no.' Jane clutched at his arm. 'Everyone would be so offended. Promise me you will not.'

'It is as you wish, my dear.' Ivo paused at the top of the right-hand arm of the staircase and looked down, seeming not to notice her start of surprise at the mild endearment. 'Wonderful banisters for sliding down, these. I used to do it daily as a small boy and got beaten for it every time my father or grandfather caught me.' He grinned. 'Not very hard, mind you. I assume they both did exactly the same in their time.'

For the first time Jane thought about children, not as an abstract concept, one that she had assumed she must forget if she was to follow her art, but as a reality. In a year perhaps she would be a mother, in six or seven years' time, a mother anxious that her children might be breaking their necks sliding down these very banisters.

Ivo's children.

Chapter Twelve

Jane was still so wrapped up in the realisation that there was rather more to marrying Ivo than the marriage bed or the servant question or even how she would continue painting that their arrival in the library came as a surprise. 'Oh! How wonderful.'

It was a proper library, a working library, not a collection of books amassed because their owner thought it was necessary for a nobleman to own hundreds of the things, all in splendid bindings. These were splendid, indeed, and the shelves were loaded, but the tables that stood around the room had piles of books, some open, some with markers sticking out of them. The atlas stands supported open volumes and the great globe had a faintly worn look to it, as though it was often spun for enquiring fingers to trace a river or a sea route or locate a mountain range.

But even better, in Jane's eyes, were the paintings. Everywhere she looked were miniatures, hung between book stacks, framed as groups, arranged in little glass-topped tables. She was nose to nose with an exquisite Elizabethan gentleman who had plumes in his velvet bonnet and a great pearl hanging from one ear when the sound of someone clearing their throat made her jump.

'Good morning, Miss Newnham.'

'My lord. Please forgive me, I did not see you there.'

'You like my collection?'

'You gathered all these?' There must be almost fifty, she thought. 'This is Hilliard, is it not?'

'Close. Isaac Oliver, I believe, although it is contested. I inherited that and about half of what you see here. The rest I have collected or commissioned.' He bent and opened one of the display tables. 'You might like this.'

Jane took the little oval that he handed her. 'It is Ivo in uniform! How very dashing you look, Ivo. Is it a Cosway?'

'It is. You have an eye for style and you know your artists, Miss Newnham. I had that painted before Ivo went abroad for the first time. Keep it,' he said when she tried to hand it back.

'Really?' It was a generous gesture and she knew she must accept with grace, but she felt almost as though she was taking it under false pretences. But at least she would not be removing it from its home, it would still hang in the house. 'Thank you, I will treasure it, my lord. I had best give it back for now, though.'

He smiled and returned it to its place. 'You go and find Mrs French, Kendall. I will entertain Miss Newnham in your absence.'

Jane suppressed the urge to grab hold of Ivo's sleeve as he turned to go out, abandoning her with his grandfather, and managed to keep a smile on her lips. The old man was as subtle as a sledgehammer and he wanted something, although she could not imagine what it was he was going to ask her. Or tell her, perhaps.

'Now this one here, this *is* by Nicholas Hilliard,' he said, moving to one of the larger miniatures, hung away from the direct light.

Jane followed him and admired the small gem, glowing in its shady corner, but she was not deceived that this was going to be a conversation about art.

'Are you in love with my grandson?' the Marquess asked.

Even braced for an interrogation, she was startled into the truth. 'No. That is to say, I like and admire him. Respect him.' She stopped rather too abruptly, but that was better than gabbling about growing desire or her anxiety over whether he truly would allow her the freedom to paint as she wished.

'Excellent. I did not think that you had foolish romantic notions in your head about this match, but one can never be certain these days. Girls read too many novels, too much poetry and that can only lead to disillusion.'

Jane bit back the retort that it was perfectly possible to read both without becoming romantically deluded. 'I am very conscious that Lord Kendall offered for me out of concern for my reputation. I would be foolish indeed to imagine warmer feelings than liking on either side.'

An expression that she hoped was approval crossed the craggy face. 'You consider it a matter of mere liking on both sides? You do not imagine that my grandson is in love with you?'

'Certainly not,' Jane said, startled into crispness. 'We had known each other for a matter of days before his proposal.' The Marquess looked sceptical. 'My lord, we have already established that I am not subject to romantic imaginings.'

'Good. Excellent, you set my mind at rest. I thought when I heard about you that you seemed to be a sensible young woman, one with some courage and resolution. Intelligence. That is what Ivo needs in a wife. But I would not have you...disappointed later.'

What on earth was he hinting at? 'I have no illusions about the nature of this match and Ivo has assured me that no other woman would be left with disappointed hopes as a result of him offering for me. Naturally, I hope and trust that affection between us will grow with time and familiarity.'

My goodness, I sound like some starched-up dowager. Oh, well, in for a penny...

'My concern is to be a support to Lord Kendall as he takes up his responsibilities at your side, my lord, but I have his word that I will be able to continue with my art.'

'Your art? Of course, you paint, do you not?'

'I paint portraits. In oils. I am not certain if you are aware of how seriously I take it?'

He beetled his brows at her, clearly not used

to pert young women standing up to him like this. 'Are you any good at it?'

'Yes, my lord.' Now was not the time for modesty.

'Convince me of it and I have a commission for you. Ah, here is Mrs French. Off you go now: I have no doubt she will show you parts of this house I have never seen myself.'

Jane bobbed a slight curtsy and turned to the woman who stood in the doorway, hands folded neatly in front of her over a crisp apron. There was lace at her collar and cuffs, a great bunch of keys hanging from her waist and a smart cap on her brown curls.

'Miss Newnham.' The housekeeper was perhaps fifty, tall, angular and plain, but her expression was intelligent and alert, her voice cool and assured. Jane had no idea whether she would prove to be an ally or an opponent, but she was clearly a force to be reckoned with. 'Lord Kendall has asked me to show you around the house at any time that is convenient to you.'

'Now would be perfect,' Jane said, relieved at the excuse to escape. She had no idea how to respond to what Lord Westhaven had said to her. A commission? Did he really wish her to paint a portrait for him, a man who could doubtless afford to have every relative he possessed painted by Lawrence, the king of contemporary portraitists? And his questions about her feelings had been even more baffling, unless he was simply very old-fashioned and disapproved of love matches on principal.

Or was he warning her against falling in love with Ivo for some reason? Why should anyone object to a wife loving her husband? Unless he feared that she would be hurt... Did that mean that he considered his grandson incapable of loving? Surely— 'Oh, I beg your pardon, Mrs French. I was concentrating so hard on remembering where exactly I was that I missed what you have been saying.'

'It is a very large house, Miss Newnham,' the housekeeper said pleasantly. 'Some confusion is only to be expected at first. But fortunately, unlike so many other old houses, it is quite straightforward in its layout. Both wings are symmetrical—in fact, they are mirror images of each other except that the West Wing has the main entrance hall and that space in the East Wing contains the music room. The only irregularity is that caused by the tower in the centre where the floor levels are different and that is compensated for by short flights of steps on either side.'

She opened a door as she spoke and Jane found herself at the top of stairs leading down to a circular room with a large hooded fireplace and a number of suits of armour. 'The tower rooms are purely to display the older artefacts,' Mrs French explained. 'They are opened when there are parties or balls and when we have visitors call when His Lordship is not at home then this is the main part of the house I show them, rather than any of the more modern rooms.'

It had not occurred to Jane that this was one of the great houses where genteel travellers might expect to call and have the housekeeper show them through the public rooms. That would be difficult to become accustomed to, she realised.

Along with a great deal else...

Mrs French took her around the East Wing because, she explained, this was now Lord Kendall's domain and would therefore be her own after the wedding. Jane found herself lost in tapestries and panelling, hangings and rich decoration and hardly dared glance through the door of Ivo's bedchamber, let alone through the one to what would be her suite of rooms next door.

'At present Their Lordships dine together every evening in the small dining room in the West Wing,' Mrs French explained as they reached the safer ground of the dining rooms. One large—enormous—and one small, which could seat fifteen easily.

There was something in her tone that suggested she did not expect this to be the case after the marriage. Jane was not so certain. It was hardly as though she and Ivo would want to be alone every evening—besides, it would complicate things for the cook.

'His Lordship suggested that you might like to view below stairs after luncheon, Miss Newnham,' Mrs French said as they arrived back in the circular tower chamber. 'Unless you are tired and would prefer to do so on another day. I am at your disposal at any time. Oh, good morning, Lady Frederick.'

The newcomer was standing at the top of the short flight of stairs into the West Wing. Jane took in an impression of elegance and height and a beautifully cut walking dress and pelisse, both in deepest black. Despite the mourning, the hat perched on Lady Frederick's dark curls was more dashing than anything Jane had seen outside the pages of *La Belle Assemblée* and the overall effect was enough to make her feel like a candidate for the post of scullery maid.

Lady Frederick...

She must be married to a younger son, presumably, but surely Ivo would have said if he had a sister? Then the other woman came down the stairs and Jane saw she must be forty, perhaps older.

'French. Who is this?' Her voice was perfectly pleasant and the housekeeper did not react to the omission of the courtesy title that even the Marquess used.

'Miss Newnham, Lady Frederick. Miss Newnham, Lady Frederick Merton.'

'Ivo's little bride? Come, let me look at you. That will be all, French, I will see Miss Newnham finds the luncheon table.'

Jane made a point of thanking the housekeeper before she turned back to the other woman.

Little bride, indeed!

'Lady Frederick.'

'I am Ivo's aunt,' she said. 'His father's sister-in-law and, apparently, the only one in the family who sees fit to wear mourning for him. Let me look at you. You look intelligent, at least, although you are a plain little dab of a thing. How satisfactory he has had the sense not to propose to some pretty spoiled chit given to high drama—presumably he has had enough of that.' It was all said with a smile and such great charm that it took Jane a second to realise that she was being insulted.

'I believe that your nephew values character over looks and, I hope, kindness over beauty.' Jane wondered what she had meant about *pretty spoiled chit*. She smiled as sweetly as she could manage at the older woman.

'You have claws. Well done.' She smiled apparent approval of Jane's retort, but the warmth did not reach her eyes. 'I suggest you do not show them to Ivo before you have his ring safely on your finger. But I forget, you have already been seen quarrelling with him in the middle of Bath. Very reckless of you. And here he is.'

Ivo came through the door and joined his aunt on the landing. 'Aunt Augusta. I did not realise we were expecting you.'

'You were not but, as by some apparent oversight I have not received an invitation to meet your betrothed, I decided to drop by. A mere twenty miles out of my way. So nice to meet you, dear, I will see you again at luncheon, no doubt.' She smiled at Jane, nodded thanks to Ivo who held the door for her and swept out.

'Ouch,' Jane said. That interview had hurt, as it had clearly been meant to. 'Your aunt is glad you have settled for a plain little dab of a thing with some intelligence as opposed to some spoiled, pretty chit given to high drama, whatever she means by that.' She felt too bruised to hide her feelings.

'Plain little dab?' Ivo said thoughtfully as he descended the stairs to her side. 'Definitely nothing little or dab-like about you. Five feet six inches, I would guess, and everything very nicely in proportion.'

Jane swallowed. If he meant her bust, then it was the first time anyone had ever said anything complimentary about it. It was there, of course, but it paled into insignificance against her friend Prue's magnificent bosom, the sight of which in an evening gown tended to reduce gentlemen to mumbling incoherence. 'Thank you,' she muttered.

'And plain? When I opened my eyes and focused on your face in the chaise I saw long-lashed hazel eyes and a face that made me think of a charming and curious cat. Charming and curious,' he repeated, tipping up her chin with one finger. 'Not some pretty little chit, but an interesting young woman.'

He was clearly about to kiss her and Jane had no intention of making it difficult for him. She swayed forward an encouraging few degrees and found herself in his arms being kissed with a thoroughness that was almost alarming. The alarming thing was how much she wanted it, how much she seemed to have learned about kissing after only a few experiments. She knew the taste of him and the texture of his lips, she knew how to stroke her tongue between them and had learned not to jump when he did the same. The heat and the intensity and the intimacy were frightening and, at the same time, so exhilarating. Her body felt alive, responsive, uncomfortably excited.

She was panting a little when Ivo finally broke the kiss.

'Are you all right, Jane? Forgive me, I was too forceful, perhaps.' His breathing sounded regular, but then she saw the pulse hammering in his throat—it was curiously exciting to realise that kissing her had produced that response.

'Yes.' She smiled at him and took a deep breath. 'I like it when we kiss and I am beginning to wonder what it will be like when we...' The dark intensity in his eyes stopped her. That last deep breath might never have been taken because her lungs felt quite empty.

'I think you will find that it is equally enjoyable, although we might not get it right first time,' he said. His hands were still on her, one at her waist, one on her shoulder, and the warmth of them was another enticement. 'We will have to learn each other: lovemaking is a skill and an art.'

'An art? I enjoy learning new things.'

Ivo found that they were smiling at each other as though sharing a delicious, rather naughty, secret and the realisation came to him that Jane, although clearly an innocent, was a very sensual one. Even as he thought it, she drew back, the colour up in her cheeks, and he told himself not to rush, not to snatch.

'I had come to find you to show you to your room if you wanted to wash your hands before luncheon,' he said, seeing her relax a little, the colour ebbing.

No, rushing would not be a good thing with Jane. It had not been so with Daphne. She had been impetuous, sensual, eager. She had wanted everything and it had called for every ounce of self-discipline that he'd had as a young man in love not to take what she offered him.

As they climbed the stairs out of the tower room he wondered why there was the difference. He did not love Jane, of course, but it struck him suddenly that it had been a rigid regard for the conventions that had given him the resolution to resist before. With Jane it was concern for her, a desire to ensure that her first experience of physical love was a good one. He had not expected to find himself so much in tune with her feelings.

'Your aunt seemed not to approve of our match,' she ventured as he closed the heavy old door behind them.

'She is opposed to the thought that I might father an heir. She would be opposed to anyone I married,' Ivo said. 'Her husband died some ten years ago and she has one son, Alfred, who is the heir presumptive. I like Alfred, he's a good fellow, although how he manages it with that harpy as a mother I do not know. There is the slight problem that he is not likely to marry and she nags him constantly on the subject.'

'Ah. Not the marrying kind?' Jane asked, sounding understanding.

'You can guess why?' He was surprised.

'My friend Prudence is a Classical scholar and encountered Greek…um…attitudes in the course of her researches and we discussed it within our reading circle,' she said matter of factly.

Ivo blinked. Perhaps he had been imagining a greater degree of innocence—at least, of knowledge—than was actually the case with his betrothed. 'Well, you may imagine the frustration of his mama who is exceedingly ambitious and doubtless sees herself as the mother and grandmother of marquesses. I always thought that she was sending a weekly remittance to Napoleon on the understanding that he direct his cannon at my head.'

'Goodness, how very Gothic! Perhaps you should employ a food taster.'

Chapter Thirteen

As Ivo waited for Jane to return from tidying herself before luncheon he found he was still amused at the thought of his Aunt Augusta, stalking the corridors bent on his destruction like some villainess dreamt up by Horace Walpole.

Jane's smile when she came back down ten minutes later was different, forced. She was being brave about something and she should not have to be, not if he could help it.

'What is wrong?'

'My suite—it is vast, I shall get lost in it. The reality of this is beginning to sink in, Ivo. I am not used to all this splendour and I am going to disgrace you by staring open-mouthed at everything like some provincial miss.'

That strange feeling of protectiveness swept

through him again and he put his arm around her shoulders and gave her a quick hug. 'Neither am I used to it again, not yet. I have been away from here a long time and most of it living rough under canvas, in half-ruined billets, under the occasional hedge in the rain. We will make our own home, Jane, and we will emerge into this other one on our own terms, when we are ready.'

She tipped her head on to his shoulder for a second, relaxed into the hug, then they were walking side by side, perfectly properly, and footmen were opening the double doors into the Small Dining Room.

Luncheon had been set out on the round table which separated Jane and his aunt. It made the meal seem more informal and he wondered if this was an example of Mrs French's tact.

With his grandfather discussing landscape gardening with Jane, and his aunt keeping her acid opinions to herself in the presence of her father-in-law, Ivo relaxed a little, took a mouthful of clear soup. He should have known better.

'That Parris girl has thrown her cap over the windmill with a vengeance, I hear,' Aunt Augusta said, with a distaste that held a trace of relish in it.

Ivo swallowed the soup the wrong way.

'Her poor father must be turning in his grave— his son dead and his daughter making a scandal of herself with a card-sharping rakehell,' Augusta went on. 'The Parris family have always been respectable, so it must be bad blood on the mother's side coming out, of course, not that anyone knows much about them, they were so obscure. One never knows with these families of no pedigree.'

Was it his imagination or had his aunt shot a glance at Jane with that comment?

'Charles Parris was my friend and an officer and a gentleman of great courage. His sister has been led astray, no doubt, but that can occur in even the best families, can it not, Aunt?'

Personally he thought that Alfred's preferences had been clear for many years and had nothing to do with the bad influences for which his mother blamed her son's reluctance to marry, but he was not prepared to let that slur on the Parris family go unpunished.

'Such a good thing that you had the sense not to marry the girl,' Augusta said, ignoring his question. 'Such a pretty little thing she was, all blonde curls and cherry lips. You were like April and May, the pair of you. I can remember saying to poor dear Frederick that, much as one deplored you being army-mad, at least it kept you away from that misalliance, at least. The girl has turned out to be a strumpet.'

Ivo heard a buzzing in his ears as he fought to keep his temper. Lady Parris had been a perfectly respectable clergyman's daughter and if he *had* married Daphne, a baronet's daughter, that would have not been a misalliance, simply not a grand match. And Daphne was not a *strumpet*. She was free-spirited, sensual, impatient and he had neglected her. Loved her and taken her for granted.

'As we know nothing of the circumstances we can hardly comment on Daphne's actions, I would have thought,' he said through gritted teeth. Out of the corner of his eye he saw Jane's look of startled comprehension then, almost as quickly as her eyes had widened and her lips parted, she was composed again.

Hell and damnation, I forget she was there for a moment.

And a moment was all it had taken for his betraying instant defence of Daphne.

'I so much admired the buildings that ornament the park, Lord Westhaven,' Jane said, apparently ignoring what Augusta and he were talking about. 'Have they been there long?'

His grandfather also showed no sign of listening to his daughter-in-law, but Ivo knew he had heard and was not pleased. 'They were erected on the orders of my grandfather,' he told Jane. 'Now the trees are becoming mature I think I may have another avenue cut and place something at the end of it. Another obelisk, perhaps.'

'Or an arch,' she suggested, sketching the shape on the tablecloth with one finger as she spoke. Ivo wondered if she even realised she was doing it.

She has quality and tact, Ivo thought as Jane encouraged his grandfather to enlarge on his landscaping schemes. *She must have guessed that Aunt was talking about the elopement that led to my beating, but she said nothing. But has she taken in what Augusta was hinting at?*

She would have to be dense not to realise that his aunt was implying that he was—or had been—in love with Daphne.

He asked a direct question about his two female cousins, Alfred's sisters, forcing a change of subject that his aunt could not avoid without her spite becoming completely obvious.

The meal was coming to its end when a footman came in with a letter on a silver salver. 'The man is waiting for a reply, my lord,' he said, presenting it to the Marquess.

'This is addressed to you, Miss Newnham,' his grandfather said after a glance at the note.

Jane took it, 'Excuse me.' She read it rapidly, then dropped the sheet. 'Oh, poor thing! My cousin Violet writes in haste to say she has been called to her sister's side. She has just given birth earlier than expected and both she and the baby are sickly. Her husband has written to Violet to say that he cannot persuade his wife to rest as she should because of her anxiety over the child. Violet is packing to leave for London immediately—she hopes to catch the late afternoon Mail coach. She says her maid, Charity, will accompany me to my parents in Dorset and she hopes your secretary can continue to look after the arrangements for the wedding that she was making.'

She pushed back her chair. 'If you will excuse

me, my lord. Perhaps someone could drive me back to Batheaston at once?'

'I will, of course.' Ivo tossed aside his napkin. 'Sir, the travelling carriage would make Jane's journey home more comfortable.'

'I think we can do rather better than that. James, send a message to the stables immediately. The travelling carriage, driver and groom to go to Miss Lowry's house. They will take the note I shall write now and perhaps one from Miss Newnham. They are to convey Miss Lowry and her maid to London and to remain at her disposal for as long as she requires them.' He stood up. 'Jane, if you will come to my study, you can write to your cousin to explain that you will be staying here. If she has one of her women pack your things, I will send a gig to collect them.'

'Stay here with two gentlemen and without a chaperon?' Aunt Augusta enquired. 'I would have thought there was quite enough talk already around this marriage without adding to it.' They all turned to her and she raised her eyebrows. 'Do not look to me to remain! I have a household and family to return to and I intend doing so immediately.'

'I would not dream of troubling you, Augusta,' his grandfather said. 'I shall send to Honoria.'

'The Dowager Lady Gravestock, my great-aunt and Grandfather's sister,' Ivo murmured to Jane. 'She lives in Bath and is utterly respectable and amazingly lazy. Do say you will stay.'

'If you really want me to,' she murmured back, warily watching his aunt and grandfather sniping at each other.

'Yes, of course, I do. Off you go and write to your cousin and please give her my best wishes for her sister's speedy recovery and that of the child.'

He sat down again as she went out, his gaze unfocused on the bowl of fruit in front of him. Did he really want Jane to be here, day and night, until the wedding? He had offered to marry her because it was the honourable thing to do. She had been severely compromised because she had selflessly rescued him from a severe beating, if not worse. And he liked her and found her attractive. But it would be a marriage of convenience, an amiable agreement. He had felt no desire to get to know her better beforehand or to let her become closer to himself either.

Marriage, surely, could be managed as a polite, civilised arrangement. She would look after the household, raise the children, amuse herself with her painting. He would manage the estates. They would come together in the bedchamber, over the dining table and on social occasions. It was a form of relationship that appeared to have worked perfectly well for his parents and his grandparents.

But now Jane *was* becoming closer. He found he wanted to be with her and discuss things. He wanted to kiss her, to do more than kiss. But that felt wrong. He did not love her and, if he allowed this closeness to persist she might grow fond of him—more than fond—and that would be unfair. Unkind. He loved Daphne and he had failed her. He could not fail another young woman who should be under his protection.

'…a word I have been saying, Kendall!'

'Aunt Augusta, my apologies. I was wool-gathering.'

'Daydreaming, more like, which is doubtless how you got yourself into this mess in the first place.' She stood up in a rustle of fabrics and gestured irritably at the footman who was a fraction too late to pull back her chair.

Ivo stood again. 'I cannot imagine to what you

refer, Aunt. May I send for your carriage in, shall we say, half an hour?'

'You may send for it now, I have no reason to dally. There is something havey-cavey about that young woman, you mark my words. She is one of the new Duchess of Aylsham's bosom friends and that was a most peculiar affair, I cannot imagine what Aylsham thought he was doing. Getting married on an island, bridesmaids and guests arriving in rowing boats, the bride a positive bluestocking? The man is becoming as eccentric as his father. Where will this girl want to be wed? In a hot air balloon?'

Ivo sank down into his chair as she swept out, the two footmen jumping to catch the double doors just in time. At least they had managed to keep their faces blank throughout that utterly indiscreet tirade, but the servants' hall would doubtless be enlivened by an account of it soon enough.

When a sufficient amount of time had elapsed after each contact with his aunt he could understand her bitterness and tolerate it. A philandering husband who had died just in time to save the family from ruin, a son who would never live up to her ambitions for him and whose lifestyle put his reputation and safety at constant risk and two mousey daughters who had so far failed to secure husbands their mama considered worthy of them: all were burdens that would have over-set a less robust woman.

But face to face, and with her cutting at Jane with every word, he found he had no tolerance at all.

'I apologise for my relatives,' he said when he emerged into the hall and found Jane coming out of the study.

'I have met only two of them and I like your grandfather very well,' she said with a faint smile that spoke volumes of her opinion of Augusta. 'I do hope I am not putting your great-aunt to a lot of trouble and at such short notice.'

'Provided everyone else does all the work and she is merely required to put on her newest lace cap and be handed into her carriage, she will have not the slightest objection,' he said. 'If I know Aunt Honoria, she will invite you to sit with her for an hour in the morning and in the afternoon. She may ask you to read to her or help sort her embroidery silks, but that is all. She will be perfectly satisfied that you are safely under her eyes and you may do as you wish for the rest of the time, I imagine. The fact that those eyes will be closed, or riveted on the latest scandal sheet or novel, is beside the point. You could take up hot air ballooning for all she would notice.'

'What on earth put that into your head?' She was laughing at him now.

He grinned back. 'Aunt Augusta. Your dreadful bluestocking friend married her duke on an island with the guests arriving by rowing boat, so it follows that you will insist on some even more outrageous venue.'

'It would rather limit the number of guests. In fact, could one fit us both, the minister and two witnesses into the gondola of a balloon?'

'I have no idea. Would you like me to find out?'

'Oh, how absurd! Would you really?' Still chuckling, even when he shook his head, she tucked her hand under his elbow and said confidingly, 'It is such a joy to find someone with whom to laugh, don't you think? Perhaps there are many of your friends you can laugh with, but I do miss mine.'

Ivo thought. He had a lot of friends, men he

could be convivial with, comrades he had fought alongside, amiable acquaintances, but none with whom he could share laughter over something absurd. Even with Daphne…

There had been laughter when they were happy, of course, but looking back he did not think she had much of a sense of humour. But then, young ladies were not supposed to have such a thing. They were supposed to be light and frivolous and take delight in happy, pretty things, not dig beneath the surface in search of satire or the absurd.

'What is wrong? Have I been tactless? Were you thinking of your friend who was killed?'

'No, not at all. I was just thinking that I should not share some of the amusing situations in my past with you,' he said, making a joke of it.

'And I should not be laughing when Violet's poor sister and her family are in such straits. I do hope it does not prove to be a malignant fever. But at least they are in London where all the best doctors are and, if anyone can rally a household in despair, it is Violet.' She gave a little sigh, almost too quiet for him to hear.

The clerk who had been assisting Violet with wedding preparations emerged from the study, hat in hand. 'I am to follow the travelling coach to Batheaston in the gig, my lord, and return with Miss Newnham's trunks and any paperwork relating to the wedding preparations. I shall instruct the receiving office to direct all post for the household to Miss Newnham here.' He clapped his hat on head and strode to the front door.

'Things happen at alarming speed when the Marquess assumes command,' Jane remarked. 'I feel dizzy.'

'Come with me to see Great-Aunt. We will take Grandfather's letter and see if we cannot coax her into the carriage.'

'With no notice? She may have any number of engagements.'

'If she cannot come, then you must stay with her until she can, because I will not give Aunt Augusta's sharp tongue any grounds for wagging. But she will agree, mark my words. She has been attempting to seduce our cook away for years without success and she will not refuse the opportunity to stay, not with the inducement of Mrs Hopwood's food at all hours, let alone the chance to interfere with all the wedding preparations and inform all her closest friends that she was critical to the successful planning. She will lie on the *chaise longue* giving elaborate instructions to everyone and then forgetting them the next day.'

Ivo seemed pleased to have her company, Jane thought when, half an hour later, they set out in a smart carriage and four to carry Lady Gravestock off in style.

'We might be back on our adventurous journey from Kensington,' he said as the carriage turned out of the gates on to the turnpike road.

'The further that is in the past, the more amusing it seems in recollection,' Jane admitted. 'Is your shoulder quite healed? I keep forgetting to ask you, because it does not appear to be giving you any trouble.' And she should have been thinking about that and not admiring his figure in his well-cut coat and tight breeches, she reminded herself.

'It is, thank you. You found the journey entertaining, did you?' His expression was rueful. 'It appeared more in the nature of a nightmare to me. Everything hurt, I had an impossible young lady artist on my hands and a hideous mess behind me.'

Jane decided to ignore the *impossible* on the grounds that it was deliberate provocation. 'I have not liked to ask because it is none of my business, but is there any news of Miss Parris? It is the same person that Lady Frederick was referring to, is it not?'

She hoped that Ivo did not realise that she had perfectly understood the hints that his aunt was throwing out. Daphne Parris was not simply the sister of his close friend, she was his youthful love. She tried to console herself with the thought that he could have married her before if the attraction had persisted, but common sense told her that a young man setting out into the perils of war would have not tied a young bride to him, or that her parents would have agreed to so precipitate a match. She tried to ignore the cold feeling deep inside, the fear that Daphne meant more to him still than a memory and a promise.

Ivo nodded. 'Yes. Her brother Charles was my closest friend—their family home is just eight miles away to the east.' He spoke easily, his long body was relaxed, almost sprawled, in the corner of the carriage, yet his gaze seemed unfocused as he stared, not out of the window, but at the empty seat opposite him.

'So you lost both your father and your friend almost at the same time and then found yourself with the impossible task of rescuing a girl who had no wish to be saved.' Jane edged towards him, wanting to hug, or, at the very least, to touch him, but there was nothing in his manner that suggested such comfort would be welcome. And if he still had feelings for Daphne, then another woman's touch would be even less so. She decided to opt for practicality. 'Has there been any word of how that progresses?'

'There has been nothing from her,' Ivo said.

'Perhaps that is a good sign. She reacted so wrongly, lashing out when you tried to help, but now she will have had time to consider and, as you are such a close friend from her childhood, surely she would turn to you if her husband proved to be abusive or neglectful?'

'I suspect that I would be the very last person...' Ivo seemed to give himself a shake and sat upright. 'The lawyers say there is nothing to be done. The Scottish ceremony appears to have been performed according to the law, there is no evidence that she was forced or deceived and the marriage has been consummated. However, with Charles's unexpected death he had made no provision for her in his will and their father's disposition still stands: she receives no dowry until she reaches the age of twenty-five unless she marries with the blessing of her guardian. And I believe her elder aunt is now that guardian. No consent was given, so Sir Clement Meredith has no money or lands from her.'

'I hope that does not make him treat her badly,' Jane said, then could have bitten her tongue. 'I am sorry, that was thoughtless. You must be so concerned about her, not just because of your promise to her brother, but because of your feelings for her.'

'My *what*?' Ivo demanded, turning abruptly on the seat to face her.

Oh, yes. I was not wrong. He loves her still.

Somehow she kept her thoughts from her expression. 'I thought you were childhood sweethearts. Your aunt implied you were.'

'My aunt is an interfering harridan,' Ivo retorted sharply. 'And I would be obliged if you would refrain from vulgar speculation.'

Chapter Fourteen

There was a deadly silence before Jane managed to find her voice. 'I beg your pardon.'

Inside, something hurt and indignant wanted to protest, *It was sympathy, not vulgar speculation. I want to help. And I am hurting, too.* But she managed to close her lips on the words. Ivo was feeling raw and guilty and, surely, bitterly betrayed by Daphne Parris's reaction to his attempts to help her.

'And I apologise, too,' Ivo said. 'You clearly meant well and no speculation was necessary when Aunt Augusta was painting such a very clear picture. I believe Lady Parris once crossed her badly in public with a witty retort to one of Augusta's nasty jibes. Those who heard it tittered. You do not laugh at her and expect it to be forgotten, I fear.'

'Miss Parris is very pretty, I gather.' Jane

hoped that did not betray the shameful jealousy she felt about Ivo's sweetheart. He *might* not love Daphne now, she still had no proof of that, and it was pathetic to care what she looked like, but Jane found herself afraid of the comparison.

And Daphne had spirit. She had gone for what she wanted, defied convention and eloped with her lover, however unsuitable he might be. Her own attempt at kicking over the traces and making a bid for freedom had run aground because she had not thought about what she really wanted and how she might achieve it. She had dreamt of the grand gesture even though it was not right for her. Ivo probably admired Daphne's courage although he deplored the outcome.

'Pretty?' Ivo seemed to be looking at some mental picture. 'She is of a type that is very much admired, yes. She has always been lovely and, as a result, she was spoiled by a great deal of admiration and indulgence.' Jane thought that was all he was going to say until he added, 'I appear to be one of the few people who does not do what she wants, when she wants it.'

There did not seem to be much to add to that. Jane let the silence hang for a few minutes, then asked, 'Your grandfather asked me about my painting and said that he might have a commission for me. Do you know what he wants?'

Ivo seemed glad of the change of subject. 'He said something about having the servants painted, all of them. He has heard about the series of portraits of the staff at Erddig in Wales that the Yorke family commissioned and was interested. Then he saw the miniatures that the Duke of Dorset has at Knole and conceived of the idea of having our own staff immortalised.'

'I have never tried miniatures.'

'I believe he wants normal-sized canvases. Think about it, because he will want to discuss it with you himself.'

How many of them were there? Inside and outside staff? Distracted, Jane pulled the little sketchbook out of her reticule and began making notes of the things she must ask the Marquess.

Perhaps half an hour later she came to herself to find that she was curled up in one corner of the carriage, feet tucked under her, shoes on the floor and a neat list of queries on the page. Ivo was asleep. At least, his eyes were closed and he seemed more relaxed than he had when they had been talking earlier. Perhaps she had been saying too much, asking too many questions, and he welcomed her silence. If he still loved Daphne—she made herself think the words even though her mind kept skittering away from them—then it must be exhausting to have the woman you were going to marry talking about her.

Jane grimaced at her reflection in the glass of the window, noticing that they had reached the City already. She was not cut out to be a silent woman, she knew that. She wanted to ask questions, make observations, exchange ideas.

As she thought it, Ivo opened his eyes. 'Why are you pulling faces at me?'

'I am pulling them at myself, thinking.'

'You think too much,' he said and moved purposefully along the bench seat until she was within arm's reach. 'If what you are thinking makes you wrinkle your nose, I shall have to take your mind off it.'

The kiss was exciting, made more so by the movement of the carriage and the fact that it had slowed almost to a walk in the Bath traffic and anyone might look in and see them. Jane clung to Ivo's lapels as he held her. It was awkward, but somehow the discomfort and the danger made it more urgent. Then they turned a corner, the carriage lurched and they fell apart, sprawled on opposite seats. Jane found that she could not look away from him.

'We are here,' Ivo said with a hasty glance through the window. He straightened his neckcloth and reached out to set her bonnet back straight on her head.

His breathing was decidedly rapid, which Jane decided to take as a compliment. 'My mind has been so far distracted that I am going to appear a complete airhead to your great-aunt.'

'You think too much,' he had said. Was that what he wanted, a compliant wife with no thoughts in her head? One who would melt in his arms whenever he felt like kissing her and then return to a state of passivity? It was not a pleasant thought. She gave herself a brisk mental shake. This was nerves, that was all. She had tumbled into a betrothal when she had no intention of marrying, she had placed her freedom to pursue her art in the power of a man and her world, already shifting on its foundations, was about to be turned upside down. No wonder she felt out of sorts. But understanding why she felt like this was not reassurance.

Jane tweaked her bonnet ribbons into order

and allowed Ivo to hand her down. They were between the Circus and Queen's Square, she realised as they climbed the two shallow steps and crossed the slab that lay like a bridge across the sunken service area. Two chairmen, labouring under their burden, trudged up the steep street behind them and she flinched inwardly at the reminder of how she had found herself in this position.

An elderly manservant admitted them, showed them through to a drawing room cluttered with china ornaments, heavily framed watercolours and much drapery, then creaked off to ascertain whether her Ladyship was receiving.

He left the door ajar so they were perfectly able to hear Lady Gravestock in the next room.

'Of course I am at home to my great-nephew, Smithers! What is the matter with you? Bring him in this moment and send for refreshments. The scones as well as the cakes and do not forget the jam.'

There was the sound of Smithers mumbling.

'A young lady? Why did you not say so? Both of them, of course.'

Jane braced herself for an irritable old lady and was surprised by the beaming welcome they received from the plump figure on the sofa. 'My dear! Come in, come in. That old fool Smithers, keeping you waiting when he knows you are my favourite great-nephew, Ivo. And is this the charming young lady who is to marry you? Come and kiss me, my dear.'

Clearly their arrival was as entertaining as a seat at the theatre. Great-Aunt Honoria gasped in sympathy at the news of Violet's family's illness, tutted in dismay at the thought of Jane being left alone in the Batheaston house with only the servants for company and protection, nodded sagely at the decision to stay at Merton Tower and then clapped her hands in delight at the suggestion that she might assist by chaperoning her.

'The very thing—how sensible dear Westhaven is, to be sure. I shall not grudge the slightest exertion in coming to your aid, my dears.'

As the exertion appeared to be entirely on the part of Lady Gravestock's maid, several footmen and a middle-aged companion—so mousey that Jane did not notice her until a good half-hour into their visit—it was easy to recognise Ivo's description of his aunt.

Fortunately the Marquess's travelling carriage

was capacious and they managed to fit in Jane, Ivo, Lady Gravestock, the maid and the companion—'Eunice, Miss Herring, my niece'—without great effort. Several trunks were loaded on to the roof and, as they set off with much groaning of springs, Ivo remarked that it was a good thing that he had eaten only two scones.

A week later it seemed to Jane that with the arrival of Lady Gravestock everything became more real. It was a strange thought—Merton Tower, the Marquess and, certainly, Ivo had all seemed very real indeed before, but somehow preparations picked up pace, acceptances were still coming in, the size of the guest list and the practical considerations all became alarmingly apparent.

Ivo's great-aunt never seemed to actually exert herself to move far from her self-appointed position on a *chaise longue* in the Chinese drawing room, but little Miss Herring was constantly scuttling about with pieces of paper or checking things off on lists.

Ranwick, the Marquess's secretary, began to enquire what Jane's preferences were on any number of subjects on which she had never before thought to form an opinion. Flowers in particular were obsessing him that morning.

'Roses?' Jane said, at random.

'For the chapel, the dining room or the entrance hall and reception rooms, Miss Newnham? The gardeners need as much notice as possible, you understand.'

'For everywhere. Roses—will we be able to get them in October? Anyway, shades of pink and some dark blue flowers and a great deal of white,' she decided, plucking colours out of thin air. 'In different proportions. More blue, white and foliage in the chapel. More pink in the reception rooms and more red in the rest. That should give both continuity and variety.'

Ranwick was scribbling. 'Excellent, Miss Newnham. Sprays, garlands, towers or formal vases?'

Jane finally escaped half an hour later, head spinning. She needed fresh air and an escape from decisions. The Marquess had told her he would like pencil sketches of some of the staff first so he could decide on style and size, so she took her sketchbook and went out on to the back lawn in the hope of finding the gardeners.

There was none in sight, but she did see Ivo walking towards the ha-ha. She thought he looked enviably relaxed in breeches and boots and what was clearly a favourite old coat. He was bare-headed and she watched him climb down a hidden flight of steps into the ditch on the park side of the ha-ha and then walk along towards a grove of trees.

Now he had shown her the way to get directly into the grounds, the idea of exploring seemed tempting. She would walk in the park around the house until she came to the front where she might find the gardeners.

Ivo was out of sight by the time she reached the ha-ha so she clambered down the rough stone steps and strolled off in the same direction he had taken, keeping the sun behind her. The long grass of the park was full of late wild flowers and the hum of bees and she wandered along in a daydream, thinking vaguely of how to compose the portraits and whether to show the occupations of the various servants plainly or just hint at them.

Then she saw Ivo and recognised where he was. That was the hermit's cell she had seen from the carriage when she arrived and the mound next to it must be the ice house. Ivo had told her the ground was boggy there, but he appeared to have crossed it with no difficulty. Perhaps with the fine weather it had dried out and, if that was the case, then the biting insects he mentioned would probably have gone, too. The overgrown path did not seem to cross boggy ground, but perhaps it drained well.

When she was closer Jane perched on a fallen tree trunk and waited. Ivo looked as though he wanted to be alone and was probably escaping, as she was, from the demands of the household. When he was gone she would explore the little folly and perhaps make a quick sketch. It might make an interesting background for a picture of the gamekeepers.

Ivo was in no hurry to move along. He was standing by the door into the little hermitage, a Gothic fantasy, built with a half-ruined turret. The roof was intact, tiled and thick with moss and, as she wondered if it was unlocked, Ivo stooped and went in. He was inside for perhaps ten minutes and she began to worry. What if there were fallen timbers in there and he had tripped and hit his head? Or a well...

Just at the point where she was about to get

to her feet and follow him he came out, stood for a moment with one hand on the door jamb, then strode off.

As she picked her way over the tussocky grass she wondered what had kept him in there for so long. Was he in retreat, not just from the demands of the household and the wedding preparations, but from her, the woman he did not love but was committed to marrying? It was an unpleasant thought.

Despite the unsettling reflections, she smiled at the detail of the little building as she came closer. There was tracery in the single window and some miniature grotesques carved under the roof—snarling beasts, strange foliage and comical characters pulling faces.

It was dimly lit inside, the sunshine filtered through a drapery of cobwebs over the window, and she wondered afresh what had detained Ivo. There was nothing to see, nowhere to sit. Perhaps he was checking its condition. She glanced down and saw marks on the dusty floor as though someone had scooped up a handful of dry dirt. Scooped it up and… She turned slowly, studying the little room. He had spread it on the window ledge.

Jane went outside, picked up a handful of grass and used it to sweep the ledge clear. Underneath were words carved into the soft stone. They stood out, white and sharp as though someone had just cleaned them with a knife, and she realised that was what Ivo must have been doing. Cleaning them and then covering them up. She almost brushed the dust back across them, some instinct telling her to leave well alone, not give in to curiosity, but the temptation was too great.

Daphne, naiad of the stream,
Beauty like sunlight,
Love me for ever as I love you.
Ivo

Underneath in a different hand, was *D.P.* and a roughly scratched heart.

Her immediate thought as she stood there was, *This is why he did not want me walking down here. This was their special place.*

Then all the hints and comments that she had been trying to ignore, pretending to herself not to understand, or consoling herself with the thought that it was all in the past, became clear. Lord Westhaven did not want her to expect love because Ivo's heart was already given. His aunt's jibes had been directed at Jane as much as at Ivo—she was being compared with the golden-haired beauty whom Ivo loved.

He had tried to save Daphne from the consequences of her elopement and she had responded by almost having him killed. The sense of betrayal must be even more acute if he still loved her. And Jane thought he must do.

She walked out of the hermitage and back the way she had come, blind now to the butterflies and the flowers, the scent of haymaking and the warmth of the sun. She sat on the bottom step out of the ha-ha, hidden from the house, and hugged her knees for comfort.

Ivo had loved—*did love*—Daphne, had tried to save her from making a dreadful mistake and had failed. In the process she, Jane, had been compromised and, being Ivo, he had proposed to her. Protectiveness seemed engrained in his character. But he had denied loving anyone else, she had asked him. She closed her eyes and thought back to the orchard and his proposal and her question.

'I am not promised to anyone. You have my word on it,' he had said. *'There is no one who has hopes of me, upon my honour.'*

But that was not what she had asked him and he had not answered her, had avoided mentioning his own feelings. He had spoken the truth, but only part of the truth. If he had loved Daphne once but no longer, then, surely, he would have said so?

If he no longer loved her, would he not have obliterated that inscription? It must have been vivid in his memory, because he had reacted instantly to dampen her interest in the hermitage, to give her reasons not to walk there. Perhaps he had gone to remove it, but could not bear to, so had covered it. *Buried it.* She shivered despite the heat.

Daphne was lost to him now, she was married, however unsatisfactory that marriage might be. From what the lawyers had said there was no possibility of an annulment and divorce was appallingly difficult even if both parties wanted it. As it was, neither of them did.

Jane blinked and looked up to find that it was raining out of a cloudless sky. Then she realised that the moisture on her face was tears.

What are you crying about? she asked herself angrily, swiping at her cheeks with the back of her hand. *You knew he did not love you.*

But you did not know he loved someone else, a harsh little inner voice whispered.

Perhaps he had fallen out of love when he had discovered that Daphne was faithless, had had him beaten, might have caused his death.

But love was not like that. Shakespeare had written, *'Love is not love which alters when it alteration finds, or bends with the remover to remove,'* and the man from Stratford seemed to know about love. Ivo might fall out of love with Daphne, but that would not happen until he saw her with different eyes and realised that he had loved someone different from the woman she had become.

Which left Jane with a question. Did she marry a man who loved another woman or call off the wedding? Her bones ached as she stood up and plodded up the steps to the lawn again, ached as though she had been ill. She put back her shoulders and made herself walk firmly.

I am strong, she told herself. *I will not weep. I will think this through and make a decision.*

She found herself by the gate into the rear yard that led to the service area and pushed it open. The yard was large and cobbled with a pump in the centre and a range of outbuildings—a wood store, an ash heap, two doors with crescents and stars cut out of them—the privies, she guessed—and some kind of workshop. Outside that was a bench and a small boy perched there, feet swinging, a row of shoes on one side of him and another row, shining and clean, on the other.

His freckled face was screwed up in concentration as he worked blacking into the shoe he was holding and the tip of his tongue stuck out. Jane sat on a stool next to the chopping block outside the wood store and pulled out her sketchbook. Drawing helped her clear her mind and it certainly needed clarification now. After a minute she picked up the stool and moved to get a better view of the lad's face. He was about eleven, she guessed, on the first rung of the servant hierarchy. Hall boy next, then under-footman.

He put down the shoe and picked up its mate and Jane moved closer again. This time he saw her and shot to his feet, dropping his brush. 'Miss?'

'I'm sorry I startled you. Please sit down again. Lord Westhaven asked me to draw all the staff— did you know?'

He shuffled back on to his seat again. 'Mr

Partridge said so, but I didn't think it meant me, I'm only Boots.'

'But that is a very important job, otherwise we would all have dirty shoes and that would be a disgrace. Just think what everyone would say if His Lordship went out in muddy boots!'

'Cor, yes.' He picked up his brush and began polishing again.

'What is your name?'

'Jem Fletcher, miss. Me dad's head groom.'

Jane wrote *Jem Fletcher, Boot Boy*, in the corner of the page. 'And you don't want to be a groom, Jem?'

'I likes horses,' he said, 'but I want to be like Mr Partridge, a butler in a really nobby house with a striped waistcoat and long tails, and sit at the head of the table in the Hall.'

'That is very ambitious, Jem, but I am sure if you work hard you will achieve your ambition.'

'That's what me ma said and I reckons if you wants something bad enough and you do the work, you'll get there.' He nodded his head emphatically. 'And Billy the hall boy is after the under-footman's place at Colne Hall, so I reckons I've got a chance there if he gets it.' He looked round, cautious. 'Do you think I can, miss?'

'Certainly I do. How would you like it if I put in a good word for you with Lord Kendall and tell him what a hard worker you are?'

His eyes were round. 'Yes, *please*, miss. Do you know him then, miss?'

'I am going to marry him,' Jane said, suddenly certain.

'If you wants something bad enough and you do the work, you'll get there' was not a bad motto and it might succeed in marriages as well as for ambitious small boys.

'Oh, heck.' Jem had gone pale. He got to his feet again, tugging at his forelock 'Mr Partridge will have my hide.'

'Nonsense. I will be talking to everyone and drawing them, too.' She looked at the sketch and smiled. She was pleased with it and she thought she would pin it up in her bedchamber for when she felt low again. 'Carry on polishing, Jem.' As he worked she drew another study, then tore it off the pad and handed it to him. 'Your mother might like that.'

Chapter Fifteen

'You are very quiet, Jane,' Ivo observed.

They were sitting at either end of one of the sofas in the drawing room after dinner. Great-Aunt Honoria was dozing in the largest, most comfortable armchair with her feet up and Eunice was diligently working on the petit-point seat cover the Dowager fondly imagined was all her own work after she exhausted herself by setting half a dozen stitches in it before dropping off. His grandfather was playing chess with Ranwick, whose dubious pleasure it was to be invited after family dinners to be soundly thrashed by his employer and then to have his every move critically examined afterwards.

'I am a little tired, that is all.'

Her smile looked forced and he felt a pang of worry for her. Her life had been turned upside down within days and although most young women would have leapt at the chance to marry an earl—any earl—he knew that for Jane this was second best to independence and her art.

'I went for a walk this afternoon and found it more draining than I had anticipated, so then I began work on my sketches with the boot boy, Jem.'

'Walk? I did not see you.' He cursed his own weakness in not obliterating that inscription, but it had seemed like the last nail in the coffin of his dead youthful dreams. He would go back tomorrow with hammer and chisel and do the job thoroughly. Unless Jane had already seen it.

'I went into the park. That way.' She gestured vaguely and Ivo released the breath he had not realised that he had been holding. She had gone in the opposite direction from the ice house and hermitage. 'The grass was longer than I had thought and harder work, but I expect the exercise did me good.'

'I will show you the best walks,' he said. 'The grounds staff scythe paths through the rough grass to make it easier. And we must begin our riding lessons.'

'Later, I think,' she said. 'I have too much to

think about without adding learning how to stay on a horse to the list.'

'Yes, of course, it is not something to be rushed into. Tell me how the sketches are progressing. Is everyone being co-operative?'

'So far, yes. I have drawn Jem, the boot boy—he is a very bright lad and he is exceedingly ambitious. Could you give him serious consideration for hall boy if Billy gets the footman's post at… Colne Hall, is it? And I sketched Molly, the new scullery maid, who is homesick but being brave about it because she knows this is a good household and Mr Evans, the clerk, who found the whole thing very embarrassing because he is self-conscious about his ears.'

'His ears?' Ivo tried to recall what Evans looked like and realised he was having difficulty.

'They stick out, so I am drawing him in half-profile and he is much more relaxed about it,' she said. 'Why are you looking at me like that?'

'In half a day you have discovered the ambitions of the boot boy and the hall boy, consoled the scullery maid and set the clerk at ease. You are going to become a much-loved mistress of the house, that is clear.' And he had not expected it and was now a trifle ashamed of himself. He had thought that Jane, not used to such a large staff, would have found the servants difficult to deal with and that she would be far too pre-occupied with her art to give much thought to household management. He should have realised that to create a good portrait one must take an interest in the person you are painting. It was he who was too distracted to pay attention to the woman who would become his wife.

'And that makes you smile? I suppose the prospect of domestic harmony must appeal.'

'It makes me smile because I am reminded once again what a very nice person you are and what a good decision I made in proposing to you, Miss Newnham.' She blushed and laughed a little and he reached across and took her hand, needing to touch her, feeling a strange sense of peace steal over him.

I have done the right thing asking her to marry me, he thought and found that the peace was disturbed by a tremor of desire.

He wanted to kiss Jane, not because she needed reassuring, or convincing, but because he wanted to. Wanted rather more than kisses.

Jane met his gaze and he saw it there, too,

an awareness, a warmth. Her fingers tightened around his and her thumb moved over his knuckles.

It was disturbing, this feeling. He was betraying Daphne by wanting another woman and yet Daphne was not his to desire any longer and she had made it more than plain she did not love him. He could not live like a monk all his life because he could not have the woman he loved and he should be a husband in all ways for Jane, not think of her as second best.

She was still watching him, her head tipped a little to one side, those hazel eyes questioning. She was warm and soft and innocent, yet there was steel within those feminine curves and an untapped sensuality that made his blood heat.

'Jane, shall we go outside and—?'

'Ha! Checkmate again.' His grandfather was crowing over the unfortunate Ranwick's latest defeat at the chessboard. 'Now, where you went wrong was in your third move. If you had only played—'

'You must not be afraid of him. He shouts and he blusters, but inside he is really not so bad,' he murmured, taking the opportunity to lean close.

'I like him,' Jane whispered back. 'He is afraid

of showing what he feels, that is all. It makes him gruff. He is so proud of you—did you realise?'

'What, proud? No, you must be mistaken.' Ivo laughed off the old hurt. 'He was angry that I joined the army. Foolish romanticism, he called it. A youthful desire to play at chivalry.'

'And that is why he can recite every battle and skirmish you have been involved in and the dates, I suppose? He knows every wound you suffered, has clippings of every mention in the *London Gazette*. He showed me and made quite certain that I knew I was marrying a gallant soldier, a hero.'

Ivo found that his mouth was open and closed it abruptly. His grandfather had followed his career, thought him *gallant*?

'I had no idea,' he managed to murmur at last. 'Thank you for telling me.' He swallowed, reluctant to expose a weakness, yet knowing he owed her honesty. 'It had hurt, I will not deny it. I never thought myself a hero, that is nonsense, I was simply doing my duty. But I thought he felt I was wasting my time, playing at soldiers.'

'Rough games to play,' Jane remarked, letting go of his hand. 'I have seen the scars.' She leaned forward, put one hand on his shoulder and kissed his cheek. 'Goodnight, Ivo. I think I will sleep well tonight.'

He stood, drawing her to her feet, and bent to kiss her on the lips. 'So will I. Goodnight, Jane.' She went over to speak to his grandfather and Ranwick, then bent to whisper to Cousin Eunice without waking his great-aunt.

Yes, he would sleep well, he thought, opening the door for Jane and nodding to the footman on duty in the hall to send a maid upstairs. But first he was taking a lantern, hammer and chisel down to the hermitage and erasing all traces of that inscription.

'Kendall!'

'Yes, sir?'

'Before you go up to bed, there is something in that proposal for the cottage repairs from Brownlow I want to talk through. Come into the study, will you.'

Jane sat up in bed, the day's sketches spread out in front of her. She was pleased with them and planned on catching some of the more senior members of the household the next day. She should be analysing these now, looking for weaknesses, but the lines kept blurring and re-forming as Ivo's face. The way he had been looking at her… The way he looked when she told him about his grandfather. Had he really had no inkling of how the old man saw him? It seemed not. Men were strange creatures, unwilling to talk about their feelings.

He was never going to tell her about Daphne, she knew that, so she was going to have to make up her own mind whether she was prepared to go ahead with this marriage or not. Marrying a man who was not in love with you was quite a different thing from marrying one who was in love with someone else, she was certain. But he was never going to see Daphne again, surely—not after the violent way she had reacted to his well-meaning attempts to help her. Daphne was married, unavailable, and she, Jane, was here with him.

Ivo liked her, he felt desire for her, although she understood from Verity and her own observations that men, the strange creatures, were quite capable of desiring women they were otherwise indifferent to, or did not even know. He was kind—he had shown her how precarious her unplanned ambitions were, but had done so without patronising her. He was brave and loyal, so he would make every effort, she was certain, to put thoughts of Daphne aside once they were married.

She trusted him, Jane realised. She had from the beginning: a large, battered, unknown male who should have been threatening, even semi-conscious. But some instinct had made her trust and she was going to rely on that now. Trust and put the work in as her youthful advisor Jem had said.

Marriage to Ivo would give her the freedom that wealth and status afforded a woman. It came at a price—she was not walking into this blindly. If she had mistaken the man, he could confine her in the rigid role of countess and mother, stop her painting, lock her in a gilded cage.

Jane gathered up the sketches and set them aside, blew out the candles and wriggled down in the bed. He had taken a chance on her, too. Ivo had rescued her from social disgrace, given her the opportunity to paint, when he must have been hurting over Daphne's betrayal. He must still be hurting, she worried as she began to drift off to sleep. Was there any hope that one day, if they both worked at this marriage, he might come to love her as she loved him.

Jane sat up, wide awake in the darkness.

I love Ivo? When did that happen?

She lay down again, shaken. This was dangerous, it made her so much more vulnerable. Dangerous, but wonderful, too.

Days passed and the frightening, glorious, reality of loving Ivo coloured every one of them. Jane did not think she betrayed herself because he certainly showed no signs of the alarm a man might be expected to feel on discovering that the other half of a marriage of convenience was inconveniently in love with him. He remained kind and amusing and, when he took her in his arms, passionate.

Responding to that passion was dangerous. She knew she was too inexperienced to hide her feelings, that she should try and remain cool and modest in her response, but it was impossible. Ivo felt so strong and solid when he held her against him, she felt safe and in peril all at the same time and she wanted the peril, wanted his heat and the urgency she could feel him controlling.

* * *

'The wedding night seems a long way off,' he said three weeks before the day, after one long, delicious kiss in the laundry where he found her after drawing sketches of the head laundry maid and her little team.

The women had trooped off to the drying yards, lugging dripping baskets of linen with them, leaving her in the steamy warmth, her hair lank and her face red. 'I look a mess,' she protested when Ivo caught her up and kissed her.

'You look flushed and lovely and decidedly wanton,' he countered, picking her up and sitting her on the long sorting table. 'I want to make you even more disordered.'

'You make me feel disordered,' she said, trying to make a joke of it. 'Ivo—what are you doing?'

'Helping you cool off.' His hands were busy with the fastenings of her bodice, then he tugged at the shoulders and she found herself sitting there in her chemise. One glance down at the thin muslin and she realised what his gaze was fixed on—the curve of her breasts pushed up by her stays.

At least I am so red in the face with the heat

he will not see my blushes, she thought as his hands fastened on her waist.

'Ivo!' The downward pressure of his hands pulled down the edge of the stays until she felt her nipples escape. It felt...

Goodness, that feels so... Touch me, Ivo, please...

As though by arching into his hands she had spoken out loud he moved in closer, bent his head and touched his tongue to the brown aureoles showing through the damp cloth, licking, fretting as she felt them harden and her breasts began to ache.

'Ivo... *Yes.*'

What do I look like? she thought wildly as she fell backwards into a pile of table linen.

Ivo was pressed between her thighs, bent over her. She could feel the hard thrust of him, intimately tight against her, even through skirts and petticoats and his breeches. Then she stopped caring about anything but Ivo and wanting him. There was too much fabric between them and she wanted bare skin, to run her hands over those muscles she had seen at the inn. Her hands made claws and she raked them down the unyielding cloth of his coat, moaning in frustration at not being able to touch him.

His right hand was on her thigh now, pushing up her skirts, and she arched against him, not knowing what she wanted, only that she needed something, needed him…

Then Ivo pushed back, pulled her upright and jerked her bodice back into place. 'Someone is coming, I heard the yard gate bang.' He looked at her. 'Oh, hell.'

'Coal store.' Jane managed to totter to her feet, grabbed at her sketchbook and ran for the door into the room where the fuel for the boilers under the coppers was stored. Did it have another door out? She was not sure, but anything was better than being caught in an amorous tangle amid the damask cloths.

They collapsed against the door as it swung closed behind them, both panting.

'There's the door to the yard,' Jane whispered, nodding to where light came in around the battered old planking. Behind them the room filled with the sound of chattering as the laundry maids trooped back in.

'Miss Newnham's gone,' one of them said.

'Fancy His Lordship wanting us all painted—never heard the like.'

'She's nice,' one chipped in. 'A proper lady, she is, interested and not talking down to us.'

'Aye, well, she'll want her washing done, just like the rest of them,' the head laundry maid interrupted. 'How's that fire, Madge? Do we need more wood under the big copper?'

There was the sound of metal rattling. Jane held her breath and felt Ivo tense beside her, then the girls called, 'No, it'll do another half-hour. I'll get these tablecloths in, shall I?'

Jane and Ivo both slumped against the door.

Just like naughty children up to mischief, she thought and was seized with the urge to giggle.

Beside her she could feel Ivo shaking, then a muffled snort escaped him. He took her hand and took three long strides to the outer door, cracked it open, peered out and then they were outside and round the corner into the shelter of the open wood store.

Jane slumped against one of the posts and gave way to helpless giggles. Ivo sat on the saw horse and laughed until the tears ran down his face.

After a few whoops he managed to get himself under control. 'Lord, I think I've cracked a rib again.' He pulled out a handkerchief, looked at Jane and passed it over, then wiped his hand over his face. When they had both calmed down he grinned at her. *"'A proper lady, she is,'"* he quoted, setting Jane off again.

'We cannot go into the house looking like this.' Jane straightened up at last, gave a last swipe at her face with the handkerchief and tried to pin back straggling locks of hair.

'The rose garden,' Ivo said, holding out his hand.

It was surprising that, after such a tumult of sensation, she could feel calm and happy and at ease with him. They strolled down through the back gate without encountering anyone and made their way round the side of the East Wing into the rose garden, sheltered by high hedges and, more importantly just at the moment in her view, secluded from most of the windows in the house.

'I am sorry, that should not have happened,' Ivo apologised. 'I am afraid my feelings got the better of me.' Something certainly had and he was not sure what it was. Desire, obviously, but there was more than that. Jane had looked content, happy, pleased to see him and walking into that steamy laundry room had felt for a second like coming home, which was ridiculous.

And then the deliciously damp and disorderly look of her, rosy and round and perfect. And her response. Even thinking about that breathy *'Ivo... Yes'* made him hard all over again. But it hadn't been that kiss or the feel of her soft and urgent under him, the promise of the heat between her thighs, that was making him feel so off balance. It was the laughter. Sharing that laughter with her, that moment when they were hiding like two naughty children and both of them had reacted in exactly the same way.

Now Jane was frowning at him, all laughter gone. 'What was wrong with it? I mean, we could have chosen a better place, somewhere that didn't have the staff walking in every few minutes, but...' She seemed to realise what she was saying, blushed, then carried on stubbornly. 'I liked it, you making love to me. I did not want you to stop, although I know you had to because it would have been embarrassing.'

Ivo was conscious of the scent of the last late roses, of the soft green grass all around them, of the high, concealing hedges, of Jane, still flushed and deliciously flustered and wishing they had not stopped—and all he had to do was take two steps and she would be in his arms and... And then a gardener would come in and start pruning, or shovelling manure on the beds or...

Oh, God, beds. Think about manure, he told himself desperately.

'You are a respectable lady. I should not be debauching you on the laundry room table. We are not married yet.'

'We are going to be,' Jane pointed out.

'Yes. In a while. Do you not want to wait until your wedding night?'

Jane broke off a rose and twirled it under her nose thoughtfully. 'Not particularly. I mean, you are not going to decide not to marry me just because you've already...' She seemed to be searching for the right phrase, then left it hanging. 'It always seems as though one has to wait because otherwise the woman might change her mind having tried it. Not that I am going to change my mind.' She smiled at him. 'I think I am going to enjoy...being with you.'

'So am I,' Ivo said, realising that he meant it. 'And not only the bedchamber parts,' he added, just for the pleasure of seeing her blush. 'It is a long time since I laughed about something like that.'

'Like that?' Her eyebrows shot up and she grinned at him.

'Something ludicrous. And you have to admit, the pair of us hiding from our own staff, caught like young lovers sneaking off to misbehave in the haystack, is certainly lacking in dignity.'

He sat down on one of the carved stone benches and she came and sat beside him, then lifted her feet on to the seat and leaned back against his shoulder. 'Nice,' she murmured and then was silent.

Ivo probed the thought that he should not feel like this, not when he loved Daphne. But he owed Jane his affection and his thoughts because she was going to be his wife. Daphne was lost to him, of her own free will, and for the first time he felt not pity and anxiety, but the stirrings of anger. If she had been unhappy, why had she not written to tell him so and ask to be released from the engagement? As a gentleman he would have had no hesitation in agreeing, however much it hurt.

He shifted on the seat so that Jane could lean

more comfortably against him and put his arm around her. Somehow he could not imagine Jane failing to tell him just what she thought and felt.

Chapter Sixteen

4th October

Dearest Verity,
The Dress was delivered today! It still needs
some alterations, but I cannot believe how
elegant I look in it.

It is of white silk with fine gold embroidery
down the front and around the hem and the
neckline.

Lord Westhaven has insisted that I wear
the most exquisite parure of diamonds and
emeralds—there is a tiara and a necklace
and earrings and bracelets. I tried to say
that it was too valuable, but he says it will
be mine to wear when Ivo and I are mar-
ried, as will all the other jewels in the fam-
ily collection, which is even more terrifying.

Did I tell you that my 'diamonds' are

paste? Goodness knows who sold the real ones—I suspect Grandmama.

Only two weeks and you and the others will be here and then I will be married. It seems that I cannot wait—and yet I am so frightened I wish time stood still.

I am falling in love with Ivo. I never expected to. I never meant to. And he loves Daphne still, I am certain. Sometimes he is so quiet, withdrawn inside himself, and I am convinced he is thinking about her.

I want to take a hammer and go back to the hermitage and smash the inscription I told you about, but then he would know that I know... And I want to hate her and I try so hard not to because that can help none of us.

6th October

Darling Jane,
He will come to love you—how could any man who is not a fool fail to once he is married to you? And you would not love a fool, so it is certain. Although I have to warn you, it might take a while before he realises it— men are not naturally talented at examining their feelings.

Besides, that silly woman Daphne is married to her rakehell husband. Will tells me hair-raising stories about the man's profligacy and debts. Your Ivo will soon come to realise that he has had a very lucky escape.

You are right not to hate her, although in your shoes I would want to give her a good shake. And push her in the lake, if truth be told.

Now—gowns. Armed with your instructions, we bridesmaids—I cannot keep serious at the thought of my being a matron of honour!—have ordered gowns in various shades of cream and emerald and will look very fine...

The day after Verity's letter arrived Jane laid out the drawings of every one of Lord Westhaven's indoor and outdoor staff on the longest library table and held her breath.

The Marquess walked slowly down, pausing at each image, then back, and then at the point where Jane had to breathe, once more. 'These are excellent,' he said gruffly. 'Quite exceptional. Partridge has informed me that the staff are very much gratified by the attention and I am most gratified with the result.' He peered at her from under beetling brows. 'It was a great deal of work, I imagine.'

'I find sketching relaxing, my lord.'

He grunted. 'Painting this many will take some time and will not be as relaxing, I imagine.'

'You wish me to paint them all in oils? I had thought uniform-size canvases would be best.' She showed him the modest panel she had selected.

'Partridge and the boot boy on equal terms, eh?'

'I thought so, my lord. I had hoped to convey the person rather than the role.'

'An interesting conceit. Very well, but begin with Partridge, Mrs French and Cook or the servants will think the revolutionaries have taken over the establishment and declared equality for all. Order what you need for supplies, Ranwick will deal with it, although I imagine you will not have time to begin on these until after the wedding.'

Jane was not so foolish as to take that for a question, instead of the command it was. 'Yes, my lord.'

The old man regarded her steadily. 'You are a good girl. Are you happy? Eh? No second thoughts?'

'No, none at all.' Just hopes and worries and awful moments when she wondered at her presumption in thinking she was ever going to be able to cope with this new life, with the man she was falling deeper in love with every day. And then, when she was ready to flee, Ivo would find her in some secluded part of the house or garden and kiss her and she had to fight the desire to drag him into the nearest bedchamber.

'You are good for the boy,' he said.

'He is not a boy, my lord.'

'No, he is not, is he? But when you are my age anyone under forty seems a mere youth.' The sudden smile was almost a grin and he looked so much like Ivo in that moment that Jane laughed. 'He is down in the garden. Run and tell him that Foskett has written to accept my offer for that land to the west of the Long Plantation. He'll need to make certain the steward marks it out accurately because I trust Foskett as far as I can throw him, the old fox.'

'Yes, sir.' Jane ran downstairs, humming under her breath. All those portraits to look forward to and the Marquess apparently approving of her. And there was Ivo leaning on the back of a garden seat and contemplating the fountain, all broad shoulders and long legs and the not-handsome face she had come to love.

'What are you smiling about?' he asked as she came to his side.

'You, looking very fine in the sunshine. What is wrong with the fountain?'

'It has two dribbling nymphs and one with a drooping spout. We need a plumber to sort it out before the wedding.'

'I agree, dribbling nymphs are not at all the thing. Your grandfather has sent me with a message about Sir James Foskett and the land he is selling, and, Ivo—he is pleased with the drawings and wants me to paint all of them in oils. Is that not marvellous?'

'It is, although there are the devil of a lot of them. He is handing you a vast task.'

Jane shrugged. 'There is no time limit set, although I am not to begin until after the wedding, he decrees.'

'And not until after our honeymoon.' The heat in Ivo's eyes fuelled the warmth inside her. 'I am not having my wife giving all her attention to the staff.' His voice dropped to a growl. 'Not when I want it all to myself.'

Jane swallowed. 'How long will the honeymoon be? Are we staying here?' It had not occurred to her that things would be different—she would be a countess, of course. Ivo would come to her bed. She would take over managing the household. It occurred to her now that those three things were not quite in the right order of importance. Not for her and, it seemed, not for Ivo.

'As long as you like and we can close ourselves off in our wing of the house or we can make an expedition to wherever you desire.'

More decisions.

'Will you tell me something, honestly?'

'I will.' His brows drew together sharply, reminding her of the fighter she had first seen. He was wary, but his gaze was steady when he said, 'I would not lie to you, Jane.'

'Are you glad that you asked me to marry you?'

'Of course.' He moved closer, took her in his arms. 'Can you not tell that I desire you?'

'That is not what I asked you,' she managed to say, although already her determination to find the truth was blurring. Her body wanted his, her mouth craved his kisses so she could believe, just for a little while, that desire was love. But it would be foolish to deceive herself.

'Yes, I am glad,' Ivo said steadily. She could not see his face, he was holding her too close for that, but she could believe him. 'You are brave, intelligent, talented. We laugh together, we desire each other, you fit here as though you were designed for this place.'

Was *'this place'* his arms or the Tower? She did not know and could not bring herself to ask. It was enough, it had to be enough, because she loved him and must hope that one day he might feel the same about her. But first they had to make this marriage work.

'Yes? What is it?'

Jane startled, then realised that Ivo was not speaking to her. Flustered she moved aside and saw Patrick, one of the footmen. He was pink with embarrassment and gazing fixedly at the fountain.

'The post arrived, my lord, and Mr Ranwick said there was a letter that he thought you would wish to see sooner rather than later.'

'Now what?' Ivo muttered. 'Tell Mr Ranwick that I will be with him shortly.'

'My lord.'

'Walk with me?' Ivo suggested, linking arms with her. 'It might be something to do with the wedding preparations and, if not and it is all about leases and field drains, you can cheer me up while Ranwick explains it all in tedious detail.'

I am happy, Jane realised as they walked up the gentle slope of the lawn towards the terrace. It was not something she had ever thought about. One knew when one was miserable or angry or upset or delighted or frightened or content—but happiness as a constant state…that was new.

Ranwick stood up from behind the wide desk in his office as Ivo held the door for her. 'My lord, Miss Newnham. The lawyers' investigations and opinion on the matter of Miss Parris's legal situation that you requested urgently, my lord.'

Jane's stomach felt as though she had swallowed a spoonful of ice cream too hastily. She moved away and sat on one of the chairs against the wall, out of Ivo's line of sight, suspecting that he had forgotten she was there.

Ranwick handed over a sheaf of papers. 'To summarise, my lord, her aunt and guardian has moved to ensure that Meredith has no access to his wife's money until she reaches the age of twenty-five in two years' time. He is threatening to take the matter to court, but, as they know he has not the financial resources to undertake such an action, they doubt it will come to anything. Miss Parris, the aunt, has promised to contact them in the unlikely situation that it should actually come to pass. However, the rest of the report is less satisfactory. Learned counsel's opinion confirms that the marriage is legal under Scottish law as we assumed and, as Lady Meredith is firm that she was neither kidnapped nor unduly influenced and deceived, there is nothing her family can do about it. Nor the lady herself, should she change her mind: it would be a question of divorce.'

He glanced at Ivo, who had made no attempt to look at the papers in his hand. 'They wish to know, at your earliest convenience, whether they should pursue the matter further as they have several of their most useful agents tied up investigating the affair and following Sir Clement.'

'Write and tell them to take no further action, but to notify me at once should Miss Parris require assistance. Thank you.'

He turned and left the room. Jane sent the secretary a harassed smile and followed him out.

'I beg your pardon, I had forgotten you were there. What a damned mess.' Ivo smiled ruefully, 'And I apologise for my language.'

'Perhaps the prospect of a fortune in two years will be enough to make his creditors step back and that will give Sir Clement the opportunity to consider his behaviour,' Jane suggested, not very hopefully.

'And my grandfather may take up Morris dancing.' He stopped walking. 'I should not have abandoned Ranwick to all that work. The poor man is attempting to teach me to be a landowner on top of his usual duties and the wedding organisation. There was the land purchase that you brought me the message about—will you excuse me, Jane?'

'Of course.'

She walked back slowly to her rooms. That news had affected Ivo to the extent that he had forgotten she was in the room, had sworn in front of her and was now making excuses not to be with her. She knew he was spending hours with Ranwick already.

Stop it, she told herself as she sat down at her writing desk. *Of course he is upset. He loves her, the treacherous little—*

She contemplated a variety of phrases that were unladylike in the extreme and struggled to find some sisterly compassion.

We all make mistakes, she thought. *But we do not all resort to violence as a result.*

Jane pulled a sheet of writing paper towards her and dipped her pen in the ink and began to write.

Dear Cousin Violet,
I do hope your sister continues to improve in health and spirits—

Twenty minutes later she finished the letter and sanded the wet ink. That was better. Talking to Violet, even at a distance, had made her feel calmer again, better able to think of things more charitably.

Daphne set those men on Ivo because she was

frightened and lashed out. It doesn't excuse her behaviour, but it does explain it. If Ivo can forgive her, then so can I.

She chewed the end of her pen.

I hope.

Ivo wrestled with the complexities of repairing leases while attempting to give his conscience a rational talking-to. If Daphne had written to tell him of her unhappiness with their engagement, he would have released her from it. Once he heard of her entanglement with Meredith he could not have got back to England any faster than he had done, so he could not have prevented her elopement. He had done all he could to clarify her legal position given that she did not want to be freed from the marriage.

He tried to imagine Jane in a similar positon and found that he could not. She would have written him a series of letters beginning with concerned enquiries about his well-being and culminating in an announcement that she no longer wished to marry him. If he had not responded, he would not have put it past her to take ship and march into camp to demand to know what he thought he was about, neglecting her.

He smiled at the thought, the lengthy legal document in front of him blurring until Ranwick cleared his throat. 'This can wait a day or so, my lord, if it is not convenient to consider it now.'

'No, I was simply wool-gathering. Explain this clause to me, if you would.' Thoughts of Daphne had never made him smile out of sheer affectionate amusement, he realised as he focused on schedules of dilapidations.

'Ouch!'

'I am sorry, Miss Newnham,' the *modiste's* assistant mumbled through a mouthful of pins.

'Do not apologise, it was my fault, I was fidgeting,' Jane admitted. She had been standing on a stool for half an hour while the seamstresses fussed around the hem of her wedding gown. First they had raised it, then, after a lengthy scrutiny involving all five of them in addition to Betsy, Jane's new lady's maid, and Great-Aunt Honoria who, refreshed by several glasses of sherry, was supervising from the comfort of an armchair, they decided to lower it by half an inch.

Jane's patience was ebbing in direct opposition to the hem. Somehow she could not imagine that Ivo was remotely interested in hemlines unless they were at mid-calf or higher. Necklines, though—that was very possible. She glanced down, smugly content that the gown showed a very pleasing expanse of bosom, daring enough to interest Ivo once she put back her veil, but modest enough to be perfectly suitable at the altar.

He was still somehow distracted after that news from the lawyers the day before, although his manner had, if anything, been more attentive to her. Men were mysterious creatures.

Her perch was in the square bay window on top of the porch of the front door. With glass on three sides it gave the dressmakers good light and gave Jane something to look at while she was poked, prodded and, occasionally, pricked. The weather was holding, the season slipping into a sunny, golden autumn and the prospect was pleasant.

She obliged by turning yet again until she faced down the driveway to the first bend which meant that she had an excellent view of the carriage as it came into sight, the sweating horses labouring in the traces.

'There is a carriage coming, Lady Gravestock,' she said.

'Who is it?' The old lady put down her sherry glass. 'Where is my stick.'

The vehicle came to a halt and a footman jumped down from the back, opened the door and let down the step. The young woman who took his hand and climbed down was petite and no one Jane recognised. Then she took off her bonnet and gazed around her, tipping her face back for a moment. Blonde, fragile, pale.

Jane stared down, feeling a sick apprehension wash through her. Could it be? She got off the stool in a scramble, hem half-pinned, and ran for the door. The railing around the open well of the hallway was just opposite and she hung over it, ignoring Lady Gravestock's demand that she came back this instant and tell her who it was.

The bell peeled and a footman strode down the hall to open the door. Jane held her breath.

The woman walked straight in. 'Lord Kendall,' she said, her voice clear and carrying and urgent.

'Who should I say, ma'am?'

'Just get him! Get him now!'

Jane heard a door open under where she was standing, the sound of booted feet on marble. 'Henry? What is going—? *Daphne?*'

Jane looked down on Ivo's head as he walked into view below her. He stopped, perhaps six feet from the woman. *From Daphne.*

'Oh, Ivo, you have to help me!' She ran, threw her arms around him and his closed about her, supporting her as she sobbed on his chest. Then she tipped back her head. 'Oh, Ivo, I have *killed* him.'

Chapter Seventeen

Jane picked up her skirts and ran along the landing and down the stairs without conscious thought. Ivo was still holding Daphne, who was weeping and clutching at him.

Who has she killed? Her husband?

As Jane thought it the realisation hit her: if Sir Clement was dead then Daphne was a widow.

But a murderess, she told herself. *He cannot marry a murderess...*

Then, *But he is an earl and earls have influence.*

The fear jolted her to a stop on the bottom step and with it came a kind of ice-cold calm. Jane took hold of the newel post hard enough to hurt her hand and focused on the pain until her breathing steadied and she was thinking clearly. She had been ready to take the other woman by the shoulders and drag her away from Ivo, ready to literally throw her out of the front door, she realised.

But someone was dead and that was what mattered in this moment, not how this might affect her. That was how a good person, an unselfish person, would think—as her nails scraped into the wax polish on the carved griffon under her hand she knew she was not that self-sacrificing.

But at least the check had given her a moment to compose herself and she had not screamed, *Leave him, he's mine!* like a harridan.

'Daphne, calm down,' Ivo said with remarkable firmness, given that a hysterical self-confessed murderess was weeping into his shirt-front. 'I cannot help you if I do not understand what has happened.'

It only seemed to make things worse.

People were beginning to appear in the hallway: staff, a strange young woman who must be Daphne's maid and Eunice, clutching a vase half-full of flowers that she had been arranging.

She skirted the pair in the centre of the space and joined Jane on the bottom stair. 'Miss Newnham? What is happening? Lady Gravestock will be very alarmed.'

'That is Lady Meredith. Please, give me that

vase, go up and see what you can do to soothe Lady Gravestock.'

Eunice blinked at her, but handed over the flower arrangement without argument, then scuttled up the stairs, much like the mouse she so resembled.

Jane walked up until she was within arm's length. 'Ivo, I would recommend stepping back. Lady Meredith, you are making yourself ill, stop this at once.'

Predictably the wailing continued.

'Ivo!'

He looked at her, startled, but did not move, so Jane tossed the flowers on to the floor and shot the water straight over Daphne's head anyway.

She shrieked and spun round, letting go of Ivo. 'Ah! You—'

'Oh, do not thank me, it was the least I could do with you in such distress. Hysteria will only make you feel worse, you know. Partridge, kindly send Mrs French to me in the Blue Sitting Room with towels and plenty of tea. Are you Lady Meredith's woman? Yes? Then come along and help her change out of these wet clothes.' She took a firm grip on Daphne's upper arm and steered her into the nearest small reception room, ignoring her gasps and struggles. Besides being compact, the room had a chilly blue and white decor and hard seats.

Let her try and cast herself into attitudes in here, Jane thought grimly as she pressed the other woman into a chair.

The little maid began to open a portmanteau and Mrs French appeared, her arms full of towels.

'The tea is on the way, Miss Newnham. My goodness, Miss Parris—Lady Meredith, I should say. I do hope you are not unwell.'

Daphne managed a tremulous smile. 'Mrs French. You are so kind.' The glance she sent Jane was wary. 'Oh, Peters, I am so cold.'

They got her out of her pelisse and gown and wrapped her hair in a towel. She snatched another and swathed it around herself.

Jane felt queasy and realised it was apprehension returning, only momentarily banished by the need for action. 'Here is the tea. Now, drink it down, Lady Meredith. I have added sugar, it will help with the shock.'

'My clothes. Please,' she quavered, ignoring the tea. 'Behind that screen.'

Peters, the maid, got her dressed while Mrs

French and Jane sat looking at each other in silence. Then the housekeeper whispered, 'What has happened?'

'I am not sure,' Jane murmured back. 'But I think some fatal accident has befallen her husband.'

Daphne finally emerged, dressed. She was pale, her eyes were wide and dark, but she looked tragic and lovely and not blotchy, red-nosed and swollen-eyed, as Jane was all too aware she would have looked after that much weeping.

'Are you feeling a little better now, Lady Meredith?' Jane asked.

Daphne sank down in a chair and picked up her teacup, holding it as though it was a shield between her and whatever awful thing Jane might do to her next. 'Who are you?'

'Jane Newnham. Lord Kendall and I will be married in ten days' time,' Jane said.

The other woman flinched, then took a gulp of the cooling tea. 'I want to speak to Ivo.'

'I am sure you do. Mrs French, perhaps you would be good enough to ask Lord Kendall if he will join us. Then I do not think we need keep you any longer—I know how busy you are preparing for the wedding. Could you take Lady Meredith's maid with you? I am sure she will want to prepare her mistress's bedchamber.'

The silence as the two women went out crackled with tension, but Jane made no effort to break it. Instinct told her that she was in the presence of an enemy and that speech would betray her weakness: that she loved Ivo and was frightened by what power this woman possessed over him.

When Ivo came in he was expressionless. Jane could see that he had changed his coat and linen.

'Ivo,' Daphne said on a breathy whisper as he sat down. She glanced at Jane, clearly hoping she would leave. Jane settled back in her chair.

'What exactly has happened, Daphne?' Ivo asked. 'We cannot help you if we do not know the facts.'

Her lips tightened at the *we*, but she dabbed at her eyes with her handkerchief and said, 'Clement is dead. I killed him.'

'When? How?'

'Where?' Jane added.

'At home, of course. Three days ago. He fell down the stairs. We had this terrible argument and I… I might have pushed him.'

'Were you defending yourself?' Jane asked.

Ivo jerked upright in his chair, but she pressed on. 'Were you?' She might dislike Daphne, fear her, but if her husband had been threatening her then she had a right to fight back.

'Ever since he discovered there was no money because Ivo had been advising my aunts and they blocked my access to it he has been so angry. Horribly angry.' She looked at Ivo, her eyes swimming with tears. 'How could you do that? You *love* me. Don't you want me to be happy?'

Ivo was sitting very still now. Jane tried to read his expression, but the set lines gave nothing away. 'I ensured that your aunts had the best legal advice. I was concerned about you and it seems I was correct in my assessment of Meredith. He could not have got the funds for another two years, Daphne. The bank would not have released them without your guardian's permission. But that is beside the point—tell me what happened.'

'He was drunk,' Daphne said. 'He has been every evening since he realised about the money. And we were at the top of the stairs and he took my arm and was shaking me and I pulled away and then I pushed him and he…he fell down the stairs. I knew he was dead, his neck was at this awful angle and his eyes were open and there was blood.'

'It was an accident,' Ivo said and Jane thought his shoulders relaxed a little. 'He was drunk, off balance and he fell. What did the magistrate and the coroner say?'

'They said they could smell the brandy on him and the servants told them he had been drinking too much.' Her gaze shifted away from his and her fingers began pleating the fabric of her skirt. 'But then I heard the two footmen whispering about how I might have meant to push him and how I would have to put up their wages so they wouldn't tell anyone. So I went down to the stables and told John to harness the team and I came away. I came to *you.*'

'Who else was there when he fell?' Jane asked when Ivo thrust both hands into his hair.

'Just the servants. They called the constable and Sir William Horton—he is the magistrate.'

'And they will have told him that it was an accident, or he would be asking more questions and the footmen can hardly accuse you later or it will be clear they are simply blackmailing you,' Jane said firmly. 'Running away was foolish, but

I suppose the magistrate might believe that you did so because you were frightened and you had never seen a dead body before. Don't you think?'

Daphne seemed to shrink into herself. 'When he fell… I laughed. What if they say that at the inquest?'

'Hysteria,' Ivo said firmly.

'What did you say to your husband?' Jane asked. 'What might the servants have heard?'

Please do not let her be guilty or Ivo will blame himself. Let her just be a foolish, head-strong girl who is in no danger of hanging. In no need of rescue.

'That I hated him. That I wished he was dead. That he had deceived me and only wanted my money. I said that I would tell Ivo I was unhappy and he would come and kill him.'

'At least you did not threaten to kill him yourself,' Ivo said. He sounded weary.

'I *might* have done,' Daphne said. 'I cannot really remember. It was *awful*.' Her lower lip trembled and tears began to trickle down her cheeks again.

'When is the inquest?' Ivo asked.

'Today.'

'But you will have been called as a witness, surely?'

'It would be horrible, I was frightened and there wasn't anyone to help me. The aunts hate me.'

'No, they do not, they—'

'There is only you, Ivo.' She looked so tragic and lovely sitting there that Jane almost wanted to paint her. Almost. 'I was so sad that you abandoned me, but I forgive you. Can you not forgive me?'

'You had him beaten by your grooms,' Jane said. 'Four of them. He could have been killed, maimed. Is that what you call forgiveness?'

Daphne turned her wide, tragic gaze on Jane. 'Oh, no! But that was not me—how could you believe it of me? Clement came home and the servants told him that Ivo had been there and had just left so he was furious, said he would deal with it. I thought he meant he would send Ivo a letter and tell him to stay away from me. Ivo, were you badly hurt? I could not bear that, I am so sorry.'

She got shakily to her feet, reaching for him, but Jane was there first. 'You must come and lie down, you will make yourself ill, Lady Meredith.'

'Do not call me that. I should never have married him, but I was so unhappy.'

Jane took her arm and steered her towards the door, suddenly conscious that she was wearing her own half-finished wedding gown.

She is not going to weep all over this and mark the silk, she thought distractedly.

'Come along, Daphne. Your chamber will be ready now.'

She handed the other woman over to the care of her own maid, closed the bedchamber door and leaned back against it, trying to find enough calm to go back downstairs to Ivo.

Daphne could ruin more than my wedding gown, she realised, looking up and catching sight of her reflection in the long glass opposite.

Daphne was beautiful, truly lovely. She was frightened, fragile and in need of help and Ivo had loved her. Must still love her, because he had always evaded the question when Jane had asked him about her feelings.

He had a guilty conscience about neglecting Daphne, he had not even been able to remove that old graffiti, and now she denied having set those men on him.

I could go downstairs, tell him that I release him. It will be an awful scandal... Or perhaps it will not be so bad if I call off the wedding now. He could not marry Daphne for at least a year because she will be in mourning. What could be more natural than that the two old sweethearts came together after all?

Jane's knees felt strangely wobbly and she realised that she was beginning to slide down the door, that she was shivering. Pride got her on to her feet again. She was not going to collapse here where anyone might see her.

I am not going to collapse anywhere, she thought, stiffening her spine and pushing away from the panels.

The man she loved was now free to marry the woman *he* loved. She had two choices: fight and insist on the wedding going ahead so she could spend the rest of her life knowing he loved another woman whom he could have married, or give him up so that he could be happy.

There did not seem to be much choice. First she was going to take off this gown and send away the seamstresses, then she was going to talk to Ivo. And break her heart.

'You want to do *what*?' Ivo demanded. 'You are jilting me?' He resisted the urge to pinch himself. This was not a nightmare, this hellish day really had become very much worse.

Jane sat down on the other side of the desk. She had found him in the midst of composing letters to the coroner and the magistrate responsible for the district around Meredith's home, promising that Lady Meredith, despite being prostrate with grief and shock, would return the next day to attend the inquest which must have been adjourned in her absence. He had just explained that Lady Meredith had fled to his grandfather, an old family friend, as she had no one else to turn to, when Jane had walked in.

She looked pale, but composed and quite rational. Certainly not hysterical or drunk—either of which would have been excusable, he thought.

'You want to marry Daphne, I want to be an artist,' she said. Her voice was wobbly, but he could understand that. It had been an effort to hold the pen straight. 'We planned to marry to avoid a scandal and because Daphne was lost to you, but now there is no need. I will break off the engagement and, if anyone wants to know why, then I will tell them that I simply do not feel fitted to the responsibilities of such rank: no one will be surprised at that. They will recognise that you did the honourable thing in offering for me. You will have to wait until Daphne is out of mourning, of course.

'Meanwhile you will lend me sufficient funds to establish myself in a popular resort—Scarborough or Brighton, I think. I will change my name and pay you back as my business grows.'

'I thought—forgive me if this sounds arrogant—but I thought you were more than reconciled to marriage with me,' Ivo said, amazed to find himself in control of his voice. 'I thought that you had recognised that setting up in business was not something you wanted after all.'

'I like you very well and I am sure we would have rubbed along together most amiably. But we do not *have* to.' She leaned forward, earnest and intent. 'We can both have what our hearts desire now. There is no need to compromise. If you will lend me money, then it will be much easier for me, I am sure I can make a success of it.'

'Jane, think what you are doing. You know you can paint after we are married, you know I will not stand in the way of your art.'

'Yes, but do you not remember that I said I never wanted to marry unless it was for love? Now I do not have to because we have this way out.' She stood up and Ivo stood, too.

He wanted to reach for her, but that would be like begging and he made himself stand still, absorbing the fact that she had not been reconciled to the marriage, that she was happy to have found a *way out* as she put it.

Jane was still talking, quite calm and determined. She seemed to have thought it all through. 'Now I am going to write to Mama and Papa and Cousin Violet and my bridesmaids and tell them that I have decided we will not suit. I fear poor Mr Ranwick will be busy tomorrow cancelling all the invitations and the arrangements.'

Ivo did not go and open the door for her, that was too much like helping her to go. As it closed he sat down again and tried to think. What had he done to make Jane believe that he still loved Daphne? Because he did not, he knew that with bone-deep certainty now and the knowledge had been creeping up on him for days. Had he ever loved her—or had he been dazzled by her loveliness, infatuated by her adoration?

He made himself finish the letters and went out to find Ranwick. 'See that these go off express,' he said, then went back to the study, pacing. He needed to do something, something physical. Get on a horse and gallop, chop wood—take a hammer and chisel to that damn sentimental carving. He had meant to do that and had forgotten it, now at least he could erase the thing and then, perhaps, he could begin to think clearly.

The tool shed beside the wood store supplied what he needed and he strode down to the ha-ha, his mind incapable of thinking about anything but the fact that Jane wanted to leave him.

The door to the hermitage stood ajar and he went in, then stopped. The dusty floor was marked with footprints: his and, overlapping here and there, the mark of much smaller shoes. The dirt he had scattered over the window ledge was not as he had left it either. He had smoothed it perfectly, now there were the marks of slender fingers raking through it.

Jane. Jane had seen this, read his words, known for certain that he had loved Daphne. And now she was setting him free.

He attacked the soft stone of the ledge with the tools, obliterated the inscription until all that remained was a ragged hole. The controlled violence was calming, he realised as he left, pulling the door closed behind him. Jane was wrong about his feelings for Daphne, but he could not be sure of her own motives. Was this gallantry of a kind he had not realised women possessed, or was she glad of the excuse to be free of him?

Jane was coming down the stairs, letters in her hands, when he came in and he had to stop himself covering the distance between them in long strides, taking her in his arms.

'Ivo, could you give these to Mr Ranwick? I'm afraid I… I would rather not have to explain everything to him.'

'Yes, of course.' He took them from her cold fingers and returned the faint smile she gave him before she turned and ran back upstairs. Then he walked slowly down to Ranwick's office, shuffling the sealed letters as he went, studying her writing as though there was some clue there.

And then he realised that there was and, for the first time since Daphne had burst through the front door, he knew what he was going to do.

'Ranwick.'

'My lord?'

'I am going to need your help.'

Chapter Eighteen

Who was going to tell the Marquess that there would be no wedding? Jane supposed it should be her because she was the one breaking off the engagement. It was much easier to focus on that, on what to say, on how she would react to the things he was likely to say in response, than it was to think about losing Ivo. She had told him that they could each have what they wanted now, what their hearts desired, but it was not true. She wanted Ivo first and beyond everything—except for his happiness.

Jane curled up in the window seat of her sitting room and tried to unravel her own thoughts and feelings. Now she would be free, with the resources to paint, unfettered by husband or parental authority, was it what she wanted?

No, she admitted to herself. She had accepted Ivo because she wanted him and there had been no conflict because she trusted him when he said he would never interfere with her art.

It was the act of creating that she craved, the possibility to grow as an artist that drove her, not the desire to be a businesswoman where time and energy must be devoted to making a living. Time and energy expended on making a life together with Ivo was one thing, but wrestling with landlords and builders, enticing clients, fighting prejudice—no, he had understood her so well. Even with money behind her, it would grind her down, take the joy out of her art.

Of her friends it was Melissa who had a burning ambition, not simply to write but to turn society on its head. Votes for women, equal rights in marriage, control over money, the right of women to be doctors and lawyers—all those impossible things for their sex were on Melissa's list of the reforms she wanted to see in her own lifetime, and the fervour she put into the debate only fuelled her novel writing. Jane knew that the fight would crush her because she did not have the limitless optimism that her friend possessed.

'Your vision is too close to hand,' Melissa had once said to her in the middle of a heated debate. 'You will fight, but only for the people you can see, the things you can experience. You will seek compromise and peace.'

And that was true. She had seen Ivo and had fought for him in Kensington and on the road to Bath. She had fallen in love with Ivo and had determined, somehow, to make the marriage work and hoped that he might come to love her, too. Now she must compromise again, seek peace of a kind for both of them. If only it did not hurt so much…

'Jane, I need your help.' Ivo's voice was so unexpected that she jumped, banging her elbow on the window frame.

'Ivo?'

'I am sorry I startled you, I did knock.'

'I was thinking that I must tell your grandfather,' she said.

Ivo waved away the rest of the sentence. 'He's gone over to the Farringdon estate, said he would probably stay the night. He and the earl have a scheme involving breeding foxhounds, I believe. I have to take Daphne home now—the longer we leave it, the worse the situation becomes. But I cannot take her by myself—think how that will look. Will you come, too? I will leave a letter for Grandfather.'

It took a moment for what he was asking to sink in through the general fog of misery. 'You want *me* to chaperon her?' But Ivo was right—if Daphne had been heard telling her husband that she wanted Ivo to save her, then the fact she had run to him was damning enough. If they travelled back alone, then it reinforced the suspicion that she had an even stronger motive for murder than a desire to be free of the baronet—and it possibly implicated Ivo in some kind of plot.

She took a deep breath. 'Very well. I can see that would be necessary.'

'I am very grateful. Thank you,' he said. 'I have asked for an early luncheon. We should set out as soon as possible and travel through the night.'

He looks grim, she thought. *Daphne's situation must be so worrying. And whose fault is that?*

It was an effort to try and be fair, to suppress the suspicions that were, surely, fuelled by jealousy.

'And, Jane, I do not think we should tell anyone outside this house about our decision not to marry. Not yet. I have seen Ranwick and he will not send out any announcements yet.'

'Of course.' Her presence as Ivo's betrothed would be an even clearer indication that he and Daphne were not conspiring together. She supposed that Ivo thought that, as she had no feelings for him, that she would not mind doing this. Her stomach felt as though she had swallowed pure vinegar. From somewhere she found the strength to stand up and speak briskly. 'I will go and tell my maid what to pack.'

Daphne, Ivo realised, was Being Brave. Had she always play-acted like this and he had been too besotted to notice? As the carriage turned out between the lodge gates and on to the highway she had her chin up, her expression set in tragic lines, her handkerchief grasped firmly in one hand.

Jane, he was relieved to see, had her small sketchbook with her and was drawing rapidly, although he could not see what her subject was. She was determined on rescuing him again, he was certain, although enough of a small, niggling doubt remained for him not to show his hand yet. If she truly would prefer to

be a professional artist instead of a countess—
his countess—then he was going to have to let
her go, just as she was determined to free him.
But he knew her well enough now to sense her
true emotions behind whatever façade she had
erected and she was not happy. He did not want
to hurt her, never that, but some part of him
hoped that he was right, that this was as hard
for her as it was for him.

'I have sent express letters to the coroner and
the magistrate, Daphne,' he said after the silence
had dragged on for half an hour. 'They should
arrive a little before we do and may help. I have
explained that you were so distressed that you
fled to the Marquess because he, a neighbour
from your childhood, was the nearest person to
a grandfather that you have.'

'But I came to you,' Daphne said, reaching out
her hand and he took it because she was swaying towards him on the seat.

Jane looked up from her sketchbook. 'Excellent,' she said crisply. 'Say that if you want to
show everyone what an excellent motive you had
for murdering your husband.' She was making
no attempt to hide her exasperation.

'Oh.'

Ivo let go of Daphne's hand and she pouted.

You came to me because you wanted to heap more guilt on my head, Ivo thought.

'You were distressed and confused and needed male guidance,' he continued, receiving an incredulous look from Jane whose views on male guidance were abundantly clear to him. 'Naturally my grandfather sent you straight back with me as escort and with Miss Newnham as chaperon.'

Daphne brightened up. 'If a marquess tells the coroner that it was an accident he will *have* to believe it.' She went back to gazing out of the window. Or possibly, admiring her own reflection in the glass.

Was she always this self-centred? He did not think so. But she had been spoiled and indulged because she was so pretty and her aunts were, as they were now ruefully realising, completely inexperienced in rearing a wilful girl. Perhaps he *was* the only person who had not given her what she wanted, when she wanted it.

They reached Kensington, and the Meredith house, at eleven the next morning, stiff, travel-worn and weary, but they went directly to the magistrate and then to see the coroner. To Jane's relief even Daphne was too subdued to complain when Jane took her arm, detaching her from Ivo for the duration of the interviews. Ivo, thank heavens, had too much sense to let Daphne cling to him, however much he wanted to support her. She had seen the way they had clasped hands in the carriage.

'That went better than I had hoped,' Ivo said when they finally arrived back and sank into chairs in the drawing room.

Both men had been stern but avuncular with Daphne and Jane realised that they had found nothing strange in her behaviour—they expected gently reared females to go to pieces in a crisis and rush off to find male aid. The inquest had been adjourned until the next day, after which, they told Daphne, she could make arrangements for the funeral.

'I will deal with that,' Ivo said. 'I will write to my family solicitor in London and he can make arrangements and sort out the will and so forth. You had best go back to your aunts while all that is going on, Daphne.'

'But—'

'That will look best,' Jane said and Daphne nodded meekly, to her relief.

She watched Ivo covertly, wondering at the alchemy that made an intelligent man fall for someone so foolish and self-centred. But Daphne was fragile and frightened and Ivo was nothing if not naturally protective and gallant. He was probably still feeling guilty about her and there remained the depressing fact that she was exceedingly lovely and beauty appeared to turn the head of even the most rational man. The magistrate and coroner, despite their age and attempts at sternness, had visibly responded to the appeal in her wide eyes, her fluttering gestures and expertly wielded handkerchief.

They ate a depressing meal, clearly scratched together from a depleted store cupboard. 'I will speak to the staff,' Jane said when Daphne showed no sign of noticing anything amiss.

'We both will,' Ivo said. 'Daphne, I think you should go and lie down and rest. You must be exhausted. Have your maid look out mourning for you.'

'Can you talk to the Cook and any kitchen staff?' he asked when Daphne had drifted off upstairs, trailed by her maid. 'I am going to make certain those footmen understand that their future prospects depend on their discretion.'

'You will threaten them?'

'I will point out that my solicitor will be writing their references. I think that will nip any daydreams about profitable blackmail in the bud.'

'A good idea,' Jane said, suddenly weary. Shock was beginning to set in and with it a very clear vision of a future without Ivo. And there was the worry about whether she was doing the right thing. Would Daphne, once she was safe and had what she wanted, become less selfish, more loving, or would it only make her worse?

But what was the alternative? She could hardly say to Ivo, *I love you and I think I would be better for you than the woman you have loved for years.* Perhaps it was she who was being selfish, finding excuses to go back on her decision.

All she was certain of was a strong desire to sit down and have a good weep. And that, she told herself sternly, would do none of them any good. But firm resolve did not seem to help. 'I will go and see Cook, she said and fled before the tears escaped.

* * *

'They believed me,' Daphne said, smiling and serene the next day.

The inquest had found that Sir Clement had died as the result of an accidental fall while under the influence of alcohol. Daphne was apparently ignoring the fact that the jury had added that in their opinion the fact that he was having a loud argument with his wife at the time had doubtless distracted him, causing him to trip when he was in no condition to save himself.

'Now all we have to do is get the funeral over and the will read and it will all be just as it was before the horrible man seduced me away.' She clasped Ivo's hand.

'Come and sit down, Daphne,' he said. 'You are over-tired and still in shock.'

She believes what she says, Jane thought with sudden realisation. *She honestly believes that none of this is her fault.*

She sat in the far corner of the drawing room, as befitted a chaperon, while Daphne and Ivo talked on the sofa by the fireplace. The tears that had threatened all day yesterday had dried up, leaving only a sort of dull misery and a nagging worry that this was not the right thing to do.

To distract herself she began to look through the sketchbook that was more than half-full now. There were the little cameos she had caught in the inquest room to distract herself—the coroner, stern and attentive, some of the jurors bored or excited, inattentive or hanging on every word. Daphne, pale and tragic in black, of course. 'It hurts so much that my last words with him were angry ones,' she had said, creating a ripple of sympathy around the court.

Then, working back, she came to the sketches she had made on the journey—little snatches of rural life, figures glimpsed at the toll gates or passing inns. There was something in the cover where she tucked spare pages that bulged a little, making the pages sit unevenly. She flipped through to it and saw a dirty, creased piece of folded paper.

What on earth is this?

Then she remembered where it had come from. This was the paper that had fallen from Ivo's coat when he had taken it off so the doctor could examine the stab wound. She had picked it up, meaning to give it to him, and had completely forgotten it because this was her travelling sketchbook and she had not used it once she had arrived in Batheaston.

Jane glanced across the room. Ivo was listening to Daphne, neither of them paying any attention to her. She unfolded the paper.

Now do you believe that I do not want you any more?
I told them to make sure you understand.
Leave me alone.
I hate you.
D.

It took her a moment to realise what this was, then she recalled one of the grooms thrusting it into Ivo's coat just before he hit him. Daphne had lied—it was not her husband who had set the four men on Ivo in a jealous rage, it was she who had tried to stop him interfering in her marriage, even if it meant he was badly hurt, or killed, as a result.

'Excuse me,' Jane murmured. 'I am going to rest.'

She went upstairs without either of them appearing to notice that she had gone. In the safety of her room she struggled with her conscience. She could burn this or she could give it to Ivo, show him the woman he loved in her true colours, finally open his eyes to her true nature.

But there was really no decision to make, she realised. There was all the difference in the world between giving up a man so he could marry the silly, pretty, love of his youth and hiding from him the proof that the woman he loved had ordered his beating and then lied about it.

A cold finger seemed to touch her as she looked at the note in her hand. Had Daphne really been innocent of her husband's death or had she pushed him down those stairs? Was she a cold-hearted murderess or simply someone who hit out when she was frightened and cornered?

Whichever it was, she had no choice. She had to give him the note and then she had to go away, otherwise he could well conclude that she was waiting for him to propose again on the rebound from the shock.

Jane wrote a note, folded it around Daphne's message and sealed it, then packed the few things she had taken from her portmanteau, put on her pelisse and bonnet and went quietly downstairs. One of the footmen was in the hall. 'Call me a cab, please.'

When he came back she handed him the note

and a coin. 'Please give this to Lord Kendall in an hour's time. Not before.'

Then she gave the driver Cousin Violet's sister's address and sat and watched as the carriage passed the Civet Cat alehouse. How many days since she had seen Ivo there and her life had changed for ever? The cab lurched and moved on and she tried to recall what Violet had said in her last letter. Everyone was well and healthy now, but she would remain for the rest of the week and be back in Batheaston just before the wedding.

Jane would not be imposing, she thought, and if she found that she was, then she would have to grit her teeth and move on to Aunt Hermione. Telling her that the wedding was cancelled would be…difficult. But not as difficult as learning to live with a broken heart, she supposed, bleakly.

Chapter Nineteen

Lady Harkness, Violet's sister, was reclining on a sofa in her drawing room when Jane was admitted. Violet, who was sitting by her side, dropped the book she had been reading aloud from and jumped to her feet.

'Jane, what on earth is wrong? Althea, dear, this is Jane Newnham, our cousin.'

'Lady Harkness. Cousin Althea, I mean.' Jane dropped a small curtsy. 'I do apologise for arriving unannounced like this, but I find myself stranded in London and I hoped Violet would assist me and that I might stay a few days. But if it is at all inconvenient I can go to Aunt Hermione.'

Lady Harkness straightened up and put her feet on the Aubusson carpet. 'Nonsense, of course you must stay. Goodness, it must be all of fifteen years since I last saw you. Ring the bell, dear, and then come and sit down and tell us all about it.'

Jane did so, but she was still dubious. 'Are you sure you are well enough for a visitor, Cousin?' Neither were wearing black, so the baby must have survived, she realised with a surge of relief. 'How is the little one?'

'So much better, thank goodness. We were in the greatest anxiety, but after a few days little Caroline seemed to rally and the doctor is confident that she will thrive now. And I am ordered to lie around and rest, but I feel quite the impostor. Since Violet has been here I have felt able to cope with anything. And I would be delighted if you will stay.'

She smiled, but Jane thought Althea looked pale. She would accept the invitation, but perhaps she could help by taking over some of Violet's tasks. 'Thank you so much.'

'But why do you need a refuge?' Violet demanded when her sister had rung for the housekeeper and ordered a room to be prepared for the unexpected guest. 'And what on earth are you doing in London?'

'The wedding is to be cancelled. The woman Ivo loves, the one he should have married, is now a widow. I... I released him from our engagement.'

'He accepted that?' Violet sounded incredulous. 'He is marrying her?'

'No. I do not think he will. But her arrival seeking his aid made me realise that I could not marry a man who still loved another woman. I believe that he may now have discovered things about her character that will change his mind about her, but...' She swallowed and made herself smile. 'It is too late. I have made it clear that I would prefer not to marry him.'

The two sisters looked at each other, then Althea said, 'Do be careful, Violet,' as though they had been having a discussion.

'Fiddlesticks,' Violet retorted as she turned back to Jane. 'Do you love him?'

'Yes. That is why.'

'Of course, I understand that,' Violet said, surprising her. 'If you both were settling for a convenient marriage based on a mutual liking and tolerance, that is one thing, but an unequal match with one party in love with someone else—even if they have been disillusioned about that person—that would be intolerable, I imagine. You would constantly fear comparisons and recoil from showing your feelings in case he pitied you, which would destroy whatever friendship and ease there was between you.'

'Oh, yes, exactly that,' Jane said. 'You understand. I was beginning to think I was overreacting because I dislike Lady Meredith so much, but Ivo is too important to me to settle for second best.'

'And perhaps you find yourself thinking less of him because he has fallen for someone like her?' Althea asked.

Jane winced. 'I suppose there is that thought niggling away at me. But she is so very lovely and men seem to be blinded by beauty.'

And I am no match for that.

'And she is in distress and Ivo has a very protective nature.' Although just how protective he would be feeling after reading that note was moot.

'What if he comes for you? Wants to marry you after all?' Althea asked. She seemed determined to pose all the difficult questions.

'He will not. I made it clear I did not want to marry him and that if he lent me the money to allow me to set myself up as a portraitist then he did not need to worry about me any further and I would have achieved my ambition.'

Both sisters stared at her, comically alike with their mouths open. 'You want to do *what*?' Violet managed.

'Be a portrait painter. But I realise that I do not, not really, not as a profession. I want the freedom to paint, yes. I want to be able to practise and improve and I thought I could only do that if I could support myself. But it would be a constant battle to keep a roof over my head and food on the table and how could I paint and learn if I am struggling all the time? I know I should be willing to suffer for my art, but I don't think my art would be much good if I was suffering.' She bit her lip. 'Which is very feeble of me.'

'It sounds clear-headed and practical in my opinion,' Althea said briskly. 'You know yourself, you understand your own strengths and weaknesses. You are not concerned with being famous for your painting, are you? No, I thought not. And—forgive me if I am prying—but I suspect you would wish to be a wife and mother as well as a painter?'

Jane nodded again. 'I have a friend whose

ambition is to be a novelist and to right all the wrongs women labour under, and she has the passion and is single-minded enough to make all the sacrifices necessary for a life like that. And I believe they would be sacrifices, because I suspect that she wants a family and someone to love. She considers men are misguided, but she does not hate them.'

'Mildred and Arthur would never be happy with a daughter who wanted to stay at home painting portraits in oils,' Violet said to her sister. 'They are ambitious for a fine marriage for her—they will be sorely disappointed that this one will not come about and life at home in Dorset will be difficult for Jane.'

'Impossible to tolerate, I would have thought,' Althea remarked.

Jane winced. 'I know. When I was explaining to him that I did not wish to marry him after all I asked Ivo to lend me money so I could establish myself somewhere like Brighton or Harrogate under an assumed name and pay him back as business developed and he agreed. I did not mean it, I knew very clearly that was not the right answer for me, but now, I wonder that he accepted it so easily. Not the idea of the loan, but my attempt to set up in business. He hardly seemed concerned about that at all.'

Which, the more she thought about it, the stranger it seemed. Perhaps he was so befuddled by Daphne's return and her predicament that he was not thinking clearly, but Ivo had shown no sign of that.

If one leaves aside his love for such an infuriating female in the first place, Jane thought with a burst of irritation.

'He knows me, that is why he did not appear concerned,' she said slowly, working it out. The thought gave her a fleeting glow of warmth.

'Frankly, Lord Kendall's emotions are the least of my concern at the moment,' Violet said. 'You will have a miserable time if you return home to your parents. Would you like to live with me? We get along well, I think, and I have found having a companion most congenial. And, naturally, I am more than happy for you to paint.'

'Or you can come to me,' Cousin Althea suggested. 'Your mama might be calmed a little by the thought of you meeting eligible gentlemen in London.'

'That is so kind.' Jane looked from one to the other, at concerned, smiling faces, the warmth in their voices testimony to the genuineness of their offers.

Violet smiled at her sister. 'We must share Jane, you know, otherwise we will be squabbling over her.

'If you think I could earn my keep, then that would make me very happy,' Jane said. 'I believe I can be of use, if you will allow me.'

Whether she could achieve happiness seemed, just now, improbable, but she could be content, she thought. She would have her painting, her friends would not shun her and her cousins, she hoped, would allow her to make herself useful to them so she would not feel too much of a charity case. Mama and Papa might forgive her eventually and the life of a spinster companion was one that was the lot of many women.

At which point something seemed to break inside, the tether that had kept her heartbreak under control, had allowed her to do what must be the right thing with some dignity, some grace. Now the misery had escaped, was choking her. 'Excuse me. I must…' Jane fled.

Somehow she managed to be coherent as she

asked a footman to direct her to her bedchamber, then she locked the door, fell on the bed and wept.

Jane had never been prone to crying. It had never seemed to make things better, whatever the cause of the unhappiness. But now she woke, rumpled, too hot and sticky-eyed to find a sort of strange calm had come over her. The misery was still there, but a settled thing now, not the internal storm that had threatened to tear her apart.

She made herself tidy, washed her face in the cold water in the ewer, then rang for the maid who, as she hoped, came with hot water and a message from her cousins.

'They say they hope you had a good rest, miss, and not to trouble yourself to stir before dinner.' She glanced at the clock. 'And that will be another two hours. I'll unpack while you wash, shall I, Miss Newnham?'

'Yes, thank you.' Jane blinked at the clock. Was that all the time was? Not yet half past five? She worked it out and realised that she had fled the Meredith house before luncheon and it had taken her only perhaps an hour to reach Cousin Althea's home. In Kensington Ivo would still be coming to terms with the proof of Daphne's betrayal and lies. What would he do? What would he be feeling? And he had no one to confide in, he was miles from home.

Her love. Her friend. The man who had protected her and who understood her. And he needed a friend now. She had found her sanctuary and the help of friends, but Ivo was alone.

'Please find me a fresh chemise and brush the skirts of my walking dress,' she said to the maid as she jammed hairpins back into place. 'I have to go out again.'

Her cousins were remarkably calm when Jane erupted into their tranquil drawing room and announced that she must have a cab, now, immediately. 'I am sorry,' she said, all fingers and thumbs as she tried to tie her bonnet ribbons. 'I will come back, although I do not know when. But I simply cannot run away—'

'Of course not,' Althea said, ringing for a footman. 'John, please have the small carriage brought round for Miss Newnham immediately. And I will tell Cook to be prepared to serve dinner for two whenever you and your young man return.'

'He is not mine.' She would not let herself

hope, it hurt too much. 'But thank you for warning Cook that I will be late back. And for lending me the carriage.'

'There is no hurry to bring it back,' Althea said. 'No hurry at all.'

If she never saw Kensington High Street again, she would be a happy woman, Jane thought, as the carriage stopped lurching over the muddy ruts of the road from Knightsbridge and hit the cobbles again. Soldiers from the nearby barracks marched past, the Mail scattered an unwary flock of chickens as it headed for the White Horse Cellar on Piccadilly, the horses sweating now on this last stage before London.

The memories this place held were too confused. Did she wish she had never seen Ivo, had missed the fight by seconds? Of course not, but…

She made herself watch the slowly passing scene. It was a busy village and it had the inns to cater for that, she noticed now—the Duke of Cumberland, the Bunch of Grapes—and the Civet Cat. Once again the carriage slowed. She peered out of the window, trying not to look at the alehouse. No collision this time, but a herd of cattle emerging from Church Lane.

A tall man was standing on the kerbside, just past the Civet Cat. Time slid backwards, then with a lurch of the carriage picking up speed she saw this was *now* and that was, unmistakeably, Ivo, arm raised to hail a cab.

Jane jerked the check cord, dropped the window and leaned out. 'Stop! Coachman, stop! Ivo, over here!'

He swung round and for a heart-sinking moment his face was bleak, expressionless, then he ran, catching the door as she threw it open, catching her as she tumbled out of the slowing carriage.

'*Ivo.*' She was in his arms, safe against the solid strength of him, and it was wonderful. Somehow she managed not to throw her own around his neck and kiss him, but turn her instinctive embrace into a comforting hug. 'I was so worried about you. Where is Daphne?'

'I sent her to her aunts in my carriage.' He looked around. 'We can't talk here—whose carriage is that you were in?'

'My cousin Althea's—Lady Harkness, Violet's sister.'

'They will not allow you to stay?' He held the door for her to climb in, then said something to the coachman she did not catch.

'Yes, of course, but I thought how awful you would be feeling when you saw Daphne's note and realised what she had done and that she had been lying to you all the time. I thought you would need…need a friend.'

'Is that what you are?' He sat opposite her and she tried to read his expression.

'I hope so. Are you very angry that I gave you the note and did not destroy it? I just felt that it was too awful a thing to have done and then deny it, that perhaps she was not at all the person you thought she was and might be… Well, anyway, I felt you had to know so you could talk to her about it.'

This was harder than she had feared. Did Ivo think she had been acting out of spite?

'You thought she might be dangerous to husbands? Frankly, I do not think she meant to kill him and I suspect that Meredith's fall was a drunken accident, not what you fear it might have been. Daphne is a creature of impulse.'

'I only thought that for a moment, but I did think you should know all the facts before you married her.' Something was hard between her fingers and she looked down, found she was fiddling with the buttons on her glove and one had come loose. She stripped off the glove before she could do any more damage and made herself sit still.

'Facts are, of course, important, but they are not everything,' Ivo said. He glanced around the carriage. 'No luggage?'

Jane blinked at him. 'What? No. I was going back to Cousin Althea, not on to my parents in Dorset. I only came to find you, to see if I could help. I should not have left like that.'

'No, I understand. It must have been difficult.' He reached out and took the crumpled glove from the seat beside her, turned it the right side out and smoothed it flat on his knee. 'Did you think of simply tearing up her note?'

'No. I knew you would find it hurtful, but some things have to be faced, dealt with.'

'You are right, facts are important, but the feelings behind them, the emotions, they matter most of all.'

'I see,' she lied. She saw nothing, understood nothing except that she should be happy that Ivo was not destroyed by the revelation about the woman he had loved for so long. She need not have come, he was quite well without her.

'Your feelings have not changed, then,' she said, attempting to put some lightness into her voice.

'My feelings for the woman I love have not changed, you are quite correct.'

'So you will marry her?'

She will break your heart. Oh, Ivo, my love, do not do it.

'I have every intention of doing so,' he said and, for the first time since she had seen him that evening, he smiled.

Chapter Twenty

Jane knew she should say something. *Congratulations* or *I am so happy for you.* Either would stick in her throat. She managed what was probably a very sickly smile. 'She is fortunate that you are so loyal.' That was ungracious, but it was all she was capable of. She wanted him to be happy. But she knew he could not be so with Daphne. She must try. 'Are you quite certain? You have thought it through?'

'Most certainly.'

'Even though she jilted you?'

'Even so.' His smile was wry now. 'That made me realise what my true feelings were, you know.'

'Oh.' She plastered the smile back on her lips and looked out of the window, bereft of things to say. The scenery in the gathering gloom was familiar, but it was not Knightsbridge. 'Ivo, where on earth are we going? This is the road out of London. In fact—Ivo, that is the Pack Horse. We are in Turnham Green.'

'Yes,' he agreed as the carriage drew to a halt. 'Shall we see if they can produce a decent glass of wine?'

'Whatever are you thinking of?' Jane demanded as Ivo jumped down without waiting for the groom to set the steps in place.

'I was thinking that an elopement has a certain appeal with the right person.' Ivo turned to speak to the coachman who was leaning down awaiting instructions. 'Take it round to the stables, rest the horses, have yourselves a drink.'

'Ivo!'

'Good evening.' Ivo was smiling at a maid who was staring back at him.

'Why, I remember you, sir. The injured gentleman and his sister. Are you well now, sir?'

'Excellently so,' Ivo said, as though he had not taken leave of his senses. 'We would like a snug private parlour and a bottle of your best claret.'

'Of course, sir. This way, ma'am.'

'Ivo.' Jane slammed the door of the snug little room—one she recognised all too well—and leaned back against it. She needed support from

somewhere. 'What do you mean, an elopement? You are marrying Daphne.'

He took her hand, led her to a chair by the hearth. 'Sit down, Jane.'

'No.'

'Please, because I am far too tempted to kiss you if you stand there glaring at me and we have things to discuss first.'

The feather cushions were large and soft and she sank into them, floundering. 'You said—'

'I said I was marrying the woman I loved. I should have added, *if she will agree*.' He sat opposite her. 'You did once.'

'Me? But you do not love me.'

'I did not when we first agreed to marry,' Ivo said. 'It crept up on me, Jane. Crept so gradually that I did not recognise it for what it was because I had never felt it before. I thought I loved Daphne, but it was not the same thing, just a shadow of it, simply calf love. If I had remained at home and not gone off to war, we would have never even thought it was more than a flirtation.'

Jane managed a sound somewhere between a gasp and a sigh. Could this be real or was she imagining it all? Had she really woken up after that storm of tears or was this just a dream?

'She was not waiting patiently and faithfully for me, so her aunts tell me now. There were more flirtations, one or two near-scandals. If I had not felt so guilty, and if I had not made that promise to Charles, then I would have seen clearly what my feelings were the moment I was confronted with her that first time.' He grimaced. 'Guilt is not a helpful emotion in circumstances like that, I find. It is like fog in the brain.'

'But when…when did the fog clear?'

'When she came to the Tower and I saw her as though through your eyes. I had been doubting for some time before that, but all I could see was Charles, dying and so anxious about her. I saw the way you dealt with her, the firm, practical kindness.'

'I did not feel kind,' Jane said with feeling. She still dared not hope. It would be too cruel if she was wrong.

'Any other woman in your position would have shown her the door. You were worrying about me, about her, and then I realised that you saw everything we had crumbling into dust.'

'Did we have something?'

'Oh, yes. I think so. Something beyond friendship, something beyond a practical agreement. And when I saw the letters you had written to your friends, the shaky handwriting, the few smudges that looked suspiciously like tears, I was almost certain you felt it, too.'

Ivo stood up, held out his hands and, as she took them, brought her to her feet. 'Jane, I love you. I want to marry you. Am I right—can you love me?'

'But you did not say.' She shook her head, more to clear it than in denial.

'You came to me and broke the engagement, seemed relieved that now you had an excuse. I was suspicious, but I had to be certain. And I could not abandon Daphne, not when she had done such a staggeringly foolish thing as to run to me. Time was short and there was none to spare for the quiet, honest conversation that you and I needed to have. We still do,' he added, smiling down at her.

'Ivo.' She found she was in his arms, tight against him, his heart beating in time with hers, fast and hard. And true. 'This is not a dream,' she said, her voice muffled against his shirt.

'No,' he agreed, somehow hearing her. 'It has seemed like a nightmare these last two days, but it is not a dream. If you want to be free, Jane, if what you told me when you released me was the truth, then say so now because I do not believe I can endure this suspense for much longer.'

'You cannot?' She leaned back against his arms so she could look up into his face. 'Neither can I! Oh, Ivo, what if I had not been passing that awful alehouse when I did? What if those wagons had not collided and held up the traffic?'

'What if you had not found a footman willing to pose for you and you had not been sent off to Bath in disgrace?' he countered. 'We were fated to meet. And now, my infuriating, stubborn, brave, adorable Jane—can you love me?'

'Yes,' she said, a second before he kissed her. 'Always,' she added when he finally lifted his head and they both could breathe again. 'Ivo, can we stay here tonight?'

His eyes were dark with a heat she had never seen before and his hands on her were possessive. For a moment she thought he was going to say yes, then, slowly, he shook his head. 'For one thing, they remember us from before and think we are brother and sister, for another, your cousins will be expecting you home eventually and, thirdly, my Jane, I suspect that when I do have you in my bed we may not get out of it for some considerable time.'

There was a knock on the door and they managed to step apart before the maid came in with the wine. Jane kept her face averted and pretended to be searching for something in her reticule although it could have contained anything from vipers to diamonds for all she could tell.

'One glass to drink to the future.' Ivo poured the deep crimson liquid with a hand that shook, just a little. That small, betraying movement made something warm and tender blossom inside her and it was an effort to keep her own hand steady as she took her glass from him.

'To our future,' she said and laughed as they both tossed off the wine. 'I am going to be tipsy, although I do not think that I actually needed wine to make me feel so dizzy.'

'We will go now, before we both become utterly irresponsible and drunk on love.' Ivo tossed some coins on the table and took her hand. 'Come with me now.' He drew her close, his voice tender. 'Let me take you back to your cousins tonight. Tomorrow I will go down to the Tower and when Miss Lowry can leave her sister you and she can return to Batheaston for the wedding.'

'But we cancelled it,' Jane realised. 'How on earth are we to explain?'

'I have a confession to make.' Ivo looked at her quizzically and tucked her hand under his arm to lead her out. 'I am going to tell you in the stable yard in the hope that you will not berate me too severely if we have an audience.'

'You may confess to almost anything except a secret wife and I will forgive you,' Jane said as they emerged into the yard.

The coachman and groom were leaning against the carriage, tankards in hand, but when they saw them they drained their ale and ran to check the harness.

'Very well,' Ivo said. 'No plans have been cancelled, no letters have been sent. The wedding is going ahead as planned. I took the risk that you might not truly wish to leave me.'

'Just because of the traces of what might have been teardrops on my letters?' Jane stopped dead and twisted round to look into his face.

'That was a hint that gave me hope. Call it instinct, perhaps, or blind faith or wishful thinking.'

'Oh, Ivo Merton, I do love you.' Jane threw

her arms around his neck, pulled down his head and kissed him fiercely, ignoring a whoop from the door to the taproom, a burst of giggling from the maids crossing the yard and an outburst of whistles from the stables.

She broke off when Ivo swept her up and carried her towards the carriage. 'Well, you had better marry me and make an honest man of me, because my reputation on the Bath Road has been quite ruined.'

She heard him say, 'Lady Harkness's residence, if you please', before the door slammed closed and they were rumbling out of the yard with her on Ivo's knee and his laughter warm on her neck.

'Tell me one thing before I kiss you all the way back to Mayfair,' Ivo said. 'Did you believe that I was still in love with Daphne when you agreed to marry me?'

'I did not know you had ever loved her until I began to understand the hints and clues. Your grandfather was anxious that I was not expecting a love match, I would have had to be stupid not to understand what your aunt was hinting so very clearly—and then I found the inscription in the hermitage. I almost called it off, I lost a lot of sleep,' she confessed. 'But Daphne was married, I trusted you to be faithful and I thought that it might be as though you were widowed and one day you might come to love me as well.' She snuggled closer and smiled to herself. 'I thought you were worth being patient.'

'And I was confusing nostalgia and guilt for love,' Ivo said. 'I think your patience would soon have been rewarded once we had married.'

'My friend Verity says men are not very good at recognising their own emotions. But poor Daphne,' Jane murmured.

'You are very forgiving.' Ivo sent her bonnet flying on to the opposite seat and was doing interesting things with the buttons on her pelisse.

'I feel sorry for her and that, I find, helps. She is not very intelligent and she had been indulged and spoilt. I do not think she has much natural empathy for other people or has ever been encouraged to look at herself through the eyes of anyone who is not besotted by her looks. She needs someone older, I think, someone who does not need her money and who admires her looks, but who has the strength of character to manage her moods and fancies. Perhaps, once she is out of mourning, she will find a beau,' she said hopefully.

'She can find him with my blessing and without our help,' Ivo said firmly. 'She is safe and you, my darling Jane, are in imminent peril of being ravished in a moving carriage.'

'Is that…possible?'

Ivo's lips were on the swell of her breasts, her bodice was surprisingly loose and his tongue was finding its way under the edge. It was difficult to breathe, let alone speak. Then the tip of his tongue found the aureole of her right nipple and she squeaked, forgot the question and concentrated in getting as much inconvenient clothing out of his way as she could.

'Perfectly possible.' To his own ears Ivo sounded as breathless as Jane was. 'I have never tried it and I do not intend doing so now, but I am powerfully tempted.' He caught her up more securely in his arms, sat back and looked at her in the shadows of the carriage as she sat, bare from the waist up, hair coming loose around her shoulders. Even in the gloom he could tell she was blushing, but she trusted him, *loved him*. The thought almost brought him to his knees because heaven knew what he had done to deserve her.

'You are beautiful,' he said, meaning it. 'Beautiful inside and out. And we are going to get you back into that gown, somehow, because the first time I lie with you, my love, I want us to have all the time in the world and every candle alight so I can see you properly.'

The effort to find buttons and tapes and hairpins resulted in laughter and teasing, for which he was truly grateful because, for Jane, nothing but the best was ever going to be good enough and he had never found his self-control so shaken.

At her cousin's house he took her up the steps and saw her in, pressed one last, lingering kiss on her hand. Then he turned to walk to the Merton town house for the night, the last time, he told himself, that he would ever walk away from his true love again.

18ᵗʰ October—Merton Tower

'You look *wonderful*,' said Verity, Duchess of Aylsham, as she tweaked the veil held in place by the wonderful Merton tiara.

'I feel wonderful,' Jane confessed. 'I actually

look…pretty?' Through the gauze her image in the mirror was a little blurred.

'No, you are not pretty,' Melissa said, frowning at her. 'You will never be *pretty*.' There was a sharp intake of breath from her other two friends, Lucy and Prue. 'You are beautiful,' Melissa concluded.

'That is love,' Jane said as she took up her bouquet. 'Come along, I cannot wait another moment to be married.'

It took more than a few moments, swishing along the corridors, down the great staircase where Mama was waiting, handkerchief in hand, to tweak and fuss.

Jem, newly promoted hall boy, was standing to attention in his smart new uniform, a big grin on his face as she passed him. Then they had reached the chapel door and poor Papa, who was white with nerves as Mama hurried past him to take her place.

There was a swell of music, the rustle of silks and broadcloth as the congregation rose to their feet and ahead of her, beyond the pools of coloured light cast by the stained-glass windows, was Ivo. He was looking at her and even at this distance she knew the expression in his eyes, the tenderness of his smile. He held out his hand and Jane, not waiting to take her father's arm, went straight down the aisle to her love.

Ivo took her hand as she reached him, raised it to his lips. 'At last,' he said.

'For ever,' Jane whispered back.

* * * * *

LET'S TALK

Romance

For exclusive extracts, competitions
and special offers, find us online:

f facebook.com/millsandboon

📷 @millsandboonuk

🐦 @millsandboon

Or get in touch on 0844 844 1351*

For all the latest titles coming soon,
visit millsandboon.co.uk/nextmonth